MOONLIGHT AND THE DUKE

The Silver Dukes
Book 2

by
Meara Platt

DRAGONBLADE PUBLISHING, INC.

Dragonblade Publishing, Inc. is an imprint of Kathryn Le Veque Novels, Inc.
P.O. Box 23
Moreno Valley, CA 92556
ceo@dragonbladepublishing.com

Produced in the United States of America

First Edition November 2024
Trade Paperback Edition

⫸⫷

Dearest Reader;

Thank you for your support of a small press. At Dragonblade Publishing, we strive to bring you the highest quality Historical Romance from some of the best authors in the business. Without your support, there is no 'us', so we sincerely hope you adore these stories and find some new favorite authors along the way.

Happy Reading!

CEO, Dragonblade Publishing

Additional Dragonblade books by Author Meara Platt

The Silver Dukes Series
Cherish and the Duke
Moonlight and the Duke
Two Nights with the Duke

The Moonstone Landing Series
Moonstone Landing (Novella)
Moonstone Angel (Novella)
The Moonstone Duke
The Moonstone Marquess
The Moonstone Major
The Moonstone Governess
The Moonstone Hero
The Moonstone Pirate

The Book of Love Series
The Look of Love
The Touch of Love
The Taste of Love
The Song of Love
The Scent of Love
The Kiss of Love
The Chance of Love
The Gift of Love
The Heart of Love
The Hope of Love (Novella)
The Promise of Love
The Wonder of Love
The Journey of Love
The Dream of Love (Novella)
The Treasure of Love

The Dance of Love
The Miracle of Love
The Remembrance of Love (Novella)

Dark Gardens Series
Garden of Shadows
Garden of Light
Garden of Dragons
Garden of Destiny
Garden of Angels

The Farthingale Series
If You Wished For Me (Novella)

The Lyon's Den Series
Kiss of the Lyon
The Lyon's Surprise
Lyon in the Rough

Pirates of Britannia Series
Pearls of Fire

De Wolfe Pack: The Series
Nobody's Angel
Kiss an Angel
Bhrodi's Angel

Also from Meara Platt
Aislin
All I Want for Christmas
Once Upon a Haunted Cave

CHAPTER ONE

Lynton Grange
Devon, England
August 1817

"**M**Y CHILDREN ARE gone?" Connor Fieldstone, sixth Duke of Lynton, had just arrived home and was given no time to dismount before the fourth nanny he had engaged in as many months approached him with her bags packed and a letter of resignation in hand. "Nanny Fuller, what do you mean when you say that my children are gone?"

"They are gone. G-O-N-E, as in gone. Fled their rooms, Your Grace. The little savages are your problem now. I am tendering my resignation effective immediately. Good luck finding them." She stuffed the resignation letter in his hand, and then climbed into a waiting wagon that would take her to the nearest coaching station.

Connor dismounted and went in search of his mother, the dowager Duchess of Lynton. Where was she? Gone too?

"She is shopping in town," his head butler said, not looking very perturbed, since the children managed to run away at least twice a week and always miraculously returned in time for their suppertime pudding.

"Thank you, Brewster. I don't suppose the children might have accompanied her?"

"No, Your Grace." He gave a sad shake of his head. "They ran off about an hour after your mother left in your carriage."

"I see." The seacoast town of Lynton was one of the prettiest places in all of northern Devon, and Connor's own estate, Lynton Grange, commanded one of its finest views. Why would anyone ever want to run away from here? Was this not an idyllic place to raise children?

Well, on a bright note, his children had not burned down the family home...yet.

Connor ordered his entire staff to conduct a search of the house from cellar to attic, and all the outbuildings. It stayed light until at least ten o'clock in the evening at this time of year, so he had hours of daylight left to find them. Still, he was worried. His boys were twelve and ten, but his daughter was only eight years old and could not keep up with her brothers.

They had done this often before, but their behavior had gotten worse these past three years since the death of their mother. He had not considered Mary a particularly good mother or wife, but it seemed even an apathetic mother was better than none at all. He supposed this was why his own—the dowager duchess who adored him and drove him mad with her meddling—was now obsessed with finding him a proper wife.

Well, one problem at a time. First, he had to find his children.

No matter how familiar they were by now with Lynton Grange and its surroundings, accidents happened. There were no guarantees they would return home safely after every escapade.

He was about to ride out with one of his hunting dogs to track them through the nearby hills, when he saw his neighbor, the lovely Eden Darrow, coming toward him in her rig. Well, he had no idea why he suddenly thought of her as lovely, for she had wild red hair and wore hideous spectacles that dulled the brilliance of her hazel eyes. Pencils usually poked out of her hair because she always carried them and a pad to jot down notes while on her nature studies.

Three smiling faces peered out from behind her, his daughter's smile the biggest and brightest of all.

"Eden, thank goodness! Where did you find them?" He hurried forward to take his children in his arms.

"Papa! We missed you," the youngest cried, wrapping her little arms around his neck as he lifted her and hugged her fiercely.

"Priscilla, you had me so worried." He kissed her pudgy cheeks with heartfelt relief.

"We're sorry," the eldest, his namesake Connor, said as he stepped down from the carriage and joined Priscilla in hugging him.

"We were about to come back," Alex, his middle child, sought to assure him as he burrowed between his siblings for a hug as well. "But it was a long walk, and Priscilla got tired."

"Then Eden found us and gave us a ride," his eldest added.

Connor felt a mix of relief and anger, wanting to hug the daylights out of his children, and at the same time spank them and send them off to bed without their pudding.

Eden watched quietly from her perch while they engaged in their joyous family reunion. "They were by the cliffs overlooking the beach. It is too dangerous for them to be playing there without adult supervision. I happened to be sketching goshawks when I saw them trying to steal an egg from one of the nests. So I brought them home with me and fed them biscuits and hot cocoa before returning them to Lynton Grange." She glanced around. "Where is Nanny Fuller?"

"Gone. G-O-N-E. Gone," he said, repeating the latest nanny's words as she left.

His children cheered. Gad, they were little terrors.

But Connor was sincerely grateful to Eden for her care of them. "Stay for supper, won't you? I'll escort you home afterward."

The children erupted in pleas for her to stay.

She emitted a soft breath. "All right. I'll stay. But the three of you had better run up and thoroughly wash your hands. Connor," she said to his eldest son, "see that Alex and Priscilla do a proper job of it. You are in charge and must set the good example. Soap and water. Hands fully lathered and scrubbed. I'll be conducting an inspection before we sit down to dine."

The children nodded before gleefully running into the house and almost knocking over Brewster in their haste.

Connor turned to Eden and cleared the lump of relief in his throat. "Thank you, from the bottom of my heart. Those little fiends are quite precious to me."

Eden shook her lovely head. "I know. They really are wonderful children. But their nanny situation is troubling. Another one lost? This is getting out of control."

He was painfully aware.

But why had he thought of Eden as lovely again? Surely he was feeling gratitude and nothing more.

"We have a houseful of guests about to descend on us tomorrow," he remarked. "There is no way in blazes I'll be able to find another nanny to attend them for the entire week this infernal house party is going on."

She laughed softly as he took her hand to assist her down from her rig. "Poor dear. That is a problem for you. Your mother seems to be obsessed with getting you married off."

"She'll never succeed. I am quite happy in my present situation." He escorted her into the parlor to await the return of his children. "Nor do I have any intention of shackling myself to a little peahen who is young enough to be my daughter."

"Ah, Lynton. You are quite deluded if you think you will stave off that determined dowager. You are, and shall forever be, her little boy. Do not judge her too harshly, however. She desperately wishes to see you happy."

He threw his head back and laughed. "I am over forty years old and have graying hair. I am no one's *little boy*."

She sighed as she made herself comfortable on the settee. "You will always be that to her. She is a good mother and loves you."

"I am too old to be mothered to death. I am a—"

"If you start spouting off about being a Silver Duke, I am going to kick you."

He sank into a chair opposite her seat, casually tossing an arm over the back of it as he stretched his legs before him and relaxed. "Why should I not spout off about it? I *am* a Silver Duke, and proud of the fact. As it turns out, I just left Bromleigh and Camborne. We stopped in Brighton to visit Bromleigh's cousin, Lady Shoreham. She happens to be throwing her own house party as we speak. Bromleigh and his cousin are determined to see Reggie Burton, his nephew and heir, married to a proper young lady."

"Married? You are pushing Lord Burton toward marriage when the three of you are so desperately avoiding it? Is that not hypocritical of you Silver Dukes?"

"Not at all. Bromleigh is merely planning ahead. After all, unless he marries and sires sons of his own—which seems unlikely at this point—it is Reggie Burton who will become the next duke. Bromleigh is determined to see him well matched."

Eden snorted. "Ah, the best-laid plans. I wonder how that will turn out."

"Fine, I'm sure. It is an excellent plan and necessary to ensure the smooth transfer of the Bromleigh title. As a matter of fact, Bromleigh, Camborne, and I were just talking about how content we are as bachelors. Silver Dukes stick together, and none of us will ever get married...or in my situation, remarried."

"Neither will I ever marry," Eden said, her manner suddenly wistful. "The last thing I want is the disaster my parents have. I did not realize two people could bear so much hatred for each other."

Lynton's heart gave a little tug, for he knew how awful Eden's upbringing had been. That she had come out of it as well as she had was a compliment to her fortitude and good sense. But it was a shame that their behavior had scarred her as badly as it had. She was kind, intelligent, and probably would have made some fortunate man a good wife.

She had rejected several offers, if the rumors were true. How old was she now? About twenty and four? Perhaps twenty and six. Not that she looked at all on the shelf.

In truth, she was quite pretty if one looked past those owlish spectacles and drab gowns that were serviceable and durable, and designed more for hiking up cliffs than sitting in parlors taking tea. They were not in the least fashionable. In fact, one might say they were defiantly *un*fashionable.

"I hate to agree with your mother about your children needing a nurturing hand," Eden said, interrupting his perusal of her features. "Priscilla especially feels the lack of a mother. Having felt it myself, I know how important it is to a child's happiness."

A wild thought came into Connor's mind, one he needed to discuss with Eden before his Mongol horde came thundering down the stairs and interrupted their conversation. "Eden, about this dilemma…and knowing how my children need a gentle hand to guide them…and seeing as how my mother is determined to put her deranged matchmaking scheme into effect starting tomorrow…"

"Yes?"

He leaned forward, quite excited about this new idea. "And seeing as I will not have a moment to myself as she relentlessly hounds me into taking a wife…we might help each other out here. Would you… Well, I know this may sound absurd to you. But would you… Seeing as my children adore you, and seeing as you would rather be anywhere but in your home whenever your parents are around… Would you consider…"

She pursed her lips and frowned. "Connor, are suggesting that I marry you?"

"What?" He sucked in a breath and his heart momentarily stopped. "Wait…no. I was asking you to be my nanny."

The air turned oppressively thick as Eden gaped at him. "Your nanny? Your *nanny*? You are asking me to look after your children while you flirt and picnic and dance, not to mention generally cavort with every peahen at your party? But I am to remain in the nursery tending to Priscilla, Alex, and Connor while you strut about like a silver cock in a henhouse? And this is helping *me* out how?"

"Um…" Well, he hadn't really thought that part through yet. "Eden, wait… Don't—"

He toppled to the ground as Eden kicked his chair out from under him.

Chapter Two

"I FIND YOUR aggression oddly stimulating," Connor—the dolt—said as he lay winded and flat on his back, looking up at Eden with brooding eyes the deep blue of a May sky. But this was what he and his friends, Bromleigh and Camborne, were—magnificent specimens of manhood, real men with fully formed musculature and faces of character. They were called Silver Dukes because they were above the age of forty and had hints of gray in their hair. Eden rather liked the way those flecks, more white than gray, salted Connor's full head of dark hair.

Eden knelt beside him, appalled by what she had just done, and also confused by what he had just said. "I stimulate you?"

He coughed. "No, that came out wrong again."

She sighed and told him to lie still another moment to catch his breath before attempting to get up. "You toppled rather hard. I'm so sorry. I behaved as badly as my parents. Thank goodness your children were not here to see my outburst. Truly, I cannot apologize enough."

He took another breath, and then accepted her offered hand as he groaned to a sitting position. "No, this was all my fault. I was in the wrong for speaking out of turn to you, Eden. I never meant it as an insult. I just saw how much my children adore you and selfishly leaped at the possibility you might help me out."

In truth, she liked his children very much and would not have minded taking them for a day or two. But an entire week seemed too much for her to manage.

"I'll figure out something else," he said, absently caressing her hand that he still held. His own was roughened and warm because of his physicality. He was no soft lord with slender fingers who never lifted anything heavier than a quill pen. His hands were big and felt divine. The same could be said for his muscled shoulders.

She tried not to look disappointed when he released her.

"This house party is doomed to be a disaster anyway," he continued. "What was my mother thinking to invite these *ton* diamonds? Some of them are barely eighteen years old. How would it ever work when I am over forty? How can I look seriously upon a young lady who is more than twenty years my junior? What could I possibly have in common with her?"

Eden helped him to his feet, feeling surprisingly small beside his large frame as they stood side by side. She was not a short woman, yet he was a full head taller than her. "Since we seem to be speaking rather bluntly to each other, why would you not want someone young and fresh in your bed?" she asked.

He righted his chair, and then turned to her and shook his head. "That is precisely the point. That young and fresh diamond is not going to want to share my bed. Oh, she might do her duty without grimacing too obviously, but I already have my children. Do I really need more? Connor and Alex are the heir and the spare, ensuring the Lynton line of succession. And I also have Priscilla, my little sweetheart. I do not need another marriage such as I had with Mary. In truth, I do not need another marriage at all."

Eden regarded him thoughtfully. "But you seemed to be a happy family."

He snorted. "Mary and I were cordial to each other, but that was all. She was kind to the children—I will give her that. But would she ever risk her own life to protect them? I'm not sure. I never saw a spark of courage in her. Nor much in the way of maternal instinct. But who knows? Through all our years of marriage, I never got to know her. And before you say anything, it wasn't from lack of my trying."

"I was not going to suggest it." She waited for him to continue because he seemed eager to get his feelings out, and she did not mind listening.

"She never expressed an opinion. She never felt passionate about anything, not even the children. Nannies took care of them mostly. I was the one who took them on nature walks, who read to them before they went to sleep, and who sat by their side if ever they were ill."

"And Mary?"

He shrugged. "I have no idea how she spent most of her day. We rarely entertained, which suited me well, since I was usually tired after long days at the Lynton farms, especially if there was physical work to be done. We had maids, a cook, a housekeeper, butlers and footmen, nannies and governesses to take care of the house and children. Mary... She was a leaf detached from a tree and floating upon a stream, just going along with the current. When she died..." He raked a hand through those lovely waves of dark hair. "Well, this is getting too personal. I've said too much already."

"You know that I will keep whatever you say in confidence. The children felt her loss," Eden said, wondering what his response had been to his wife's passing. Had he shed a tear? He wasn't a bad man, but she did not think he missed her very much, because he had never achieved a closeness with his wife that he might have done in a love match.

Not that she wished him to be unhappy and desperately mourn his loss. But was it not better to experience perfect happiness for a short while rather than never have it at all?

Was this not the very thing she was struggling with now?

She was beginning to think she had made a mistake in rejecting all those offers of marriage during her first few Seasons. Some of the gentlemen were honorable enough, and they might have made a go of it.

But she had been too scared to try because her parents had such a horrible marriage. She did not want to repeat their mistakes.

For this reason, she had shunned entering into that same sort of unholy alliance and suffering their sad fate. Considered a diamond in her day, she had turned down plenty of offers. Most of her suitors were more in love with her dowry than with her.

But was it not possible that a few actually liked her, too?

Well, it did not matter very much, since none of the gentlemen courting her had ever left her breathless or made her heart flutter. None of them would have been a love match.

But so what? Where had all her caution gotten her?

She was now the ripe old age of seven and twenty, and firmly on the shelf. Not that she was miserable about it. She had made a good life for herself here in the town of Lynton. Connor was a good neighbor. He and his mother, Duchess Evelyn, were always welcoming whenever she stopped by. Even his children tended to be on their best behavior whenever she came around to visit, although their best wasn't always very good. She never minded their antics and enjoyed spending time with them.

She owned her own home, Chestnut Hill, that she had inherited from her grandmother, along with a sizeable trust fund that came under her full control two years ago. Indeed, that inheritance had left her quite wealthy in her own right. For this reason, there were always men willing to step forward in the hope of seducing her into marrying them.

She was too cynical to fall for their obvious ploys.

"Uh oh. I hear the thundering horde," Connor jested.

Their conversation ended when the children came bounding in. The discussion now shifted to queries about supper, because these growing sprites were starving.

Eden noticed how Lynton's face lit up when his children swarmed around him.

Yes, this was what she was missing—children of her own. But would she be a good mother? Or was she doomed to become the banshee that her own mother was? Her father was little better, always provoking his wife because the two were like oil and water. Mother was always in a crisis over the smallest problem, and Father was a walking testament to every bad habit invented to date.

How had they ever been a match?

This was why she enjoyed Chestnut Hill so much. Her parents spent most of their time in London while she resided here, well out of their reach. This was *her* home, *her* sanctuary, and they rarely bothered to come here because it was so out of the way.

Not that she ever minded their visits. Separately, they were tolerable. Together, they were a disaster.

One would think they might have learned to stay apart by now. But they seemed to love confronting each other, and each got wicked enjoyment out of ruining the other's day. Eden was tired of their shouting matches and their hurling vases, cushions, and any other objects close at hand at each other. Mostly her mother tossed them at her father, and he usually ducked in time to avoid getting hit.

Neither parent ever cared whether she was present and watching their theatrics. Quite often, they forgot she existed.

Lynton broke away from his children and took her gently by the elbow, his touch shaking her out of her thoughts. "The Mongol horde is too hungry to await my mother's return."

Eden regarded him with some surprise. "But will she not be put out? It would be rude of us to proceed without her. What if we merely sat with the children while they ate?"

"And then dined with my mother? I have no idea when she'll be back."

At that moment, Brewster strode in. "Your Grace..."

"Yes, Brewster. What is it?"

"Your mother just sent word that she will be dining in town this evening."

Connor frowned. "Did she provide any explanation?"

Brewster nodded. "Apparently, Sir Nero Arnulfson is giving a lecture at the Lynton Literary Society, and Duchess Evelyn has decided to host an informal supper at the Lynton Hotel for the members afterward."

"Oh, the society meeting," Eden muttered, feeling a bit guilty that she had declined the invitation. Sir Nero was a pompous bag of wind, and a lecherous old man to boot. He had twice pinched her bottom, and she was not about to give him the opportunity to do it again.

"Then it is just us and the children," Connor said with a surprisingly affectionate smile.

They dined on the terrace overlooking the magnificent Lynton gardens and an expansive view of the ocean. The terrace was in shade at this hour, providing a perfect way to enjoy a meal on a hot day like this one. A gentle breeze blew off the water and carried the scent of salt, sand, and waves toward them. As the wind swirled and shifted, it also carried the fragrant scent of garden roses that were presently at their magnificent peak.

Priscilla sat beside her, looking up at her with such happiness on her adorably round face that Eden's heart gave a lurch.

Would it be so terrible to have these children with her for the week?

Their chatter was constant and lively. The children told their father about their day. To his credit, Connor listened attentively and made suggestions for activities they might undertake once the onerous week of his house party was over. "But that is a whole week away," Priscilla grumbled. "What are we to do while you are busy finding us our new mama?"

Connor paused as he was about to take a sip of his wine. "I am not finding you a new mama," he muttered between clenched teeth. "Who said I was?"

"Grandmama Evelyn said you were going to meet her this week," Alex said.

"Well, your grandmother is wrong," he replied. "I am quite content with you three and do not need anyone else."

"Other than Eden," Priscilla said, taking her hand with her sticky fingers in a sweet gesture meant to ease any insult in leaving her out of this happy family grouping. "We need Eden, don't we?"

Connor smiled and raised his glass to her. "Yes, Eden is included."

"I am honored," Eden said with a soft laugh, raising her glass of cider in turn.

The children cheered.

Eden was appalled to find herself tearing up. She quickly turned away and masked this unexpected bout of sentimentality by pretending to sneeze. "Oh, do excuse me."

Connor stared at her. "Are you all right?"

She nodded. "Just something in the air. It tickled my throat."

"If you say so." Connor did not take his eyes off her for the remainder of the meal.

The children continued to chatter, and only fell silent upon Connor's discussion of what tomorrow would bring. "I'm sure we'll have time for a morning hike and perhaps a walk down to the beach right after luncheon," he told them. "Guests will start arriving by early afternoon, so I may not be able to take you to the beach. I cannot promise that."

"Then who will take us?" Priscilla asked. "Eden, would you?"

"I..." Eden stared in dismay at Connor, then sighed and nodded. "I would love to take you. How about we make it a picnic on the beach? This way your father might be able to join us for the picnic, even if it is only for a little while before he must return to greet his guests."

That brought another round of cheers.

But the two boys quickly sobered, and the eldest asked, "What about the rest of the week? I can take care of myself, but Alex and Priscilla need supervision."

"I do not need super...super...what you said!" Alex retorted. "Priscilla is the baby."

"I am not a baby!" Priscilla promptly burst into tears.

Eden took her onto her lap and hugged her. "Want to know a secret?"

The girl nodded, but was still wailing in that fake little cry that children sometimes evoked when they were indignant, and shouldn't a parent notice? Eden easily spotted the fakery because she had often attempted it herself as a child when hoping to gain parental notice. But it had never worked because her parents cared more for hurting each other than loving her. "Your father is Duchess Evelyn's baby. Did you know that? And I am the baby in my family, too."

Priscilla looked up at her, no longer crying. "You are?"

"Yes," Eden said, although being an only child made her the youngest, eldest, and any other label one wished to put on a child. "So you should take it as a mantle of pride to be the youngest and adored by everyone."

"Do your parents like you best, Eden?" Priscilla asked.

No, her parents did not care one way or the other about her. She could slip off the face of the earth and they would not notice.

"Each child has their own special qualities, Priscilla," Connor said, coming to Eden's rescue when he noticed the perplexed expression on her face. He had been her neighbor for a long time and knew very well how little her parents thought of her.

"What's mine?" Priscilla asked, forgetting her tears for now.

"Oh, let's see. There are so many." Connor frowned and put a hand to his chin as he gave the matter serious contemplation. "But what is your best? I know, it is your kissable cheeks."

Priscilla was appeased. She scooted off Eden's lap and clambered back into her chair, then cast everyone a smug look before sticking her tongue out at her brothers. "What is Eden's best quality?" she asked.

"I know that one," Alex immediately replied. "Kissable lips!"

Connor coughed. "What?"

"That's what I heard Sir Nero tell Squire Hartley, and the squire agreed."

Eden felt her cheeks heat. "They said that about me?" *Those dirty old men.*

"I think Eden's best quality is that she is kind," Connor hastily added. "And fun to be around."

His eldest agreed. "You always have something interesting to say or show us whenever we go exploring with you, Eden."

"That is because I enjoy nature. If the weather holds, we can make a daily outing of it. I'll take you all hiking around the area while your father is off wooing the sweet young things your grandmother has invited for the week. In fact, I am making a journal of my findings, and this is something we can all do. Connor, would you be able to equip your children with binoculars, pencils, and writing pads? A picnic lunch, too." She grinned at him. "While you are engaging in your matrimonial endeavors, your children and I shall be discovering new birds and plants, and making a scientific record of them."

The children cheered.

Connor's eyes were alight, and he cast her a surprisingly soft smile. "Thank you, Eden. That sounds perfect. But are you certain?"

She nodded, now feeling quite remorseful for kicking his chair out from under him earlier. Spending time with his children was a nice idea. "Yes, I am looking forward to it."

"Then the motion passes," he said, casting her another soft smile. "All in favor, say 'aye.'"

"Aye!" his three children exclaimed with enthusiasm.

"Motion has passed." He turned to her, his expression noticeably wistful. "In truth, I wish I could ignore all my guests and join you for the entire day."

>>><<<

LATER THAT EVENING, once they had put the children to bed, she and Connor returned downstairs. He ordered her rig brought around. "I'll drive you home and then walk back here. It's a nice night, and I'll have enough of the fading light to see my way home."

The sun never set before ten o'clock in the evening at this time of year. Eden knew there would be little danger in his walking back to Lynton Grange, since their homes were not far from each other. There were several shortcuts available either through the woodlands or down along the beach. In the wintertime, she could see the Lynton Grange chimneys and the upper part of the magnificent manor house from her bedchamber. But the trees were lush in summer and obscured her view.

Once her rig was brought around, Connor assisted her in before climbing into the driver's seat beside her. He gave the reins a light flick to get her sprightly roan to a trot, and then waited until they were out of hearing distance of his staff before he turned to her. "Eden, did you mean it about taking my children on daily expeditions? I feel as though I have coerced you."

"No, it is my pleasure," she said with a firm shake of her head. "I wouldn't have offered otherwise. Truly, I am looking forward to spending time with them. I think it will be fun for all of us, and it will keep them out of your hair for much of each day. Assign a maid or two to assist them in getting ready in the morning and preparing them for bed in the evenings."

He nodded. "That is easily arranged."

"Being outdoors all day ought to wear them out. More important, it will keep them out of mischief. I shudder to think what dirty tricks they might play on your guests if they are stuck at home, bored and restless."

Connor threw his head back and laughed. "Well, that is one way to scare away the peahens and their matchmaking mothers. Honestly, the week you have planned for the children sounds wonderful. I'll join you as often as I can. It seems much more fun than what is in store for me."

"Ah, poor Connor. All those beautiful women tossing themselves at you," she said with mock sympathy. "How will you ever endure it?"

"Do not tease me, Eden. Being accosted at every turn is not fun at all. I am nothing more than a target for their own selfish advancement. Everyone lies to me in the hope of gaining my favor. If I crack a stupid joke, they will all declare it is hilarious and I am a wit for the ages. I could spout the most inane drivel imaginable and still be proclaimed brilliant. The only reason women toss themselves at me is because I am a duke. It is the title they love... That is all I am to them. That is all I ever was to Mary, too. The best that can be said is that she did her duty and gave me sons."

She regarded him thoughtfully, surprised that his late wife had not been more devoted to him, because he truly was a good man who valued his family life.

Not to mention he was handsome as sin. But it was his strength of character that made him worthy husband material.

That and courage. He had been away from home for long stretches at a time while fighting Napoleon on the Continent. Even while he was in England, his duties often kept him in London for sessions of Parliament. For years this had been his routine. War. Parliament. Home.

Mary and his children would only have him for a month or two before the cycle started again and he returned to the Continent.

"Ah, I am doing it again," he said, sounding apologetic. "I don't know why I find it so easy to talk to you." He turned to study her again as her horse trotted along the familiar path between their homes, requiring little prompting. "Perhaps it is because you actually listen and care. You would be amazed how few people ever do."

"In many ways, we are in a similar position. It is easy to understand and sympathize." The fact that he was handsome, wealthy, and titled added to his allure, but Eden could not see herself marrying someone for those qualities alone. She was an heiress and did not need to secure a man with deep pockets for her survival.

Her problem was similar because of her own wealth. How could she be sure a man would love her for herself? It was easier to assume they all wanted her dowry and simply trust none of them.

When she turned silent, Connor continued. "Will any of these peahens be any different from Mary? They'll pretend to like me in the hope of gaining an offer from me. The smarter, more calculating ones will also pretend to like my children because they'll understand that no one will get that marriage proposal out of me unless my children approve of them too. Connor, Alex, and Priscilla come as part of the package. I will not compromise on that."

"Nor should you. They are wonderful children."

"Even if they are scheming devils?" He laughed affectionately, but his mirth did not last very long, and he sobered. "How soon after the wedding will the fakery cease? Care to place bets on when my new wife will demand that my children be sent off to boarding school?"

Eden's heart lurched at the mere thought of poor Priscilla being sent away. No, the sweet child so desperately needed to remain at home and be surrounded with love. Eden's parents had sent her off to boarding school when she was quite young, and she still felt anguished just thinking about it.

Perhaps it would have been different if her parents loved her and had come to visit her, or welcomed her home with gushing displays of joy and love. But no, it had never happened. She was the product of benign neglect.

"I understand how one can feel so cynical about finding the right match," she said in commiseration. "I was an awkward girl of nineteen when I made my London debut, all skinny arms and legs at the time. But you would think I was as renowned a beauty as Helen of Troy by the way these bachelors flocked to me."

He frowned. "But Eden, you are beautiful."

"Maybe, back then. I had a line of gentlemen callers outside our townhouse on the days we were at home to visitors. Of course, my parents took turns chaperoning me because they could not stand to be in the same room together. They could not look at each other without breaking into a fight. But they called a truce and set up an attendance schedule in the hope that prospective suitors would not be scared off by the tavern brawl that was their marriage."

"I know you had many offers. Was there no one who caught your fancy?"

She shrugged. "Some were decent men, I'm sure. But back then, I did not know whom to trust. So I trusted no one."

He glanced at her as the rig continued along the familiar path between their homes. "Do you now regret refusing all offers?"

She nodded. "I am twenty-seven years old and my parents are still fighting. Is this how I am to face my old age? Once they are gone, as imperfect as they are, I'll be all alone and have nothing to show for my time on earth other than chairing a few ladies' societies and occasionally giving alms to those in need." She paused and let out a wistful sigh. "I think I may have made a wrong choice in discouraging every suitor."

Connor tugged on the reins to slow the horse in order to prolong their conversation. "You were young and scared... Not scared exactly, but inexperienced. And you had no one wise to counsel you. In that situation, you might have made the wrong decision in a spouse. That would have been disastrous."

"Yes, that is true. My husband would have had the power to burn through my funds, and I would have been helpless to stop him. I know you were not content in your marriage, but you did not face this same risk. Men do not give up control of their assets. Mary might not have been the wife you wished for, but you have three beautiful children to show for your union."

"Three heathens," he said with a laughing groan. "I do love them. They are my pride and joy, although I dare not let on just how much I love them or they will run roughshod over me."

"Oh, they already do. You are soft as pudding when it comes to them." She wished her parents would have shown her some affection...just once. Even the smallest recognition of pride in her accomplishments. A smile. A pat on the head. A kiss on the cheek. "But Connor, no. You must always tell them how you feel. It is a horrible thing to wonder whether anything you do will ever make a parent love you."

He reached for her hand. "Eden, I'm so sorry. Here I am spouting off about my children and not thinking at all about how you must be hurting."

She liked the solid warmth of his hand wrapped around hers. "Don't ever be sorry about talking about them. In truth, I love how good you are with them. It gives me hope that the world will not fall to pieces because some people are not the vain, indulgent, inconsiderate..." She groaned. "My parents should never have had children. But here I am, unfortunately."

He gave her hand a light squeeze. "Not unfortunate at all. I could not ask for a nicer neighbor. My children certainly adore you."

She nodded. "Because I am still much of a child, and they see this in me."

Connor cast her a wicked grin. "No, Eden. You are very much an attractive woman. But I'm sorry those arses, Sir Nero and Squire Hartley, spoke that way about you. You've done nothing to merit such disrespect. They ought to have kept their thoughts to themselves."

She shrugged. "It is better than not being thought of at all, I suppose. Hartley hides his leering better. Sir Nero is a nuisance, though. He is always trying to pinch my bottom."

Connor drew up on the reins. "He does what? Are you serious? I'll lay him low if he tries it again. Eden, just come to me and I'll—"

"You'll what? Protect me?" Warmth curled in her belly, for it did feel nice to know someone was looking out for her.

He muttered under his breath and cast her a remarkably determined look. "Yes, I will protect you. Is this not part of my duties as Duke of Lynton? There is a reason the town of Lynton is named after my family. All who live here are under my protection, most of all you."

"Why most of all me?"

He took her hand again. "Because if I do not look after you, then who will?"

Her expression turned pained. "Well, I have looked after myself for most of my life. I think I can manage."

"A moment ago, you were expressing your regret about not having married." He turned in his seat to fully face her. "Eden, why don't you stay with us for the week? I know my mother has invited you to all the entertainments she has planned."

"I politely declined."

"And yet you are now willing to care for my children? You were right to kick the chair out from under me. I had no right to ask such a thing of you. However, if you are serious about finding a husband, why not join us for the entire week? Do not worry about occupying the children. I'll put a rotation of maids and footmen to guard them, if I must. The little scamps will survive the week, and who cares if they get up to mischief?"

"I couldn't disappoint them, not now that we have started making plans for each day."

"They are resilient. Aren't all children? It is more important that you look out for yourself. I will not be the only eligible gentleman present. Join us, why don't you? I'll let you know which ones are bounders and which ones to trust."

She would have agreed without hesitation if not for the fact he would be searching for a wife as well. She did not think she could endure watching as the fresh young things flocked around him.

Was it wrong of her to be glad he was a Silver Duke and determined never to marry? No wife of his would ever allow their friendship and easy rapport to continue. Then who would she have to confide in? The wife would probably bar her from seeing the children, too.

Eden silently chided herself for being too softhearted. If she were more calculating, she would sabotage Duchess Evelyn's plans to see Connor married.

But she could never do such a heinous thing. She wanted him to find true love and be happy.

As for herself, did he really think anyone other than fortune hunters were going to flock around an aging spinster? No, she had lost her opportunity for love and marriage. "Connor, do not worry about me. I'll take your children, although I cannot promise it will be every day, since I am not going to take them out in the pouring rain. Nor am I going to stay over at Lynton Grange when my own home is only twenty minutes away."

"Eden, why are you being so stubborn about this?"

Because she was old and on the shelf. Did he not see what she was?

"There is only one thing that will change my opinion," she declared. "Well, probably two things."

He arched an eyebrow. "And what might those be?"

"First, my house burning down. But as you can see, Chestnut Hill is still standing proudly." She pointed into the distance and the rooftop of her stately home that was now in view.

He smiled. "And what is the second thing?"

"Both of my parents arriving here to plague me with their idiotic tantrums. But they are in London, as far as I know. I hope they stay there and leave me in peace while they continue on their quest to make each other miserable."

But as they turned up the drive to her charming manor house—this home where she found comfort and solace—she noticed two carriages in the courtyard. "Oh, no," she said in a broken whisper, and clutched Connor's arm. "How could they? No, it cannot be."

The front door was open.

She and Connor would have had to be deaf as posts not to hear her parents screaming at each other. Obviously, they had chosen to get out of London at the same time. Well, it was not a surprise, because the unpleasant odors and overbearing heat in that city chased everyone away. And now they were here and already fighting over who was to remain with her.

Her stomach tightened painfully. She did not want either parent staying with her. To have both was completely intolerable.

She heard the sound of glass shattering, soon followed by her father's bellowing.

Connor covered her hand with his. "Eden..."

More glass shattered.

"Dear heaven," he muttered. "Care to reconsider my offer?"

Eden swallowed hard, trying not to cry. "Will you wait for me while I pack a few of my gowns?"

"Yes," he said with aching tenderness before hopping down and then coming around to assist her off the rig.

His gaze on her was intense and fiery as he kept hold of her for a moment longer than necessary. "I'll always be here for you, Eden. Whatever you need. Whatever I can do for you."

She cast him a wan smile.

Did she dare believe his words?

CHAPTER THREE

C ONNOR'S CHILDREN CHEERED when they awoke the
following morning to learn Eden was to stay over for the
entire week. "Oh, Papa! How did you ever convince her?"
Priscilla was a frothy bubble of cheer as she scampered onto his
lap to give him a hug.

He ought to have corrected her behavior, for a proper young
lady should be taking her seat at the breakfast table instead of
leaping onto her father's lap and kissing him all over his face.

But it was just the five of them for now, so what did it matter?

In truth, he liked that breakfast was always a bit chaotic, and
adored the informality of having his children with him. Unfortunately, the upcoming week would turn his routine upside down.
The children would have to take their breakfast in the upstairs
classroom in order to keep them out of the way of London's *ton*
elite. He was not enamored of this change in routine, but neither
could he have his little heathens disrupting everyone's meals.

He wrapped his arms around his daughter and grinned over
her head at Eden, who was smiling back at him as she sipped her
tea. His mother had not come down yet, since Sir Nero's lecture
and the supper celebration afterward had gone well into the
evening. For this reason, he and Eden were the only adults
present at the breakfast table.

He rather liked looking over at Eden's smiling countenance.
Her hair looked amazing in the morning sunlight, a rich red that

resembled dark silk as the sun's rays struck it. She had on her spectacles, but there was no hiding the beauty of her hazel eyes that he swore had a sparkle to them.

Her gown was another of those unfashionable outfits designed for durability—and perhaps for camouflage when she was out in the wild, since it was a deep forest green that would blend perfectly with the surrounding shrubs and woodlands. Yesterday's gown had been a drab shade of gray that blended with the nearby coastal cliffs.

Priscilla scooted off his lap and then ran over to Eden and clambered onto her lap. Eden accepted her as though it was the most natural thing to do.

Yes, this was what he liked so much about Eden. She had a natural kindness along with a strong dose of patience, no doubt developed over years of coping with her combative parents. He liked that Connor and Alex were also politer than they would have ordinarily been were she not here. Indeed, they quite surprised him by how considerate they were toward her.

It was odd to see his heathen sons behaving like gentlemen around her.

"Eden, would you care for a scone?" Alex asked, rising to fetch one for himself from one of the silver salvers on the sideboard.

"I would love one. Thank you, Alex."

"My pleasure," he said, placing the scone on her plate.

Connor stifled a grin. Who was this stranger? Had he accidentally walked into the wrong house?

His eldest was also attentive to Eden. "What should we pack for our morning hike, Eden? I can help Priscilla and Alex gather their supplies. Priscilla, if your pouch is too heavy, I'll carry it for you."

"That is very considerate of you," Eden replied. "I have kept the list of supplies to a minimum. But we must pack some of these delicious scones along with lemonade to drink. We won't venture too far today because your father must return in time to greet his guests. So, a short morning hike, then a picnic on the beach. Maybe we'll remain on the beach and collect seashells if the weather is not too stifling. There ought to be a cooling breeze off the water."

"Can I take off my shoes and dip my feet in the water?" Priscilla asked.

Eden nodded. "Oh, yes. It is a requirement. One must dig one's toes in the warm sand and then dip them in the cool water. But you must remember always to wear your sunhat in order to protect your skin."

Priscilla pouted. "I don't like hats."

"You don't? But you look so pretty in them." Eden pretended to study Priscilla's features. "I have the perfect hat for you. It is identical to mine. We shall look like twins. I hope you don't mind, or else we—"

"I don't mind." Priscilla's eyes lit up and she cast Eden the biggest smile Connor had ever seen on his little girl. Now content, she took her own seat and finished her breakfast.

Connor was not sure what had just happened. All this fuss over a hat? And now his daughter was thrilled she was going to look like a miniature version of Eden? All she would lack were the spectacles.

Well, he wasn't going to question it. His children were happy.

They all ran upstairs to prepare for their hike, and met downstairs fifteen minutes later. Eden and the children were equipped with their small pouches containing pencils, pads, and binoculars, while he carried a larger pouch filled with food that Mrs. Ward, his longtime cook, had stuffed to the brim.

Well, his boys were at that growing stage and ate like rabid wolves. Within the hour, there would be nothing left in the sack but crumbs.

The sun shone on their faces as they stepped outdoors to begin their hike. Connor allowed Eden to take the lead, since she was the nature expert. Besides, his children were never going to listen to him. Why should they? He was merely their father and a powerful duke, while Eden was fun and filled them with excitement as they set out on their adventure.

He quietly studied his children, his heart filling with pleasure as he saw they were smiling from ear to ear.

And behaving! If Eden said to turn right, they turned right. If Eden said to stop, they stopped. If Eden put a finger to her mouth and whispered for them to be quiet while they studied a family of geese, they immediately quieted.

"Watch where you step," he reminded his children, because geese were notorious for leaving trails of droppings wherever they waddled.

"Hush, Papa!" they all urgently whispered.

"Eden told us to be quiet," Alex admonished him.

"Oh, they've flown away," Connor's namesake grumbled, frowning at him. "See what you've done?"

Priscilla, whose big eyes looked enormous under her hat, also berated him. "Papa, did you not hear Eden tell us to be quiet?"

Eden could not suppress her chuckle. "Do not be so hard on your father. He is new to these adventures. We'll encounter these geese again now that they have settled here for the summer. As your papa said, they leave their droppings everywhere. We'll have only to follow their trail to find them again. I am fairly certain we will come upon them here every morning."

"Unless Papa chases them away again," Priscilla muttered.

"Blessed saints," Connor said with a laughing groan, and held out his arms in surrender. "My apologies to all. What next, Eden?" In truth, it was refreshing to feel like the goat when everyone else who ever came around him acted as though he were a sun god.

"We'll head over to Finch's Meadow," Eden said. "The morning mist should have lifted by now, and the deer ought to be feeding. We might even spot rabbits or a fox on the open ground."

One would think they were about to discover dragons, faeries, and sea monsters. Connor looked on in amazement, for his children were enraptured.

Fragile streaks of mist lingered amid a copse of trees they had to walk through on their way to the meadow. Connor took Priscilla's hand as those wispy tendrils floated around them, and he was concerned his little sweetheart would be scared. It did not help that his boys were making ghostly sounds and telling poor Priscilla that trolls were going to jump out of the trees and eat her.

"No one is going to eat you," Connor assured his daughter, at the same time frowning at his boys. "I'll chase them all away."

"Thank you, Papa," Priscilla said, burrowing closer to him.

Eden smiled at him to acknowledge his protective gesture, and then paused a moment to point out several nests hidden amid the tree branches. "Does anyone know which birds built these?"

Connor remained silent as his children gleefully tossed out guesses.

"Dove!" Priscilla called out.

"Good guess. You are very close," Eden said.

"Cirl bunting!" Alex cried.

Eden shook her head. "Those are only common in South Devon."

"Ouzel!" said the younger Connor.

Eden shook her head again. "Close, but those birds will more likely be found in Dartmoor."

"Wren!" Priscilla tried again.

Connor listened as his children continued spouting names of birds, including several he had never heard of before. What amazed him was their knowing as much as they did. Had Eden been teaching them? It certainly hadn't been any of their wretched governesses.

Pied wagtail. Curlew. Snipe. Merlin. Bullfinch.

"Robin!" Alex finally blurted after several failed guesses.

Eden clapped her hands. "That is correct! Excellent, Alex." She then briefly commented on the pale blue eggs lying broken on the ground. "The wind might have blown them out of the robin's nest, or a goshawk might have swooped down and taken a few. Nature is beautiful, but it can also be vicious. That is why we must always be careful and use common sense wherever we are."

As they passed onto the roadway, Eden pointed to a riot of flowers growing amid crevices in the stone fences along the way. They stopped to observe the bumblebees and butterflies that came to rest upon those flowers. "There is an organization to nature," Eden said, pointing to the bees and butterflies. "Every time they alight on a flower, the pollen sticks to their feet and wings. This is how flower seedlings are spread. Same for trees. Take the mighty oak, for example. A squirrel might carry off its seeds—the acorns we often find on the ground—and bury them elsewhere."

"The bees are drinking from the flowers," Priscilla remarked.

Eden nodded. "They sip nectar from the flowers. The nectar sustains them, and they turn that nourishment into honey when they return to their hive."

"There's the beehive," Priscilla pointed out.

Connor's boys immediately picked up stones and were about to hurl them at the beehive dangling from one of the tall oak trees in Finch's Meadow when Connor growled a warning. "Alex! Connor! What in blazes do you think you are doing?"

Eden calmly took the stones out of their hands. "The hive is their home and their source of life. How would you feel if someone destroyed your home and chased you down to hurt you?"

"I would feel sad," Priscilla said, taking hold of Connor's hand once again. "It would be terrible, wouldn't it, Papa? We shouldn't hurt the baby bees."

"Yes, love. I think this is what Eden is trying to teach us, that all living things have a place in nature. We are all much alike. A papa deer will look after his children just as I always look after you."

"But he is with them all the time," Alex remarked, "and you are not."

That wounded Connor. "I try to be, Alex. But the Lynton holdings are vast, and I need to travel oftentimes to make certain all is running smoothly. Also, I have parliamentary duties that I cannot shirk. I know we live far from London. But as you get older, I will be able to take you with me and show you the sights."

"Why not now, Papa?" Priscilla asked, her voice sweet and plaintive.

He knelt to her level. "Because you are still too young to attend the balls, soirees, and other entertainments offered."

"Eden didn't like them," his eldest remarked when Priscilla began to pout. "So I don't think we are missing out on much, Priscilla."

"Why didn't you like London?" Alex asked her.

She shook her head. "It is a lovely city, and there is plenty to see and do there. But it was the endless round of parties and being put on display that I did not like very much."

"Like the house party we are about to have?" Priscilla stared up at her.

Eden nodded. "A house party can be just as cutthroat as any London ball. I am not very good at dancing. And I am not a good flirt. Most young ladies and bachelors are there because they want to find someone to marry, so everyone is always putting on a show."

"Like a peacock showing his tail feathers to attract a female?" young Connor asked.

Eden nodded again. "Yes, exactly that."

"Don't you want to marry?" Priscilla asked.

The questions seemed to be getting quite personal, but Eden did not appear to mind that Connor's children were interrogating her. She took their questions quite seriously and pursed her lips as she gave each one thought before responding. "Back then, I did not want to find a husband for myself."

"What about now?" Alex asked.

She shrugged. "I don't know. It feels like a great effort to find the right gentleman now. I am very independent and have grown used to having things the way I like them. The man would have to be someone very special for me not to mind all I would have to sacrifice when entering into our marriage. I would only ever marry for love. He would have to love me, too."

"My papa could love you. And we would love you, too," Priscilla said earnestly.

Eden hugged her. "As I love you. I have always said I have the best neighbors. But I think your father's choice is his own to make. I'm sure that if he chooses to take a wife, she will be someone quite special whom you are all going to adore."

Priscilla appeared determined to pursue her questions, but a stag chose just that moment to leap into the meadow and distracted her. Then several does came to forage among the underbrush, and the conversation was forgotten as the children turned their attention to the family of deer.

Eden took out her notebook and pencil in order to sketch the stag. The children all had their binoculars out and were scouting the meadow scrub and brambles for all the animals they could find. Connor helped them by taking on the role of note keeper, making a list of all the hares, deer, foxes, chipmunks, and birds they spotted.

His heart melted over their innocent excitement. He loved being a part of this moment.

Eden glanced over and smiled at him.

This was all because of her.

He smiled back, wishing there was some way to properly thank her for bringing this about. She had done it effortlessly. And wisely, too. How did she know his children would enjoy this adventure so much? Perhaps she was taking them on all the things she wished she had done as a child with her father.

Gad, what rotten parents she had.

He returned his attention to his children once the deer ran back into the copse to find shade as the sun climbed in the sky. The meadow was in full sun now, for the last of the mist had burned off even from the little stream that ran through it.

"All right, time to head to the beach," Eden announced.

Everyone packed up their binoculars and other supplies and started off toward the beach. This time, Priscilla held on to Eden's hand as they marched at the head of their family queue.

Connor watched them as he took up a position at the rear of their line, smiling as a gust of wind caught Eden and Priscilla's identical straw hats. They each stuck a hand to their head to keep the floppy hats from flying off, even though the hats had ribbon ties on them to keep them secure. But the combination of flimsy ribbons and broad brims were no match for the force of that gust.

Eden immediately helped to right Priscilla's hat, and then fixed her own. The two held hands again as they proceeded on their way.

When had Mary ever done this with Priscilla? He could not recall a single time his wife had ever gone exploring with their children. His mother, even in her vaunted position as dowager duchess, might have done it were she a little younger. But she saved most of her running around for shopping excursions along Lynton's high street.

When the beach came into view, he and his boys ran ahead. The day had grown hot and they needed to cool off. Of course, they could not shed all their clothes, so they merely dumped their pouches, took off their hats, boots, and jackets, and then raced into the water, diving in wearing their shirts and trousers.

His housekeeper, Mrs. Dayton, was going to box his ears. But surely she could get salt water out of their clothes with a thorough washing. Of course, he would have to sneak back into the house through the servants' entrance, for his mother would also box his ears if he showed up sopping wet to greet their guests. But there was still time before the first of them arrived, wasn't there?

He glanced over to the shore and saw Eden and Priscilla gather their discarded garments and place them in an orderly pile near the shaded beach stairs. Eden then helped Priscilla off with her half boots and afterward took off her own. They did not jump in, but frolicked at the edge of the water, raising their skirts as the waves broke at their feet.

Some waves came in stronger than others.

Connor tried not to gape as Eden raised her skirt to her thighs when a particularly strong swell surprised her and Priscilla. They shrieked with glee and darted back onto the sand, but not before he had caught a glimpse of Eden's legs.

Was that his heart exploding in his chest?

He had seen feminine legs before. But Eden's were surprisingly fine.

"Papa, look out!" his boys cried as a wave crashed atop him and carried him back to shore. The waves were not all that strong, but he had been too busy ogling Eden to pay attention, and it had knocked him over.

Eden and Priscilla hurried to his side as he washed up like a piece of driftwood upon the sand. "Are you all right?" Eden asked, kneeling beside him.

He sat up, laughing and sputtering as he brushed his hair off his face and raked it back with his fingers. His shirt was now pasted to his chest, but there was nothing to be done about that. Nor could he take it off without shocking Eden. That they were even at the beach together would be considered scandalous by London *ton* rules. Fortunately, the rules were not nearly so strict out here. "Yes, fine. The wave caught me while I wasn't looking."

"Papa, you have to pay attention or you might have drowned," Priscilla admonished him.

He tried not to laugh as the little sprite wagged her finger at him. "No, love. I'm too big and strong to drown. But let this be a lesson to you and your brothers," he said as the boys scampered out of the water to join them. "The forces of nature are powerful, especially water. Always be cautious, and never go swimming immediately after a storm, even if the sun is shining and the water appears calm. There will often be dangerous currents that can pull you under. Not even I am strong enough to swim out of those."

"You went down like a skittle," Alex remarked, mimicking the motion of a ball rolling toward a pin and knocking it into oblivion. "Pow! It crushed you."

"Thank you for that observation," Connor said dryly.

Now thoroughly drenched and having taken sea water up his nostrils, he decided it was time for all of them to move into the shade of the beach stairs. So they did. The children looked on while he set out the tablecloth and then peered into the pouch that Eden had opened. "Fruit, cheese, bread, and scones," he called out as he rustled through the contents. "Priscilla and Eden, you choose first."

Quite predictably, his boys then pounced on the remainder, grabbing food by the fistfuls and devouring it like the ravenous little beasts they were. "Gad, were you never taught manners?" Connor laughingly remarked, knowing it had been his duty to raise his boys properly.

They ate like savages, but all in all, he liked the way they were turning out. Should boys not be allowed out in the wild on occasion? That they had behaved like gentlemen around Eden for most of the morning proved they were coming along just fine as young men.

Eden handed one of her scones to him because his boys had not considered that he might want something to eat. They probably assumed he, as lead wolf of their pack, would fall upon the food just as they had done, and grab whatever he wanted for himself.

Eden had tucked her spectacles in her pocket, no doubt taking them off so they would not get damaged by the sun, water, and wayward elbows because they were all seated so closely together.

He tried not to get caught staring, but he had a hard time taking his gaze off her.

Eden was beautiful.

Why did she always hide behind those owlish spectacles? No wonder young men had lined up outside her townhouse during her debut London Season. Her mother probably hid those spectacles from her so she could not wear them while in company.

Without them, Eden could not hide the beauty of her face.

"Here, Papa. You can have my cheese," Priscilla said, sticking some revolting clumps of something soft in his hand.

"Thank you." She had given the cheese to him upon deciding she did not like it. But who was he to complain about his little sweetheart? Those clumps did not look appetizing at all. He would probably end up with a dose of food poisoning if he ate it.

He let the clumps fall in the sand as soon as Priscilla turned her head away, and quietly buried them deep, where they might be lost for all time or washed away in a winter storm.

Eden cast him a conspiratorial grin when she realized what he had done. He winked at her and grinned back. The children now moved on to build a sandcastle.

When had he spent a gentler, more enjoyable day?

But it quickly came to an end as Brewster called down to him from the top of the beach steps. "Your Grace, I have been sent to fetch you. The first guests have arrived."

Connor felt a bitter disappointment. He sighed as he rose to gather his boots and garments. "Eden, thank you for a lovely outing. I cannot recall ever having a more pleasant morning. Alas, duty now calls."

She nodded. "I know. We enjoyed having you with us. I'm sure Duchess Evelyn is eager to have you join her in greeting your guests."

"Too eager," he grumbled. "Bordering on the obsessive."

"Poor you," she teased.

"Make sure you join us for tea this afternoon. In fact, come back with me now, if you like. The children had a perfect adventure and should be fairly restrained if we all walk back together now."

"No, they are having too much fun to be pulled away. They still have a sandcastle to build and seashells to collect. We'll return in an hour or two. I'll be there for teatime."

"All right, if you say so." He glanced down at himself, soaked to the skin and probably looking quite a disheveled fright after being shoved down by that wave. "What do you think, Eden?" he asked, holding out his arms. "Will those peahens flutter around me?"

She rolled her eyes and tossed a seashell at him. "Go! And stop bragging about your prowess."

He reached over and tweaked her nose. "It is all a complete waste of time. I am not going to marry again."

But as he spoke the words, an odd feeling came over him.

He could not credit it and refused to credit it because... No, it was too far-fetched.

Eden?

CHAPTER FOUR

E DEN STARED UP at Connor, her nose still twitching because he had just given it a playful tweak. He cast her a smile that melted her heart, leaned temptingly close, and asked whether she thought the London diamonds would flutter over him.

What conceit! He knew they all would.

Even she could not stop gawking at him while his shirt was pasted to his broad chest and she could make out every muscle and sinew of his magnificent body. His shirt, that gloriously wet shirt, had become practically transparent, and she saw every ripple along the flat planes of his stomach and noted every flex of his powerful arms.

Oh, my.

His trousers were made of sturdier material, so there was no transparency there—and thank goodness, for that would have been quite the scandal. But the dark fabric clung to his long, well-shaped legs. The legs of a warrior, hard and muscled.

Good grief.

He was called a Silver Duke for a reason. These men were unattainable gods.

"Yes, Connor. Those peahens will flutter around you, as you well know. Now go on before I toss a hunk of moldy cheese at you."

He laughed, gave her a light kiss on the cheek, and then took himself off.

Her own heart did not merely flutter but took flying leaps the moment his warm lips pressed softly against her cheek.

This was not good.

She did not want to have feelings for Connor beyond the longstanding friendship between them. They had developed a pleasant and easy rapport over the years. She adored his mother and his children.

Having feelings for him would complicate everything.

And now her parents had arrived to add to the complications.

She would have found an excuse to leave the party and return home had they not shown up, but their presence had chased her out of her own house. This was a nightmare for her. She could not abide their constant battles. All their refined airs and social graces were forgotten whenever they faced each other. Why did they always have to fight in front of her?

Rather than endure them, she had chosen to spend the week at Connor's home. But how would this be any easier for her? She could not deny that her feelings toward him had changed recently. Their friendship was evolving in a new and dangerous direction, as far as she was concerned.

Could she stop herself from falling in love with him?

Sighing, she watched him disappear up the row of stairs and follow Brewster back to the house. Once he was out of sight, she returned her attention to his children. For now, they were playing nicely together while building their sandcastle.

Eden stowed their food in the pouch—not that anything remained other than a morsel barely enough to feed a mouse—and then joined them in their project.

"What did you do with your spectacles?" young Connor asked when he realized she had taken them off.

"I tucked them away to keep them safe. The metal frame heated under the sun and became too uncomfortable on my nose."

He cast her an approving stare that was far too grown-up for his young years. "You look nice without them."

Alex and Priscilla agreed.

"Well, I need them to see in the distance or else everything looks a blur," Eden said, trying to sound sensible when she was still reeling from the casual kiss their father had planted on her cheek. Had he thought twice about the gesture? She doubted he was even aware he had done it.

The remainder of the hour passed enjoyably as they built their castle quite high until it was as tall as Priscilla. When the tide began to roll in and wash away their castle, they decided to go in search of seashells. They found several beautiful ones that Eden rinsed clean of sand and bugs, and then placed in her pouch.

They had enjoyed a good dose of the outdoors by the time they returned to Lynton Grange. It was about three o'clock in the afternoon and Priscilla was noticeably tired. The boys were still full of vigor, but Eden thought they had run around enough to keep them suitably subdued for the rest of the day. She hoped they would behave like polite boys instead of zoo animals when introduced to Connor's guests.

"We had better go in through the back way," Eden said, for none of them were presentable. Their clothes had dried out but were full of sand that they could not completely shake off, no matter how hard they tried. The children all had dark hair like their father, but their glorious curls were wild and unbrushed.

His had looked magnificent even after that wave knocked him over. He did no more than rake his fingers through it to look like a dark-haired Adonis once again.

She did not want to think about her own hair, that unkempt red mass atop her head she could hardly keep in order on the best of days. "Yes, we must go in through the back," she insisted. "We don't want to scare off your father's guests."

"Yes, we do," the three of them blurted at once.

Eden sighed.

Mrs. Ward and her scullery girls were hard at work preparing for afternoon tea and the supper feast that was to take place tonight. "Do not let us disturb you," Eden said as they made their way through the bustle of activity.

"Ye're never a bother, Lady Eden," the kindly cook replied, her cheeks pink and perspiring from the heat of the hearth fire. "Look at all of ye. Ye're nothing but a bunch of heathens," she teased. "I'll have milk and cakes brought up to the classroom for ye, children."

At Eden's urging, they politely thanked her.

Priscilla gave Mrs. Ward a wide-eyed stare. "My papa is going to choose a new mama for us. That's what Grandmama says."

The woman wiped a beefy hand across her forehead and nodded. "I'm sure he'll make his own decision, and when he does, it will be a good one. No one's going to push yer father into doing something he is not ready to do. Run upstairs, love. Put on a pretty frock because he might call ye down to meet his guests. Ye want to make a good impression, don't ye?"

"No," Priscilla said with brutal honesty. "We want them all to go away. We like things just as they are."

The boys agreed.

Mrs. Ward cast Eden a helpless look.

Eden merely shrugged in response, and then turned to address the children. "You mustn't rush to judgment. Your father would be most disappointed if you did not give any of his guests a chance. You might surprise yourselves and find a lovely lady among his company. Keep an open mind. You want to see your father happy, don't you?"

The three of them reluctantly nodded.

"But he already is happy," Alex insisted. "He has us."

"And you," Priscilla added. "He always smiles when he sees you."

Eden bustled them upstairs, since this was no conversation to be having in front of the duke's household staff.

Two of the younger maids, Sarah and Millie, joined her as she marched them up to their rooms. "His Grace said we were to take care of his children for the rest of the day," Sarah, the senior of the two, said. "Lady Eden, he would like you to join him in his study once you have changed out of your hiking clothes."

"All right." Eden made certain the boys were going to wash the salt water off themselves, then headed to her guest chamber.

Connor had given her the most beautiful guest room of all, and refused to listen to her protests when she suggested it was too fine for her. He had insisted on his housekeeper settling her in there last night. "Pay no attention to Lady Eden," he had told the ever-efficient Mrs. Dayton. "She is to have the best of everything, whether she wants it or not."

"Beast," she had laughingly retorted.

But his humor had won the day, and she stopped griping. After all, it was a charming room decorated in light floral colors and had a view of the garden and the ocean beyond with its constant roil of blue, green, and gray waters. The varying shades depended on the weather. It was a mix of deepest azure and moss green today, and streaks of white foam caps sat atop the waves. She also had a private balcony.

What was not to like?

He ought to have given the room to one of his grander guests, perhaps the Earl and Countess of Lothmere, who had been invited along with their daughter of marriageable age. They also had a son expected to be in attendance, a man of almost thirty years who was not yet married.

Eden had seen Duchess Evelyn's guest list before the invitations had gone out and knew there were several eligible bachelors among them.

To her surprise, another of the household maids was waiting for her when she walked into her room. She recognized Delia, who was Duchess Evelyn's own lady's maid. "I ordered a bath for you," the sweet-looking girl said, pointing to the tub positioned by the hearth. Light wisps of steam curled up from the water. "I was afraid it would grow cold by the time you returned. But the timing is perfect. It was just brought up."

Eden closed the door and then turned to smile at the girl. "Thank you, Delia." She knew just about everyone who worked at Lynton Grange because many of them were related to her own staff at Chestnut Hill. She had even grown up with many of them, and they all attended church regularly at St. Matthew's in Lynton. "I had better decide on what to wear."

Delia cleared her throat. "Lady Eden, I took the liberty of sending down your green silk tea gown to freshen. The one with the under-layer of cream silk overlaid in dark green tulle, and a band of gold silk that belts just under the bodice. Duchess Evelyn suggested it. She thought it would be perfect for the occasion."

Eden grinned as she removed her garments and slid into the warm water. She watched as Delia poured scented oils into the bath. "Duchess Evelyn's idea too?"

Delia smiled as she nodded. "Her Grace was quite specific in her instructions to me."

Well, why not allow herself to be pampered? Eden washed her hair, since it had gotten quite windblown and knotted down by the beach, not to mention the grains of sand that had settled in it and now had her scratching her scalp. She washed it twice and rinsed it three times just to be thorough. The curls would dry quickly in this heat. At least, she hoped they would, because she had very little time before the tea bell chimed to summon them all downstairs.

Connor had requested that she meet him in his study as soon as she was ready. She did not know what he meant to say to her. Perhaps he wanted to hear more about his children, or ask for her advice on the young ladies present at the house party.

No, why would he need her opinion on that? He was a grown man and experienced enough to fend for himself.

As for her, she did not know how this week would turn out. She dreaded most of it, but did look forward to seeing more of him throughout the house party. Hopefully, they would have many opportunities to talk to each other. His children would certainly give them lots to discuss.

She stepped out of the tub, dried herself off, and donned her robe. She then sat on her small, private balcony to soak in the warmth of the sun and allow the light breeze to dry her hair while she brushed it.

She was lost in her reverie, and only came out of it when a pebble suddenly dropped at her feet. A moment later, another pebble landed in front of her. "What the…?"

She peered over the balcony railing to see where they had come from, squinting because she had not bothered to don her spectacles.

Someone waved to her. She recognized the blurred outline of Connor standing with his hands on his hips and his legs astride. "Why did you toss those stones at me?" she called down to him. Even blurry, this man was handsome.

"It was just a few small pebbles, and you would not look over when I tried to gain your attention. You appeared lost in dreams. Where are your spectacles? Well, leave them off. You look great. I did not realize your hair was so golden red. It's nice, Eden. What's taking you so long to get ready?"

She pointed to the fiery tumble he had just commented on. "I had to wash the sand and grit out of my hair."

He grinned. "Looks spectacular. Too bad it isn't fashionable to leave it down."

"I wish I could, but it would be considered quite brazen and scandalous. I'll simply braid it tomorrow when I take the children on their next nature walk. One long braid down my back," she said, not that it mattered or that he really cared.

He moved closer to stand immediately under her window. There was a rose trestle leading up to her small balcony. For a moment, she thought he might climb up it. No, that would be too much like a scene out of *Romeo and Juliet*. Perhaps romantic. Certainly too scandalous and brazen. Besides, she had no desire to end up like that love-crossed pair. "Where do you think to take them tomorrow?" he asked.

"The nesting grounds. I think the children will enjoy learning about all the birds in our area. We'll probably run across a few wild ponies, too."

"Sounds great. Mind if I come along?"

She pursed her lips. "No, but your mother is going to be livid if you shirk your duty to your guests."

He shrugged. "All right. We'll figure it out later. Maybe I'll organize a hike for all of us. Those guests who do not wish to walk can ride in a wagon."

"I don't think that is a very good idea."

"Why not?"

She sighed. "We'll discuss it when I come downstairs."

"Then hurry up. I'll be in my study waiting for you."

It did not take her long to dress. Delia styled her damp hair so that it would softly frame her face as the curls dried.

Connor was pacing in front of his desk when she hurried in.

"I peeked in the parlor and was surprised to find it empty," she remarked, wondering where all his guests had gone. She had expected many of them to be seated in the parlor or in here having drinks with Connor. But it seemed everyone was still upstairs preparing for the tea that would be served in about half an hour.

He strode forward to greet her. "Gad, you smell nice."

"That is your mother's doing," she said with a soft laugh. "I was given fragrant oils for my bath."

He laughed too. "I'll have to thank her for it. What is that scent? Apple? Vanilla? A hint of jasmine? No matter—it smells great on your skin. Your hair looks nice, too."

She put a hand to it and gently patted it. "Also your mother's doing."

"I heartily approve."

"What? You don't like the pencils usually poking out from my curls?"

His affectionate grin had the butterflies in her stomach aflutter. "Those pencils are a hazard. One is likely to get stabbed in the eye if one gets too close to you. Who did your hair?"

"Your mother's maid, Delia. She is a wonder at styling hair."

He had not stopped grinning with approval. "Where are your

spectacles?"

She sighed. "Delia suggested I leave them atop my bureau."

He nodded. "Smart girl. I ought to give her a raise in wages."

"Honestly, Connor," she said with a roll of her eyes. "Do I always look so awful that you should make such a fuss over me now?"

He reached out and tucked a curl behind her ear. "No, you always look lovely. In a cute, owlish way. But you look particularly breathtaking just now. A true *ton* diamond. In truth, better than any *ton* diamond I've ever met, and I've met more than my share. You are going to make all the young ladies jealous when they meet you. You really look stunning, Eden. I mean it."

She blushed. "Why did you order me down here so urgently?"

"Just wanted a moment to catch up about my children and tomorrow's plans. They had so much fun with you today. Would it be so awful if I arranged for all of us to join you on your morning hike tomorrow?"

"Yes, it would," she said with a light frown. "The entire point of having me here is so that I can keep the children out of your way while you charm the young ladies. Your children are little saboteurs and will not give you the chance to flirt with anyone. So, let us stick to the original plan."

He did not appear happy with her suggestion. "All right. I'll take the men out for a morning ride, but I'll stay behind and walk with you and the children if we happen to cross paths."

She folded her arms over her chest to indicate her exasperation with him. She did not mind that he was stubbornly objecting to marriage because... Well, it did not bear consideration. But she had no desire to be surrounded by baby faces and made to feel like an old lady. "No. Do you or do you not wish to meet these young ladies?"

"I do *not*. Have I not been clear about this all along?" He mimicked her stance, crossing his arms over his massive chest. "This is my mother's foolish idea, not mine."

Eden sighed again. "You are the duke. You are their host. Just be cordial. You do not have to court any of them. But do not insult them after they have traveled all the way here. Attend to your duties and leave the children to me."

"Maybe," he grumbled. "I'm not sure I am happy with this arrangement."

She arched an eyebrow. "Are you or are you not the one who dreamed up this plan in the first place?"

"If I recall, you did not much like it. You knocked me out of my chair and called me an idiot."

"I do not recall accusing you of being an idiot."

"You were thinking it, not that I blame you. But my point is, this is an opportunity for *you* to meet someone special. Seriously, Eden. You look beautiful. Do not pass up the chance to meet a young man who could be a potential husband for you. Lothmere's heir is here. So is the Marquess of Rathburne and his eldest son, Damien. Rathburne has given him the courtesy title of Earl of Hawley."

"And you think the sons of Lothmere and Rathburne are interested in a spinster of seven and twenty years?"

"Is this how old you are?"

"Yes. Do you not recall pulling my powdered bottom out of your fishpond when I was a plump two-year-old and you were a ruggedly handsome lad of fifteen?"

"I'll never forget it," he said with a soft laugh, arching an eyebrow as he subtly inspected her. "In fact, you still have a lovely, plump bottom. No wonder Sir Nero is always trying to pinch it."

"Connor!"

"Truce!" He laughed and spread his arms in a sign of surrender. "My point is that you don't look above twenty."

"Thank you, but why are we speaking of me? Lothmere and Rathburne's daughters are here, too."

"I've met them," he muttered, not sounding excited at the prospect of spending time with either of them. "As for their brothers, they are both men of good family and of an age to marry."

She pursed her lips, something she did out of habit when she was not happy or wanted to be stubborn about a thing. "You complain of your mother being meddlesome, but how are you any better? I have no intention of getting married, so put aside whatever plots you are concocting in your head."

"Now you are just being difficult, Eden. Did we not speak of this very thing only yesterday? Your regret in rejecting all suitors. Well, here's your chance to try again. Do not retreat into your protective shell."

"And what about you? Aren't you doing the same thing?"

He shook his head. "Not at all. Our circumstances are quite different. I have been married already…unhappily, as you now know. But I have my children, who are the light of my life. I am not going to be forced into an unwanted arrangement with a peahen half my age because everyone else believes I am pathetic and lonely."

Eden felt those words like a physical blow. "Is that what you think of me? Pathetic and lonely?"

He seemed surprised by the notion. "Not at all. Weren't those the very words you used when we spoke yesterday? You are beautiful, Eden. No one will ever mistake you for pathetic. I was using it to describe me. Is this not how those young peahens will view me?"

"You are daft, Connor. You have the Silver Duke aura. It is quite annoying how the air around you seems to shimmer silver in your presence. Those peahens will fall at your feet in raptures."

He shrugged. "I hope not. I'll be spending the week avoiding those sweet young things as much as possible and steering them toward the other bachelors in attendance. I'll do it subtly, of course."

"Your mother will box your ears when she realizes what you are doing."

"Only if she finds out. You're not going to tell her, are you?"

"Not going to tell me what?" his mother asked, blowing into the room at that untimely moment in a swirl of magenta silk and a hideous lace cap perched stylishly atop her white-haired head. "Why should I box your ears?"

Eden smiled and kissed her cheek because his mother was daring and slightly outrageous, and Eden adored her. "Your timing is perfect, Evelyn."

His mother kissed her back. "It always is. I'm so glad you've changed your mind and decided to join us for the week, my dear. Not that you really had a choice. I hear your parents are at Chestnut Hill and have forced you to flee your own home. Well, it is a happy circumstance that you are with us now, whatever the reason. And don't you look lovely?"

Eden laughed. "Are you surprised about my appearance? You brought this about. Choosing my gown. Sending Delia in to style my hair."

"Adding fragrant oils to Eden's bath," Connor chimed in. "The men are going to be sniffing her all night long."

"Ugh!" Eden said. "I don't want their noses anywhere near me."

But his mother's eyes brightened. "Ah, you noticed her transformation?"

He grinned. "Hard to overlook."

Duchess Evelyn's eyes were now trained intently on her son. "So, what is it you plan to do that will have me boxing your ears?"

He glanced at Eden as he raked a hand through his gorgeous mane of hair, and then turned back to face the daunting dowager. "You are my mother and I love you dearly and sincerely, but this does not give you dominion over me. I am not in agreement with your scheme to marry me off. It is a futile endeavor. But now that you have brought these peahens and their families here this week, I am going to make the best of it."

"What do you mean?" his mother asked.

"We are not going on the marriage hunt for me, but for Eden. There are eligible bachelors in attendance. Present them to her. Encourage them to get to know her."

Eden frowned at him. "Traitor."

His mother smiled. "I heartily approve! It is time Eden chose a husband for herself."

"I think it is a terrible idea. Evelyn, you needn't be deliriously pleased about this disaster of a suggestion." Eden continued to frown at Connor.

The dowager duchess cast her an affectionate smile. "Nonsense—it is a grand idea. You are such a lovely thing, Eden. We all want to see you find the happiness you deserve. Isn't it true, Connor? Don't you wish her every happiness possible?"

"Yes, I do. With all my heart. I am glad we are allied in this." Connor tossed Eden a triumphant smirk.

"It is a cheap trick to deflect attention from himself and dump all attention on me, Evelyn Do not allow him to do this. We must not lose sight of the reason these peahens are here."

"We mustn't refer to them as peahens, Eden. Though I will admit some of these girls are lacking in maturity."

"And brains," Connor commented wryly.

His mother scowled at him again. "Ignore my loutish son, Eden. Do not judge these young ladies too harshly or be swayed by his rude comments. I'm sure several of them are quite accomplished."

Connor groaned. "I hate that word. *Accomplished*—defined as something none of these young ladies are, having done nothing during their short, overly protected and pampered lives."

"There may be a bluestocking or two among them," Duchess Evelyn insisted, ignoring her son's comment. "Although I doubt any are as smart as you are, Eden. But I have the perfect resolution to this dilemma. Connor insists that I put my efforts into matching you. And you insist that I keep my efforts on matching him."

"And?" Connor prompted her.

"I shall make it my goal to see *both* of you happily matched."

"What?" Eden said in dismay.

"No," Connor said between clenched teeth.

"Oh, yes. The game is on. I shall see the two of you wed before the end of the summer. Is it not fortuitous that both your parents are here to partake of the happy event? Well, they are a bit of a nuisance, aren't they? Still, they are your parents, and you should want them at your wedding." Having issued the challenge, Evelyn walked out of Connor's study and shouted insistently for Brewster. "Ah, yes. Good man. Fetch me my betting book. My friends and I shall be placing wagers."

"On what shall you be wagering, Your Grace? If I may be so bold as to ask?"

"Indeed, you may. It is to be an entire list of bets. First and foremost, whether my son shall marry. Second, whom he shall choose to marry. Third, whether Lady Eden shall marry. Fourth, whom she shall marry. Fifth…"

She peered into the study to check whether either of them were listening to this conversation. Both were.

"Come along, Brewster. The fifth bet is not for their delicate ears." She then muttered something about setting up the tea service outdoors, since there was a lovely breeze off the water and the terrace was in shade.

This left Eden facing Connor. "This is your fault."

He had his arms crossed over his chest again. "Don't you want to be married?"

"Not to some bachelor Evelyn coerces into courting me. Oh, I'm certain several of them will find my wealth irresistibly attractive."

"Well, we are both stuck now. Won't be too bad if we put our heads together and come up with a plan to counter her schemes," he assured her.

She regarded him thoughtfully. "What kind of plan do you have in mind?"

"The simplest one is to set my children loose on our guests if things become too oppressive. Mayhem is quite their specialty."

Eden laughed. "Oh, dear heaven. You are wicked, and your

children are already plotting this very thing. Don't you dare encourage them."

"All right, but don't you dare hide behind them."

"I am taking them to view birds and perhaps ponies, that is all," she said with a dismissive wave of her hand, and strode out to join the other guests now gathered in the parlor. The windows had been opened wide to allow in a summer breeze, and many had already drifted over to the terrace where the teapots and cakes were being laid out.

Connor followed close behind her, taking a moment to lean forward and whisper in her ear, "Don't hide your loveliness, Eden. Promise me."

She frowned at him and stepped away as several young ladies charged toward him, Lothmere's daughter in the lead. The girl was quite pretty and did not waste a moment before flirting with Connor. Eden expected he would quickly be won over by her, since she was all smiles and giggles, and quite sparkly.

Her brother was handsome, Eden had to admit. Connor's mother led him straight to her. They reached her side before she was able to make her escape.

Eden knew Lothmere's daughter was called Persephone, but she had yet to learn anything about the brother. "Trajan," he said, introducing himself as the dowager duchess proudly looked on, "better known as Viscount Aubrey."

"That is a most interesting name," Eden said, curious to learn how both Lothmere children got their names.

He cast her a warm smile. "Awful, isn't it? Persephone is not thrilled with hers, either. My parents are enamored of ancient history and mythology. Persephone was the love of the underworld god, Hades. Trajan was one of the most successful Roman emperors, known for his long reign, most of which was peaceful. It was between that or Zeus for me. Fortunately, my father happened to have a horse named Zeus at the time and decided it would be too confusing to have both son and horse given the same name."

Eden could not help but laugh heartily. "Do forgive me. I like your name very much. I have no idea how mine came up with Eden. It is also a little bit out of the ordinary."

"As are you." The viscount eyed her with unmasked interest.

Oh, good grief.

Were the oozing compliments to start already? Was he eyeing her for marriage or merely speculating on his chances of a dalliance? Well, Evelyn would not have brought him forward unless she thought he was honorable.

He certainly was handsome. Tall and blond. Green eyes that regarded her warmly, but she sensed they would turn quite frosty if he were ever crossed. Probably about the same age as herself.

She was determined to remain polite but maintain a cool distance until she got to know him better. He seemed nice enough, but weren't all these bachelors on the hunt for a fortune polite and charming at first glance?

"It seems I have not impressed you," he said, remaining by her side as more guests arrived. Most huddled around Connor, but Viscount Aubrey seemed to have placed a claim on her, his mere presence keeping other gentlemen from approaching—including the Marquess of Rathburne's son, Damien, who was circling her like a buzzard.

The viscount, who apparently had no intention of ceding her to his rival, prepared a plate of sweets for her, and then took the seat beside hers. "Do you mind terribly that I am dominating your attention?" The footmen began to come around to pour tea into their cups. "Tell me truly, Lady Eden."

She was about to take a sip of her freshly poured tea, but set it aside. "No—whether it is you or Lord Rathburne's son flirting with me, it is all the same to me."

"Ouch. I do believe I was just handed a scathing set-down."

"Forgive me if I come across too harshly. It is just that I like to get to know people better before I allow them close."

He arched an eyebrow. "Am I getting too close?"

"You know I don't mean physical proximity, although there is a little of that, too."

She thought he would now make some inanely flirtatious remark, but he surprised her by suddenly turning thoughtful. "I was not eager to come here," he admitted. "My parents are determined to see me and my sister married off. I suppose it is obvious."

"I think Duchess Evelyn is just as obvious in hoping to match her son to one of the debutantes here. Your sister seems lovely."

"Actually, she is not all that lovely a person at present," he said. "My parents did her no favors by spoiling her shamelessly. She has been impossible now that she is out in Society. An absolute terror in her first year. But she will come around in time and mature into the elegant woman I know she can be. Still, I think Lynton will always be too old for her."

Eden took a sip of her tea, one of Evelyn's treasured specialty blends that slid soothingly down her throat like warm honey. Well, there was a hint of honey in this particular blend. It was delicious and did not require sugar or cream to make it palatable, although cream tea was all the rage. "I hear she is only eighteen."

"Yes, and Lynton is above forty. Knowing my sister as I do, I think that is a bit too much of a gap in their ages. But she is keen on becoming a duchess, and Lynton is well preserved for a man of his years. So it might work out."

"That is a rousing recommendation," Eden said dryly. Was this not precisely what she hated about these house parties and other events designed to throw couples together? They were all about securing titles and wealth, and not about finding love.

Well, she knew her ideas on this were unpopular.

"Are your parents here, Lady Eden? Would you introduce me to them?" the viscount asked, drawing her out of her musings.

"They... Um." She could not blurt that they were next door at her beloved Chestnut Hill trying to kill each other. Nor did she have the slightest interest in introducing this charming viscount to them. She sighed. "They are not here. Nor would you enjoy meeting them, to be frank."

He arched an eyebrow. "Why not?"

"Because they are horrible people."

He laughed in surprise. "You do not mince your words."

"I am merely stating facts. Surely you must have heard gossip surrounding the Earl of Darrow and his wife? I will not be offended if you now politely excuse yourself and run for the hills."

He laughed again. "On the contrary—I think I will enjoy learning more about you."

"Oh, I doubt it."

He held out his arm to her once they had finished their tea. "Care for a walk in the garden, Lady Eden?"

Was he serious? Perhaps another hour in her company would scare him off. "Why not? I would be delighted."

Damien, Earl of Hawley, a courtesy title granted to him by his father, the Marquess of Rathburne, had by now stopped circling her and settled beside a young lady dressed all in pink that he was pretending to worship and adore, if her giggles and fan fluttering were any indication.

Gad, could he be more obvious? At least Viscount Aubrey was subtler while laying on the charm.

They strolled down the terrace steps at their leisure, keeping to the shaded paths since the afternoon sun was quite strong at this time of day. It did not take the viscount long to start asking questions about her and her family. "I have not seen you in London. I'm sure I would have noticed you. Do you not enjoy the balls, soirees, and theaters?"

"In truth, I do not. I am much happier here in the country-side."

He frowned. "But your father is an earl. Is there a reason why he did not sponsor your come-out?"

"Oh, but he did. I endured three Seasons before he and my mother gave up on me."

"Gave up on you?" Now he looked confused. "How can that be? Someone with your pleasant appearance and secure fortune ought to have been snapped up in her first Season. Yes, I am aware you are an heiress. I'm certain you received countless offers because of it."

"I did," she admitted as they continued to walk along the garden path. The roses were in bloom and on colorful display, as were many other flowers featured in their natural splendor. Sweet Williams provided a striking crimson border while tall hollyhocks and delphinium anchored the back rows.

Eden loved the soft pinks, vibrant blues, and sunshine yellows that abounded in Connor's magnificent garden. She had always thought this was Mary's pet project and had admired her for her vision. Mary had never denied it, but Eden later learned it had been Connor and his mother who designed the flowerbeds and worked with their gardeners to turn it into the magnificence now on display. Mary had not so much as trimmed a rose or planted a cutting.

Lord Aubrey cleared his throat. "I have been back from the Continent for several years now that Napoleon's threat is vanquished. I returned in late summer of 1815, a full two years ago. When were you out?"

"My first Season was about nine years ago and my last about six years ago."

He pursed his lips. "How can this be? You do not look above twenty."

"Is that your roundabout way of asking my age?" Eden was not particularly shy about it. Why not be honest and put an end to his interest before things went further? "I am seven and twenty. Quite the spinster."

"Securely ensconced on the shelf?" He grinned. "I would never have guessed it, and I doubt anyone would consider you on the shelf no matter your age. I think the country air must be good for one's complexion. Yours is flawless."

She laughed. "I think you are in need of spectacles if you believe that."

"No." He shook his head emphatically. "I see you quite clearly. I am nearing thirty, by the way. Do you usually wear spectacles?"

She nodded. "You've noticed me squinting. Duchess Evelyn is determined to have me walk around in a blur. I am told they make me look quite owlish."

He smiled. "I love owls. They are such fascinating birds of prey. Do not let on to others, but I am an avid bird watcher. In fact, I was going to ask Lynton about the more popular walks around here where I might spot plovers, grebes, merlins, and—"

"Are you serious?"

"Yes," he said with a nod. "I've even brought along my binoculars."

She considered inviting him on tomorrow's walk with Connor's children to the cliffs, where they intended to study the nesting birds. But she had only just met him and did not think it prudent to invite him along upon so short an acquaintance.

Besides, they planned on leaving early. He looked the sort who preferred early morning rides to walking, and had probably planned to ride out tomorrow morning with Connor and other early risers.

She would extend the invitation another day, once she learned more about him. He seemed almost too good to be true. In her experience, such men were *always* too good to be true. Something would eventually come up to reveal his true motives.

But Eden had to admit she enjoyed their conversation. Lord Aubrey proved to be intelligent and well versed on many subjects. They spoke for quite a while before turning back to join the others. To his credit, he made certain always to remain in full view of those on the terrace.

Once they were back among the other guests, Eden assumed they would part ways. Although he had told her the family emphasis was on advancing his sister's marriage prospects, his were also in consideration. She expected he would now mingle with the other young ladies present in order to check out all the available options. Several of them were heiresses, so she did not think he would need to waste more time with her.

But he held her back before she had the chance to excuse herself and move on. "Is the supper seating to be formally arranged, Lady Eden? Do you know whether we will be given the chance to sit wherever we like?"

"Knowing Duchess Evelyn as I do, I doubt she will leave anything to chance. I am fairly certain our seats have been selected for us."

"Then I hope she has placed me next to you. In any event, may I escort you in to supper?"

"Yes, that would be delightful." She cast him a friendly smile, although she was not certain she liked the idea. The viscount was a pleasant man, but it had been so long since anyone courted her. She had grown quite comfortable in her daily routine. Yes, she had become restless lately and was giving serious thought to marrying and raising a family.

However, now that the opportunity was suddenly being thrust at her, she was not ready for it.

But, ready or not, should she not grasp the chance for happiness? Or at least explore the possibility?

Whatever the possibility, it would not ever be with Connor. Neither he nor Duchess Evelyn had remarked on the most obvious possibility of all—that she and Connor be matched.

He hadn't said it. His mother hadn't said it.

What other conclusion could she draw but that neither of them wanted her?

CHAPTER FIVE

C ONNOR APPROACHED EDEN the moment Lord Lothmere's son left her side. "I wondered where you had gone."

"Just walking in the garden with Viscount Aubrey," she replied, wondering why he was frowning. "Is something wrong? Are the children all right?"

"They're fine, I'm sure. The maids assigned to them have not run downstairs screaming. At least, not yet. Of course, this assumes the children have not already bound and gagged them."

Eden laughed. "The children are not nearly as bad as you make them out to be."

Amusement shone in Connor's exquisite blue eyes. "Oh, they are. Never trust their sweet smiles. It means they are plotting something dastardly. However, they always seem to be on their best behavior around you. What is your secret to making them behave?"

She shook her head. "I have no idea."

"Too bad. I was hoping you had it all figured out. They certainly do not like me."

"Nonsense, they adore and worship you. This is why they miss you so much whenever you are away. But you mustn't worry about them. I'll take good care of them tomorrow. They'll be in good hands with me."

"I know, Eden. There is no one I trust more than you. But I did not approach you to discuss my children."

"Oh, is there something else you have in mind?"

He raked a hand through his hair. "No, I just wanted to make certain you were having a nice time. I'm sorry I have not been as attentive as I should have been."

"I've had a most enjoyable time without you," she assured Connor, tossing him an impudent smile.

They were still on the terrace and had walked closer to the balustrade for a little separation from the other guests. Connor now leaned his elbows atop the stone balustrade and peered out across his garden as he spoke. "Well then," he said with a light chuckle, "I'm glad one of us has survived this excruciating nonsense. I really am too old for this."

Eden regarded him sternly. "You are not a decrepit old goat, so stop griping. Do you realize how many young men would leap at the opportunity to be in your position? How awful for you, to be accosted by England's most beautiful and accomplished young ladies."

"That is exactly the problem. *Young* ladies. I feel as though I am robbing a nursery. Many of them even talk like little girls, with their high-pitched squeals and irritating titters. Gad, it was all I could do not to cringe."

"My goodness, perhaps you really are an old goat. These young ladies are all above eighteen years of age and fully out in Society. You are not robbing any cradles. Lothmere's daughter was particularly attentive to you. She's a beautiful girl."

"Persephone? Lord, save me." He cast her a wincing grin. "She is the worst of the lot. A complete and utter peahen. I don't care if she is above eighteen. She has the mind of a twelve-year-old and did not stop fluttering her eyelashes or cooing at me like a demented bird. She made my eye twitch. See? It is still twitching."

"It is not." Eden laughed. "You are hopeless."

"And what about you? I noticed you spent quite a while with Lothmere's son."

She shrugged. "I may be hopeless, too. Perhaps a little afraid to open myself up to someone I hardly know. What have you heard about him?"

Connor's brow furrowed as he gave her question some thought. "I've heard only good things about him around my clubs. He is a cautious man and rarely gambles. When he does, he usually wins. But he also honors his debts when he loses. He's discreet when it comes to the ladies. I haven't heard him mentioned in any scandals."

"Hmm."

"I cannot say whether he would keep to his marriage vows. But his father is not a hound. It appears he has kept faithful to his vows. Perhaps Lothmere and his wife were a love match. It has been known to happen. It could be that the apple does not fall far from the tree."

"So you think the son will follow his father's ways and not run around or take on a mistress?"

Connor's eyebrows shot up in obvious surprise. "Is it that serious already, Eden? You've only known him for an hour."

She waved her hand in dismissal. "Dear me, no. But this house party is all about forming serious connections, is it not? All I am wondering is whether I should dismiss Lord Aubrey out of hand or not."

"I'll try to find out more about him for you—just do not let down your guard around him."

Eden emitted a shaky breath. "This is me you are talking to, Connor. When have you ever known me to be unguarded? I have spent my entire life constructing those high walls around my heart. But even a seasoned spinster like myself cannot mind dusting herself off and stepping down from her shelf to enjoy a mild flirtation."

"Eden," he said with a soft growl that shot tingles through her, "stop referring to yourself as that. You are the prettiest girl here. Do you not realize it? Stop talking about yourself as though you have dried up. You are not a prune."

"But this is exactly what I am...or will soon be. You needn't offer to comfort me as I pity myself."

"Is that what you are doing?" He straightened to his full height. "Every bachelor here would leap at the chance to meet you. Lothmere's son, Lord Aubrey, seems to have grabbed the advantage, but others are eager to speak to you and get to know you better. Shall I introduce you around?"

"No, your mother has already seen to it. You needn't worry about me."

"But I do, Eden. You are under my care, and I am not going to allow anyone to hurt you. So, do not give me a scowl and accuse me of being highhanded and overly protective. Who is going to look out for you if not me? Your parents certainly don't give a—" He groaned and stopped abruptly. "Sorry, but they make me angry."

She gave a mirthless laugh. "I am angry with them too. Look at what they have done to me. They've left me unable to trust. I am so scared to give my heart to anyone. And yet I ache for it. What a mess I am."

He looked as though he wanted to pull her into his arms and hold her. But Eden knew better than to believe it meant anything beyond his protective instincts. "Eden," he said with aching gentleness, "no decisions need to be made this week. Just enjoy yourself. Make new friends. If something more serious develops, then come to me and we will talk about it."

"What about you?"

He stared down at her, his gaze hot and intense.

A Silver Duke's gaze. Seductive and alluring, but never ready to commit to any woman.

She knew what his response would be before he ever spoke it.

"Why are you asking about my marriage prospects?" he said with a shake of his head. "I am not ever going to propose to any of those peahens. Nor am I in danger of falling in love with any of them. Have I not been clear about this? There is nothing to talk about with regard to me."

Teatime was almost over, and most guests were now return-ing to their guest chambers to rest and prepare for tonight's feast and entertainments. Eden decided to run upstairs and see how the children were faring.

Connor took her hand to hold her back a moment. "Let me escort you in to supper."

She smiled at him. "My valiant protector. You cannot help yourself, can you? But you needn't worry about me. Lord Aubrey has already claimed the honor."

He seemed surprised—and not very happy. "He did? And you accepted?"

She nodded. "I saw no reason to refuse him."

"Right. Of course. He is a decent fellow. Well, just let me know if ever you are in need of an escort or a dance partner…or a cards partner."

Eden felt warmed by his concern. More than that, she liked that he was looking out for her. His manner wasn't cloying or overbearing. It was just…nice. "Will you choose me for your team during our lawn sports?" she teased.

He cast her a disarmingly affectionate smile. "You'll be the first one I select. Is there a doubt?"

They parted ways, and she hurried up to the children's nursery. The boys were too big for her to refer to it as a nursery. Even Priscilla was getting too big for that. Eden needed to start referring to that large space around which their rooms were situated as their classroom or their wing of the house. She could not refer to it as a playroom, either. The boys would be offended and claim they were not babies.

Were the maids assigned to attend them still surviving?

To her surprise, no one was around when she entered their upper-floor quarters. She checked all the cupboards to make certain the poor maids had not been trussed and stuffed in them. She then checked all the bedrooms and peered under their beds. "Where did you go, you little heathens?"

She had just finished her search and was about to leave Priscilla's room when one of the maids ran in.

"Oh, Lady Eden!" The poor girl's eyes were wide, and she

was obviously worried.

"What is it, Sarah? Have the children run off again?"

She nodded. "They tricked us. Oh, His Grace is going to sack us for certain."

Eden took the girl's hand. "No, he won't. When did you last see them?"

"About twenty minutes ago. Millie," Sarah said, referring to the other maid assigned to watch the children, "went downstairs to fetch them more milk and ginger cakes. Then—oh, I cannot believe I fell for it—Lady Priscilla began to cry and said she forgot her storybook in her father's study, and that her father would be so angry if he knew she had left it on his desk. She described it to me in tearful detail. So I ran down to find it."

Eden groaned. "There was no book, was there?"

"No, Lady Eden. I am ashamed to say I was tricked by an eight-year-old child. She had me completely convinced. By the time I hurried back upstairs, they were already gone. Millie and I have been hunting for them ever since. I think they must have run out of the house."

"I'll find them. Just give me a moment to put on my walking boots and change out of this gown. I think I know where they are."

Sarah let out a breath of relief. "You do? Oh, thank goodness. I'll come with you."

"No," said a deep voice from behind them that Eden immediately recognized as belonging to Connor. "I'll go with Lady Eden to search for them. They're my little heathens, after all. Gad, can they not behave for a single day?"

Eden winced as she cast him a sympathetic look. "Apparently not."

He sighed. "I'll wait for you in the entry hall. Hurry up and change out of your finery. Where do you think they've gone?"

"Remember the geese from this morning?"

He groaned. "The ones I frightened away with a mere comment?"

"It is unfinished business for them." She nodded. "Wait for me. I won't be a moment. Sarah, come with me. I'll need help slipping out of this gown."

She thought she noticed a flicker of heat in Connor's eyes when she mentioned taking off her gown. But she dismissed the possibility. His expression was unreadable now.

Why would he ever care about her in that way?

She hurried to her bedchamber, changed into more practical attire, then found her spectacles and put them on before rushing downstairs to meet Connor. She was back to her usual form, except her hair was more attractively styled than usual. She hadn't bothered to undo it, since there was to be supper and entertainments this evening and she needed to look sophisticated and alluring for that.

Connor smiled as she approached. "There's my girl," he said softly.

She grinned back at him. "Your owlish neighbor."

He took her hand in his. "We had better hurry before the geese attack them. Gad, I hope they are there and not poking their faces or their fingers into a fox den."

"I'm certain they have more sense than that." She also hoped the boys would not throw stones at the geese and antagonize them as they had tried to do this morning. Although she did not have any brothers, she had been around Connor's boys often enough to understand how young boys thought and acted. They would think it was a fun game to hit as many geese as they could while those poor birds were feeding in the pond. Of course, Priscilla, being the youngest, would likely be the slowest to run away when the angry birds hissed at them and retaliated by pecking at her legs.

Connor had ordered his rig readied while waiting for her, and it was there when they stepped out the front door. He wrapped his hands around her waist to help her into the passenger seat. "I hope they are there," he muttered.

"I'm sure they are." She forced herself to stop tingling. The mere touch of his firm, roughened hands on her body put her senses in a roil. Butterflies fluttered in her stomach. Her heart was fluttering, as well.

He hopped up beside her and flicked the reins, spurring the horse to a fast trot.

Eden held on for dear life as they moved fast and seemed to hit every rut along the way. Although she did not complain, Connor must have noticed her hands turning white as she gripped the seat to keep herself from flying off. "Shift closer to me, Eden."

"What?"

He placed an arm around her waist and hauled her up against his magnificently hard, fit body.

Dear heaven.

Was it wrong of her to hope it would take hours to find his children?

They reached the pond just as the little heathens burst out of the bramble bushes that surrounded the pond. They heard goose honks and angry hisses mingled with Priscilla's shrieks and the boys' laughter.

"Devil take it," Connor muttered, pulling up hard on the reins.

He handed them to Eden, and at the same time hopped down to run to his daughter, who had tripped and fallen. Poor little Priscilla was crying out for him as her bottom was about to be pecked by two large, enraged geese. With truly protective fatherly instinct, he placed himself between the angry geese and Priscilla, then hauled her into his arms. "Get in the rig. Now!" he growled at his boys, who needed no prompting and were already racing to it.

The geese were now biting Connor's legs. But he was wearing boots, so they merely got a mouthful of leather, which made them angrier. They fluttered their feathers and hissed some more.

Connor ignored them and ran to the rig with his precious daughter clasped to his chest. Why could Eden's own father never be like this?

She shook out of the thought. She was all grown up and on her own now.

But for a moment, she wished to be in Priscilla's place. The little girl had her arms firmly wrapped around Connor's neck and was clinging to him for dear life. His arms were like steel bands around his little girl, and he would not let go of her until she was safe.

Eden scooted over to the driver's seat and motioned for him to climb in beside her. She wanted to help him with Priscilla, but the child was too scared to let go of him, so he managed to hop in while she stuck to him like a barnacle to the hull of a ship. In the meanwhile, the boys had scooted onto the bench behind them.

Eden took care not to harm the charging birds as she gave the reins a flick and urged the horse forward. But the geese were undaunted and scared the horse by charging at it. Finally, she managed to maneuver the rig away from those angry birds and avoided trampling any of them under the horse's hooves as she drove away.

Priscilla remained clinging to her father the entire ride back to the manor house. The boys were silent as the rig clattered along the well-worn path.

Connor was fuming. Eden could almost see the proverbial steam pouring from his ears.

As they left the pond in the distance, Connor finally turned to the boys and unloaded his wrath on them. "What in bloody blazes were you thinking? And to bring Priscilla along with you? Obviously, you *weren't* thinking. What did you do to the geese to get them so angry? Is this the way I raised you? To be wild as wolves? Did you hurt their goslings?"

He took a deep breath and silenced them with a glower when they mistakenly thought he wanted to hear their answers. He was not yet finished lambasting them. "Did you think twice about Sarah and Millie or what I might have done to them because they failed in their efforts to watch over you? Did you even think *once* about Priscilla getting hurt?"

"It was Priscilla's idea," Alex said lamely.

"Did I give you permission to speak?" Connor roared at his son. "And this is the pathetic excuse you give me? If Priscilla told you to jump off a cliff, would you do it?"

He now directed his rage to his eldest boy. "And you, Connor? My namesake. My heir. Is this how carelessly you will undertake your duties? Need I tell you everything you did wrong?"

"No, Papa."

Connor told him anyway. "First, you listened to Priscilla's stupid idea."

Priscilla wailed. "Papa hates me!"

"I don't hate you, my little sweetheart. But it was a very foolish thing you did." He turned back to his eldest. "Second, you placed Sarah and Millie in danger of losing their positions in the household by sneaking away."

"Don't sack them, Papa! It was all my fault, and I take full responsibility for deceiving them," young Connor said, sounding truly remorseful.

"Third, you placed Priscilla in danger. You both ran off and left her behind. *You left her behind*," Connor repeated. "You are her older brothers. You should have been protecting her."

Now Alex began to cry. "We're sorry, Papa."

"Fourth, you stole off and no one knew where you had gone. Anything could have happened to you. You could have been eaten by wolves. Bears."

"There is no dangerous wildlife in the area," his eldest meekly dared to point out.

"How can you be certain? A jungle cat might have escaped its cage from a passing circus. Pirates might have abducted you. Priscilla cannot swim. Would you have noticed if she fell in the pond?"

"Alex was watching her," young Connor assured him.

"I thought you were watching her," Alex said.

"Dear heaven," Connor muttered. "Priscilla might have drowned."

"But I didn't, Papa. I was afraid to go near the water."

"Good girl." He planted a kiss at the top of her head. "At least you showed some good sense. But you are still punished."

Priscilla was about to wail again, but a stern look from Connor had her quickly rethinking that plan.

He turned back to the boys. "If not for Eden's intuition, I might have been searching for you all night long. I have a blasted house party going on. I cannot be constantly on the hunt for you when I have a house full of guests to entertain.

"Fifth," he said as they approached the manor house, "I now have to decide on a suitable punishment for you. If I confine you to the house, that would be punishing my loyal staff more than you three. If I send you up to bed without your supper, you'd probably sneak down to the kitchen and bring up a bloody feast for yourselves. If I cancel tomorrow's outing with Eden—"

A chorus of "No!" from all of them interrupted him.

He arched an eyebrow. "Even you, Eden?"

She might have shouted the loudest. "They need to be outdoors or it will go worse for all of us. Besides, we are going on a bird-watching expedition. Before we head to the cliffs, I think we must stop at the pond so they can apologize to those geese."

"Apologize to geese?" Connor asked, sounding quite dubious.

Eden nodded. "Yes. And may I suggest a suitable punishment for today's escapade?"

He nodded. "Go right ahead. I'm all ears."

"I think they each must write apology letters to Sarah and Millie asking for their forgiveness in putting their positions in the household in jeopardy. They must also write apology letters to you showing an understanding of what they did wrong and what they will do to better themselves in the future."

His eldest groaned. "Papa, just take us to the woodshed and thrash us."

"Thrash you?" Connor growled. "When have I ever laid a

hand on you?"

"Never," his eldest admitted. "But I'd rather take a beating than spend the night writing letters."

Eden turned away so the children would not catch her struggling to hold back her giggles.

She heard Connor's soft rumble of laughter as he struggled with the same. "Oh, no," he said, taking a moment to clear his throat. "The suggestion is perfect. You'll each write your letters this evening. No pudding for any of you until all three of you are done."

"But we still get to go exploring with Eden tomorrow?" Alex asked, no doubt wanting to firm up the terms of their punishment before they put quill to paper.

"Yes, you go with Eden tomorrow as planned."

The children cheered.

When Eden drew the rig up in the courtyard, the boys leaped off. Priscilla tried to imitate them by leaping off Connor's lap. Fortunately, Brewster had come out of the house in time to catch her when she lost her footing.

Connor groaned. "Thank you, Brewster." If not for his reliable butler, she would have tumbled headlong onto the stone.

The little sprite also thanked Brewster for his timely catch. "You are most welcome, Lady Priscilla," he replied.

She smiled at him, and then ran into the house after Alex and young Connor, shouting at them to wait for her.

"I'll make certain Millie and Sarah are aware the children have safely returned home," the kindly Brewster said, and hurried back into the house.

Eden and Connor were left alone in the rig for the moment. He spread his arms across the back of their seat bench, lolled his head back, and emitted a hearty groan. "Are they too young to be married off? Let them be someone else's problem? Gad, Eden, they were out with you all day and still managed to get up to mischief. Do they never stop?"

"I'll try to run them around harder tomorrow."

He arched an eyebrow. "Do you think you can? I fear they will exhaust *you*."

"Perhaps. They seem to be boundless wells of energy. But even the most resilient children can be controlled." She emitted a soft trill of laughter. "The threat of having them write more apology letters ought to keep them in line."

Connor chuckled as he climbed down. One of his stable grooms now came running toward them to fetch the horse and rig. Connor strode around to her side and placed his hands at her waist to effortlessly help her down before the lad led the horse and carriage away.

To Eden's surprise, Connor did not immediately release her. "Eden, I cannot thank you enough for...just everything. You seem to understand my own children better than I do. And the punishment you devised is diabolically brilliant. Writing apology letters. The boys were willing to endure a beating rather than have to compose an essay."

He still held her about the waist as he smiled at her. She sensed he wanted to kiss her cheek again, but she was wearing her spectacles, so why would he ever be tempted? Indeed, she was probably the opposite of tempting.

But to her surprise, he did give her a tender, lingering kiss on the cheek. "Thank you, Eden," he whispered, reluctantly releasing her as his groom drove the rig away and they were left standing alone in the courtyard.

She blushed. "I had better get changed for supper."

He glanced down at himself. "Me too."

They hurried up the stairs together and parted ways at the landing, since his ducal suite of rooms was off to the right at the very end of the hall and her guest chamber was the first door on the left.

Eden realized Duchess Evelyn must have been watching for them, because she sent Delia minutes after Eden returned to her room. She had taken off her gown because it was one of those designed to easily slip on and off without laborious tapes or lacings, and had just moistened a washcloth to clean her hands and face when the girl entered.

"Let me help you, Lady Eden," Delia said, and dashed to her side.

"I'm almost finished," Eden assured her. "But I still must select a gown to wear."

"Oh, that is already taken care of. I took the liberty of having the rose silk freshened for this evening. Her Grace thought these diamond earrings would go nicely with the gown." Delia reached into her pocket and withdrew two shiny objects.

Eden was surprised because Evelyn was very careful with her things. "She is lending me her earrings?"

Delia nodded. "I mentioned that you had not brought yours along with you."

Eden nodded. "I did not think of it at the time."

She had been in too much of a hurry to gather the bare necessities and leave her own home rather than endure a moment longer with her battling parents. The pair always tried to suck her into their disputes, always making her choose which one of them she loved best. In truth, she loved them both...but also heartily disliked their selfish ways. They should have been the adults, but they acted like spoiled and inconsiderate infants.

Somehow, she had taken on the role of parent. She did not mind it with young Connor, Alex, and Priscilla because they were children. But her parents? When were they going to grow up?

"I'll thank Duchess Evelyn when I go down to supper. This is very thoughtful of her."

"She likes you, Lady Eden."

"The feeling is mutual. She is a lovely person." In truth, she wished her mother was more like the duchess. Over the years, it had been Duchess Evelyn who took her in and gave her maternal hugs whenever she needed to get away from her parents. There were times when she would come to the duchess in tears.

Now that she thought about it, where had Mary been all the while? In those years, Connor had been off fighting Napoleon.

His military service had lasted through much of the war, but he also had constant disruptions because his duties as Duke of Lynton had forced him to sail back and forth too often from the peninsula. Not to mention his duties to the Crown required him to sit in the House of Lords whenever Parliament was in session. His children had grown up hardly knowing their father.

Finally, upon Mary's death, he had reluctantly bought out his commission and returned to England permanently.

In all that time, it was Duchess Evelyn who cared for the children and brought them over to Chestnut Hill whenever Eden had her neighbors over for tea. It was Evelyn who sat in the shade of the terrace watching the children as they toddled around the garden. Of course, they each had a nanny attending them, too.

Where had Mary been even then?

Not that it mattered now. She was gone and the children were left without a mother's touch. But they certainly had a wonderful grandmother who was doing her best to raise them with love.

Before heading downstairs, Eden took a moment to knock at Duchess Evelyn's door. "Do come in, Eden dear," she said, opening the door herself. "Don't you look lovely?" As she spoke, she whisked the spectacles off Eden's nose. "But you won't be needing those tonight." Delia had followed her in, and the dowager handed Eden's spectacles to her. "Put those back in Eden's bedchamber."

Delia bobbed a curtsy and hurried out before Eden could grab her spectacles back. "I won't be able to see a thing," she muttered.

"You'll see just fine. You aren't out hunting quail or dueling at fifty paces. You need only look at your dinner companions immediately to the left and to the right of you."

"I would enjoy seeing the food on my plate," she muttered.

"Whatever for? It isn't going to crawl away," Evelyn retorted. "My dear, you will survive the evening."

Eden laughed. "All right. But do not berate me if I squint."

The dowager tucked a finger under Eden's chin while studying her features. "You are going to leave the gentlemen breathless. Walk downstairs with me. I'm sure some of the guests have already gathered in the parlor."

Eden had barely taken two steps into the parlor before Lord Aubrey came to her side. "May I be so bold as to remark how radiant you look, Lady Eden?"

Duchess Evelyn nodded in approval. "I told the dear girl the very same thing only moments ago. Do you believe me now, Eden?"

Eden blushed.

Damien, the Marquess of Rathburne's son, appeared about to approach her, noticed Aubrey already at her side, and veered off toward the very giggling and fan fluttering Miss Margaret Wallingford, the heiress in pink he had fawned over at afternoon tea. She seemed to adore the color, since she was once again wearing pink from head to toe.

Connor strode in moments later and immediately approached them. No doubt he only meant to dutifully greet his mother, but Eden caught his appreciative smile as he studied her.

Was she mistaken, or had his gaze lingered on her?

Lord Aubrey stepped between them and took her arm in his. "Your Grace, if you will excuse us. My parents are keen to speak to Lady Eden."

"Of course," Connor said, his voice more of a grumble. "You look lovely tonight, Eden."

"Thank you." She felt her cheeks heat again, because it had been quite a while since two handsome men had squared off against each other, seeking her attention. This had happened on occasion during her first few Seasons out, but she'd experienced nothing like this in years.

Not that Connor had any serious interest in her, but it did warm her heart to know he was not completely immune to her charms.

She had no more time to think about Connor now that Lord Aubrey escorted her to his parents. Lord Lothmere and his wife were friendly and interesting to talk to. They had traveled extensively on the Continent this past year. Eden listened as they told her about the canals of Venice.

"Quite beautiful," Lady Lothmere said, "but I do not recommend visiting in the height of summer. There is a foul stench that pervades the city on the hottest days."

They then spoke of the damage done on the Continent during the years of war. "My regiment was mostly based in Belgium," Lord Aubrey said. "In truth, we were primarily reserve units until Waterloo. We were in the thick of it then. A terrible loss of lives on all sides. But people are ever resilient, quickly rebuilding what was destroyed. And there was much destruction, but also many places that remained untouched and beautiful."

"I haven't traveled outside of England," Eden admitted. "But I have read much about Greece and Italy and the majestic Alps."

"I enjoy a good book myself," Lord Aubrey said, "but it is not the same as actually seeing the sights. You ought to travel, Lady Eden. Who knows? Perhaps after you are married."

"Well, I don't know about that," she said, blushing as he cast her a meaningful smile.

Was he suggesting he would marry her?

She glanced away to avoid his smile.

Out of the corner of her eye, she noticed Lord Aubrey's sister, Persephone, was chatting with Connor and his mother. Eden heard the girl's youthful laughter and wondered whether Connor was warming up to her. There was no doubt these Lothmeres were a handsome family. Both the son and the daughter would make profitable matches, especially since they both seemed quite efficient in the manner in which they approached this house party. Lord Aubrey had homed in on her while his sister had shot like a bullet to Connor's side.

Eden had grown wary over the years and was not so swept away by Lord Aubrey's rakish smiles and doting attention. In all likelihood, he was more enamored with her wealth than with her. The same might be said for his sister, who was all giggles and coquettish smiles for Connor because he was the duke. He was the prize.

Despite his repeated declarations that he had no interest in remarrying, could the astute Persephone persuade him that a young wife was exactly what he needed?

CHAPTER SIX

"LORD AUBREY SEEMS to have taken a serious liking to Eden," Connor's mother remarked later that evening while Connor was dancing with her. This was no formal ball; however, Connor chose to claim his mother for the first dance in order not to give any particular peahen his preferential attention.

They were all too young for him, giggling like schoolgirls because that was what they had been until they were pushed out into the world earlier this year.

He, just like his mother, had noticed Aubrey hovering over Eden, quietly circling her like she were prey. The viscount had a good reputation and could be a potential match for Eden, but Connor simply did not know enough about him to pass judgment. "Yes, his attentions are hard to overlook."

He tamped down the uneasy feeling now churning in his gut. What was it about Aubrey that bothered him? Why should Eden not find happiness with him?

Well, she had only just met the viscount. Eden was a practical woman. Connor would never consider her a gushing romantic. She wasn't going to leap into a commitment as important as marriage with just anyone, and certainly never upon so short an acquaintance.

He shouldn't make too much of this Aubrey chap.

"I think Eden looks particularly lovely tonight, don't you? Lord Aubrey cannot take his eyes off her," his mother remarked.

He growled at her—dear heaven, growling at his own mother—as he led her in a twirl. "Why the sudden fascination with Eden?"

She looked up at him innocently. "I am merely remarking on how pretty she is."

He snorted as he led her in another twirl. "I could have told you that. She hides behind her spectacles, but her beauty is obvious for anyone who bothers to look beyond them. By the way, why isn't she wearing her spectacles? Did you hide them from her?"

"I merely insisted that she not wear them tonight."

"She wasn't wearing them at this afternoon's tea, either. Why?"

His mother cast him an admonishing look. "Need you ask? I want her to be seen in her best light. None of these men will look at her if they think she has spent her life buried in books."

"Has she asked you to match her with anyone?"

"No. However, I have taken it upon myself to match her with someone I deem quite suitable. The dear girl may be smart as a whip, but she does not always know what is best for her."

"And you do?" Connor tried to stifle his annoyance. Why was his mother meddling in Eden's life? She ought to respect her privacy. After all, Eden was no child who needed to be led about by the hand. She was a vibrant and intelligent woman who was capable of making her own decisions.

Apparently, Eden's first decision was to dance with Aubrey. They seemed to be enjoying themselves.

Connor did not like this at all. Wasn't that bounder moving too fast? Connor was going to have a talk with him, make certain his intentions were honorable. He would pound Aubrey to dust if he meant to take advantage of Eden.

In truth, Connor would pound him to dust even if his intentions were honorable, although he did not want to consider the reason why. He was too old and set in his ways to be jealous.

Nor did he quite understand the sudden proprietary interest

he had taken in Eden. Perhaps it was merely that he did not wish to see her hurt.

Yes, that was certainly the reason.

"You haven't selected Lord Aubrey for her, have you?" He growled again at his mother. "You cannot push them together until we know more about him. Eden is…"

Gad, he was going to say that she was *his* to protect. Not Aubrey's.

"What, Connor? You were going to say something about Eden."

"Never mind."

The dance came to an end, and he quickly escorted his mother to her circle of older friends. But he had no sooner unloaded her than the peahens began to flock around him again. "Oh, joy," he muttered before cracking a smile and enduring their fake adulation.

As the evening wore on, Connor decided his head was going to burst if he had to listen to one more inane conversation or the endless giggles from these debutantes being thrust at him. Persephone in particular was giving him a blistering headache.

But she was not the only one. The heiress in pink, Margaret Wallingford, was going to do permanent damage to her eyeballs if she did not stop fluttering her lashes or sending him suggestive gazes behind her fan that she was constantly flipping open and shut.

Damien, the marquess's son, was scowling at him because he had diverted the girl's attention from him. The fool was drinking too heavily and also tossing him looks. Challenging looks, as though Connor was infringing upon his territory.

He was more than happy to shove Miss Wallingford at Damien. He could have Persephone, too. He could have all of them.

Just not Eden.

No, Eden was…

Gad, he had almost thought Eden was *his*, as though rescuing her from a fishpond when she was two years old had formed an irrevocable bond between them.

Perhaps it had. That was twenty-five years ago. Hadn't he kept an eye on her ever since?

Finally, as midnight approached and the moon shone like a silver ball upon an ink-dark sky, he managed to slip onto the terrace for a breath of air.

Others were on the terrace as well. To avoid them, he strode down the steps and made his way toward one of the quieter corners of his garden, not far from the infamous fishpond where the young Eden had taken a dive. But when he got to the spot, he noticed a slender figure sitting upon a stone bench overlooking the rose beds.

He immediately recognized the young woman illuminated by moonlight. "Eden?"

He heard her soft gasp and then her release of breath. "Connor, I did not hear you approach. Thank goodness it's you." She slid over to allow him room beside her.

His shoulder grazed hers as he settled his large frame by her side. "Who did you think it would be?"

"Lord Aubrey, if you must know. He has been...relentlessly attentive to me all evening."

"And you felt the need to escape him?"

She nodded. "I like him. He has been charming and not at all boorish, but it feels too much. Or perhaps it is me who is hopeless."

He sighed. "I know what you mean. I felt the same need to escape. One can hardly breathe from all the attention. Aubrey does seem to be genuinely interested in you."

She gave a light snort. "Interested in my funds, more likely."

He took her hand, although he probably should not have done that. Still, he was not going to let her go just yet. Her hand felt soft and little in his. "No, Eden. Never say this is all he cares about. You are beautiful and smart. Not every man is after you for your wealth."

She let out a ragged breath. "Oh, Connor. Yes, they are. Perhaps at one time I might have found a man who loved me for myself, but that time has come and gone. I only have myself to blame for rejecting everyone. I was a coward, afraid to be wrong and lose everything. And I seem to have lost the most important things anyway."

Her voice was shaking as she continued, and he knew she was going to cry.

Groaning, he put his arm around her. "Eden, I cannot bear to see you this unhappy. Why will you not believe a man can love you for yourself?"

But he knew the answer already. This girl had been raised unloved.

"Let's not talk about this here and now. It is too painful, and I am already struggling not to turn into a watering pot." Her voice was thin and punctuated by sniffles.

"All right, love."

Gad, why had he let that slip out?

He had hired an orchestra for the evening, and they were now playing a waltz. The strains drifted on the wind to their private corner of the garden. "Come on, Eden." He tried to nudge her to her feet, but she resisted.

"What are you doing?" she grumbled. "I don't want to go back inside yet."

"I have no intention of taking you back inside."

"Then what are you doing?"

"You'll see. Trust me." He took her hands in his, drew her to her feet, and then wrapped an arm around her waist.

He was pleased when she made no effort to extricate herself from his grasp, especially since he had drawn her closer than was proper. "I still don't understand what you are doing," she muttered, her voice a soft whisper against his ear.

He inhaled the scent of her skin, that mix of apple and jasmine or cinnamon that was so intoxicating to his senses. "The orchestra is playing a waltz. I am standing in a moonlit garden with the prettiest girl at my party. I am going to dance with that girl. Is it not my privilege as host?"

Moonbeams reflected off her eyes and made them sparkle. "You genuinely want to dance with me?"

"Yes. What is wrong with that?" He placed his palm flat across the small of her back and took her hand in his. "Any objections?"

She laughed softly, her melodic lilt falling gently upon his ears—a welcome relief from the inane giggles he had endured all evening long.

"Have you ever danced in the moonlight before, Eden?"

"No, this is my first time," she admitted, easily following his steps as he guided her with expert skill around the flowerbeds.

"My first time, too," he said.

She looked up at him. "Really?"

"Yes—why are you so surprised?" He kept to an easy pace as they twirled in time to the music. There were a few torches lit in the distance that were meant to keep the garden moderately illuminated. Nights were dark out here, even when the moon was bright. Quite often, a mist or clouds obscured the moon.

But not tonight. It was a perfect night. Moonlight seemed to follow Eden with her every step.

He wanted to kiss her. He wanted to kiss her soft mouth and never stop kissing her.

"You are a Silver Duke, Connor."

She gave her lip a light nibble that had the alarming effect of shooting flames through his body. "And your point is…?"

Another soft nibble like that and he would lose all control. Fortunately, she stopped.

"You have a rakish reputation," she said, pursing her lips.

This was almost as bad as nibbling. He wanted to kiss her more than ever.

"Do you expect me to believe you have never danced with a woman in the moonlight? Among all the ladies you have met and seduced in London, are you going to tell me not one of them has ever danced with you like this? Well, I suppose they have done more than merely dance with you."

"Eden, when I slip away to an elegant garden, it is merely to get a breath of air. I am not saying I am a monk, not at all. I just… Hell, we should not be talking about this."

"No, I am curious. Please go on."

"I had better not. It is highly inappropriate for your delicate ears."

"Connor, I am going to step on your foot if you repeat that stupid remark."

"All right, spare my feet. But my exploits are not nearly as exciting as most people think. That London set is more about ballrooms, boudoirs, and hallway niches. They are not keen on the outdoors."

"I love the outdoors."

"I know, but I am not talking about the respectable activities you engage in when out among nature."

The women of his acquaintance were like indoor cats. They liked their creature comforts. They liked engaging in the sort of dances one performed in the bedroom. Sometimes, they liked it up against a wall. Or on a desk. On a floor. Just not outside, where one's naked arse might get bitten by a gnat or crawled on by something hidden in the grass.

And when the deed was done, in whatever manner it was done, they liked the man to leave. No arms around each other or cuddling in bed or whispering sweet nothings in one's ear—which suited him just fine, because there was no real intimacy involved. Deed done. Get the hell out.

"Honestly, Eden. Can we not just leave it at that? You are the only woman I have ever danced with in the moonlight. Why do you look disappointed?"

"Not disappointed, merely surprised."

He twirled her around slowly. "Well, there you have it. Our rakish reputations are exaggerated. Have I not always said so?"

She nodded. "But it is hard to believe when everyone idolizes you."

"We encourage the naughty rumors, I suppose. But I give you my oath that I have never danced with a young lady at midnight, or any other time of night, in a garden. Nor have I ever kissed a young lady in a garden. Nor—"

"Not even kissed a woman in a garden? Connor, how can this possibly be true?"

"I don't know. It just is." He twirled her again, but they got too close to another couple who were in the throes of a dance of a very different sort. He heard their moans as they were reaching their climax, and quickly steered Eden away. "Nor have I ever done *that* in a moonlit garden."

Eden buried her head against his shoulder and smothered a laugh. "I should be shocked," she said, still chuckling. "I wonder who—"

"We are not going to pry," Connor warned her. "I had better escort you back inside."

"But the waltz hasn't ended yet."

"You still want to dance with me?" He was surprised, but it could be he was overly protective of Eden's sensibilities. She was an intelligent woman, not an ignorant girl. Although she would never engage in such behavior, was it not condescending of him to think she would have a fit of the vapors over catching another couple in the act?

She sighed. "You don't have to dance with me if you are tired of my company. But I'd like to sit out here on my own a little while longer."

"Then I'll stay too." He made certain to move them away from the other couple, who seemed to have finished now, if their moans and groans were any indication.

He settled with Eden back on the stone bench where he had found her. He watched as she closed her eyes and embraced the music. Was this not the perfect moment to kiss her?

Yes, he was going to do it. Bother the consequences.

What was the worst that could happen? A compromising situation? Forced to marry Eden to protect her honor?

In truth, he would not mind this at all.

He was about to lower his head to hers when his mother's stern voice cut through the night. "Connor!"

Hell in a handbasket.

Eden's eyes had been closed and now flew open.

"Connor! There you are. I—" His mother came to an abrupt halt when she noticed Eden seated beside him. "I…I…"

When was the last time his mother had been left speechless?

Eden rose and stepped away from him. "Your son was kind enough to dance with me out here, Evelyn. It was a lovely, romantic gesture."

"Dancing with you? Is that all he was doing?"

Connor growled. "What the hell else would I be doing?"

He sensed Eden's hurt as she said, "Evelyn, this is me out here with him. He was only being nice. You know he has no interest in me."

His mother put an arm around Eden. "Come inside with me, my dear. Lord Aubrey is looking for you."

"Aubrey?" Connor growled again. "Don't you think he is a bit too ardent?"

"No, I don't," his mother shot back. "Some men believe in the institution of marriage. Why should he not reach for a good thing when he sees it? He is only here a week. Why not spend his every waking moment getting to know Eden better? Eden, did you know he is an avid bird watcher?"

"Yes, he told me."

"Ah, good. Then you won't mind that I suggested he join you and the children tomorrow on your outing."

Connor wanted to wring his mother's neck. "You invited him to go with Eden? They are my children. Should you not have asked me first?"

"Why are you in a dither about a harmless outing?" the wily dowager replied as though she did not know full well why he was irritated, though she must have seen him about to kiss Eden.

It was a stupid idea for so many reasons.

First, Eden had her eyes closed and had no idea he was about to kiss her. At the very least, he ought to have made her aware of his intentions and given her the chance to decline.

But this was his Silver Duke arrogance. The possibility that she would not want to kiss him had never entered his mind.

The second reason kissing her was idiotic was that Eden was looking after his children for the week. Well, it was not exactly her job to do so, but she had volunteered. He did not want her distracted or made to feel uncomfortable because of a kiss.

Would she not be just as distracted by Aubrey romancing her in front of his children? It was completely inappropriate.

Eden must have heard his low growl, and spoke up before he had the chance to erupt. "Evelyn, I will explain to Lord Aubrey that he cannot join me and the children. I shall invite him to join me another day. You see, I promised the children this outing would be special and just for them. I think they will be hurt if others come along and steal my attention. I'll propose something for the day after tomorrow. Something that others might enjoy and wish to come along."

"Very well, my dear." Connor's mother patted Eden's hand and then led her back inside.

Connor remained standing on his own in the dark. He quickly followed them back inside because he did not want to be caught out here by one of those peahens who thought to lure him into compromising her.

Eden was different. He trusted her wholeheartedly never to scheme or manipulate. Nor would he hesitate to do the honorable thing if he somehow compromised her reputation.

He walked back into the ballroom in time to see Aubrey take Eden's hand to lead her in another dance.

His mother returned to his side as he watched. "What now, Evelyn? Have you not meddled enough?" he asked.

"Oh, I don't think so. Lots more meddling in me still."

"Oh, joy," he muttered sarcastically.

"Connor, we need to speak seriously."

"About what?"

"Do not play innocent with me. I know you were about to kiss Eden. And you have not taken your eyes off her since returning to the ballroom."

"Only because I am worried about her. She cannot hike with my children all day long and then dance the night away, too."

"Yes, I see your point. She will exhaust herself. Might I make a suggestion?"

He arched an eyebrow and glanced at his mother. "Why bother to ask me when you are going to speak your mind even if I forbid it?"

She smiled. "Eden's plans are set for tomorrow. But I think you should take your children the day after that. Give Eden time to spend with Lord Aubrey."

He was about to growl again, but held off. "Me? Take the children? Without Eden?"

"She is not your nursemaid, Connor. Why are you so reluctant to give her a chance at happiness?"

"With *him*?" He nodded toward Aubrey, who was fawning over Eden and had eyes only for her.

That wretched wolf.

That Connor was doing the same thing was immaterial.

"Yes, with him," his mother intoned. "What right do you have to interfere when you have no intention of marrying her? Will you ruin her life because she is convenient to have as your neighbor? Will you turn her into a mere bed partner? That is too cruel of you."

He strode away from his mother, not caring that he was being unpardonably rude. The thought of Eden married was a blow straight to the gut.

Eden married and lost to him?

No, he could not imagine it.

Eden married to Aubrey?

Over my dead body.

He would marry her before he ever let—

Gad, what would his fellow Silver Dukes say if he decided to take the plunge?

Not that this would stop him from taking the drastic step if he believed it necessary to protect Eden. They had a deep and abiding friendship. Could it not turn into a love match? Well, it was something to keep in mind if Eden ever needed him.

He had resolved never to marry merely for the sake of duty. He would never do this again. Love and nothing less.

Yes, he could see himself falling in love with her.

Eden regained his attention as she twirled past him and laughed at something Aubrey had said.

What was it about Lothmere's son that Connor did not like? Was it just his imagination? Or was he jealous?

He strode into his study to steal a moment alone and pour himself a brandy. After pouring perhaps too much in his glass, he settled in one of the leather chairs by his hearth and began to contemplate his feelings.

Gad, he hated these changes. Why could his life not go on exactly as it was now?

But he knew it could not. His children were growing up. His mother was aging, although she seemed to be managing it with far more grace than he was.

And Eden was ready to move on, aching to take the leap and finally marry. He knew this because they had spoken openly about the risks and benefits—especially the risk of trusting the man she married not to steal her wealth.

It was a serious risk, but he had heard no rumors about Aubrey or his family being in desperate need of funds to save the Lothmere holdings. Quite the opposite—they had impressive wealth. He was familiar with some of their business interests and knew they were profitable and well run.

Knowing this, was it fair to discourage Eden when she had the seemingly perfect suitor?

But this was what troubled him most, this apparent perfection in Aubrey. What would stop Eden from accepting the man if he proposed?

And what of himself?

Connor took a healthy swig of brandy as he morosely contemplated his life without Eden.

What if he declared himself and asked her to marry him?

He was a short-tempered duke with three demon children and a meddlesome mother. Not to mention he was already over forty, and his hair—which he still had, thank goodness—was starting to turn gray.

Why would she ever choose him over Aubrey?

CHAPTER SEVEN

EDEN KNEW SHE had overdone it last night and was going to regret not getting to sleep until the wee hours of the morning. She never stayed up this late but was glad she had done so this time, because she never would have gotten her moonlight dance with Connor if she had retired earlier.

Yes, completely worth it, she decided, even though her head was pounding and her legs felt like lead weights had been attached to them.

She hoped her stamina would last into the afternoon. She and the children intended to return to Lynton Grange before the four o'clock hour, when tea was served.

She could skip it and grab a much-needed nap instead. Yes, that was a workable plan.

After preparing herself for the day with Delia's assistance—it seemed Duchess Evelyn was going to send her maid to Eden every morning and throughout the day in order to keep her as stylish as possible, even while on her bird-watching excursion—Eden went upstairs to fetch the children.

She had allowed Delia to fuss over her hair and attire without complaint, but one thing she would not compromise on was wearing her spectacles, which were now firmly ensconced on her nose.

She was just about to enter Priscilla's room when she was brought up short at the threshold. Connor was there, bent on one knee beside his daughter while he plaited her hair and tied it with a bow. Eden's heart did leaps and flips as she watched him. "Oh," she said when he suddenly looked up and saw her standing there.

"Good morning, Eden." He rose to his full height now that he had finished his task, and smiled at her.

Had a handsomer man ever existed?

"Good morning," she replied. He must have just returned from an early ride, because he was dressed quite informally. In truth, he looked dashing in a white lawn shirt that stretched across his broad chest and caressed the rippling muscles of his arms.

He had held her in those arms last night. Danced with her under the moonlight.

"Um, I see you have been out riding." She tried not to blush as she perused the rest of him. He wore buff breeches and had on some old brown riding boots. His hair was slightly windblown, and a few curls clung to his damp neck in sinful temptation.

"Yes, my usual morning routine. I saw no reason to change it."

"Of course... Did others join you?"

"Surprisingly, no. Everyone seems to be sleeping in except for us." He was eyeing her with amused detachment, no doubt sensing her discomfort after he had held her in his arms last night.

"They appear to be more sensible than we are." She then turned to Priscilla. "Don't you look lovely? And your hairstyle is sheer perfection. Your father did an excellent job. I love the pretty bow he tied in your braid."

Priscilla took hold of her father's hand, because this little girl was not keen on his leaving. She truly looked adorable. But then, all of Connor's children had his good looks. She smiled proudly. The girl was little and sweet, as cuddly as a precious lamb.

Connor gathered her hiking gear. Eden's heart melted as she watched him prepare his little girl for their outing. He slung her pouch over her slight shoulder, placed the binoculars to hang from her neck, and put the sunhat Eden had let her borrow atop her head. All one could see peeking out from under the hat was Priscilla's big eyes and little cherry lips.

"I wanted to kiss my children and wish them all a good day," he explained, although he really did not owe Eden a reason for visiting his own offspring. They were his flesh and blood. *She* was the interloper among them.

"And compliment them on the fine letters they wrote?" Eden suggested, since the boys and Priscilla had truly agonized over that punishment. But they took it seriously and wrote surprisingly touching letters. Sarah and Millie had shown her the ones written to them.

Connor smiled. "Yes, I was about to do exactly that…now that you mention it."

He knelt again so that he was once more at Priscilla's eye level. "I am so proud of you, sweetheart," he said with all the warmth of his love. "You wrote beautiful notes of apology."

"Thank you, Papa." She threw her arms around his neck, lunging at him so that he almost fell over.

He laughed and kissed her on the cheek. "Promise me you will behave yourself today. Stay close to Eden and do what she tells you."

Priscilla nodded. "I will."

He had a similar conversation with the boys, who beamed with pride as he spoke to them. Of course, one could only hope the exercise had made them more thoughtful, and they would not get into mischief again. Eden did not know if the letter writing had been *that* successful. It was too much to hope they would suddenly change their devilish ways.

After all, the point was not to turn them into obedient drones. They did not live in a beehive. They were meant to be spirited and adventurous.

Eden decided to take them in the rig because it was simply too hot to walk all the way to the cliffs and back. They would do plenty of running around as they climbed the slopes searching for nests. Of course, they would do nothing dangerous, because

Priscilla and Alex were too young to be taken on any serious climbs. They would be safe enough keeping to the beach and looking up at the birds nesting on the lower cliff ledges.

It was a good way to teach them about hierarchies that existed everywhere in life—among men, birds, and all living things. By now they understood that their father, being a duke, was on the top rung of English society.

Connor escorted them as they marched downstairs. His eldest son climbed into the passenger seat beside Eden while the two younger children scampered into the back.

Eden could tell by the wistful look in Connor's eyes that he ached to join them. But she knew he could not. He had young ladies to woo.

"Be careful," he said, still reluctant to let go of them. "Do you have everything you need?"

Eden nodded. "We have our hats, binoculars, pads, and pencils. We also have a week's worth of food packed in the picnic basket."

He glanced at his boys and then turned back to her with a smile. "A week's worth? Let's hope it lasts beyond an hour."

"We'll forage for wild berries if we must," she teased. "See you at teatime."

Their first stop was the pond, where Eden lectured the children on showing kindness to animals. "But Henry Bright," Alex said, referring to the Lynton Grange gamekeeper, "will just shoot them for our supper. Why be nice to them when we are just going to eat them?"

Eden had no answer for that. "Well, just do not torment them before they die. Would you want to be tormented even if you were going to be eaten in a month's time?"

That led to the boys teasing their sister about eating her up.

"Don't eat me!" Priscilla wailed, and burst into tears.

Dear heaven. Time for Eden to rethink this idea.

How had she botched this so badly? Perhaps because she was lecturing them instead of allowing them to reach the right conclusion on their own. Of course, this assumed they would reach it and not resort to hurling stones at the geese again.

Their time by the cliffs was much more productive. They were not climbing to the top but mostly exploring along the beach and lower cliff ledges. The azure sea was to the left of them, the soaring red cliffs to their right as they trod through the sand. They set up watch on a low ledge and observed the birds flying in and out of their nests immediately above them. They also watched as several birds circled over the water. The boys cheered when a kestrel dove in and then flew back up with a fat fish wriggling in its beak.

They spent hours walking, observing, and even drawing what they saw. When the boys claimed they were hungry, they made their way back up to their rig. Eden had led the horse to a nearby stream and let him drink his fill before they went off on their explorations. He was loosely tethered in the shade beside some forage shrubs that he could munch on when he got hungry.

Thankfully, the rig was still there when they hiked back up. The horse was once again drinking contentedly by the stream, lapping up the cool water with his thick tongue.

Eden and the children settled under one of the larger shade trees and shared the pasties, fruit, bread, cheeses, and strawberry tarts Connor's cook had packed for them. Bottles of cider and lemonade had also been provided.

The boys did not stop eating or guzzling their drinks until the basket was completely empty. They were going to grow as big as Connor, and that required quite a bit of nourishment to reach their full height.

As the sun began its descent on the horizon, Eden decided it was time to return. By the position of the sun, she judged it was nearing three o'clock in the afternoon. Since they still had almost an hour's ride home, they quickly packed up and hopped in the rig for the return trip.

Eden took the front passenger seat this time and allowed young Connor to drive. Alex and Priscilla jumped in the back.

They hadn't gone very far before Priscilla stretched out and promptly fell asleep with her head on her brother's lap.

Alex absently stroked his sister's curls and did not fidget even once, because he did not wish to disturb her. These boys could tease their little sister mercilessly but also be kind as anything to her, as Alex was now.

Eden loved this about siblings and wished she had some of her own, even if they had only been her father's by-blows. Kin was kin, was it not?

Her mother and father hated each other, so there were never going to be any legitimate children arising from that union after her. Yet she doubted there were any illegitimate ones, either. Not that her father was a saint. He certainly was not. However, it was not like him to be discreet about *anything*, not even his misbehavior. She would have known if there were any Darrow by-blows out there.

They had just reached the manor and drawn up to its courtyard when Connor dashed out of the house toward them. "Thank goodness you're back. I was just about to ride out to find you."

Eden's heart tightened. "What is the matter? Is Duchess Evelyn all right?"

Sarah and Millie had rushed out immediately behind him. "Evelyn is fine," he assured her.

Eden emitted a rush of breath. "Thank goodness."

The two maids led the boys and a groggy Priscilla, who had woken up only minutes earlier, up to their quarters.

Instead of allowing her to return to her own guest chamber, Connor held Eden back. "Come with me."

He led her into his study. A woman was seated on the settee and appeared to be crying.

Eden's eyes widened. "Mama?"

Well, she was not entirely surprised to find her mother here, because it usually took no more than a day or two for one of her parents to come running to her, demanding she choose sides in their latest battle. But to see her mother crying *this* hard? Those were genuine tears she was spilling.

Eden rushed to her side. "What happened, Mama?"

Her mother merely wailed into her lace handkerchief.

Dread suddenly filled Eden. "Has something happened to Papa?"

Her mother nodded.

Connor closed the door but remained in the study with them. He drew up a chair for Eden and took one for himself beside her. "As far as I can tell, your mother thinks she might have killed your father."

She gasped. "What?"

"I hit him harder than usual," her mother explained between bouts of tears and hiccups. "The dolt did not duck in time."

Eden ground her teeth. "You should not have hit him at all. Are you certain he is dead? Have you summoned a doctor?"

"Do not lecture me, Eden. Your father is a maddening boor. Why should he be the one to stay with you when I rode all the way from London just as he did to be with you? If he were a gentleman, he would have removed himself and settled in one of the lovely inns in Lynton."

"As you could have done," Eden muttered. "Or the two of you could have behaved like responsible adults and simply avoided each other. It is a big house. Plenty of bedrooms. You could have kept to opposite sides of the house. But Mama, how has it been left? *Did* you summon the doctor?"

"Ugh, Eden! You are still lecturing me. Stop being as insufferable as your father."

"Well, he won't be all that insufferable if he is truly dead," she muttered, her voice shaking with anger at both of them. It was bad enough they had invaded her home at the same time, which was the reason she was here and forced to watch Connor find some adorable young thing to marry. If not for their untimely arrival, she could have been moping around her own home and left in peace while she wallowed in her misery. Chestnut Hill was her home. *Her* home. Owned by her outright.

Her parents had no claim to it, and yet had chased her out of it.

Of course, she welcomed each of them to visit her whenever they wished. As miserable as they were, they were still her parents. But when the two of them descended on her together? It was utter chaos.

She still could not wrap her brain around the possibility that her father was dead or that her mother had killed him. "Mama, tell me exactly what happened. How did the accident come about?"

"It was no accident. I purposely threw your candelabrum at him. He just stood there like the dolt he is...was... Well, you know what I mean. The gall of that man. He did not bother to block it. The thing hit him squarely in the head. And now I am sure he is dead and it is all his fault."

"*His* fault?" Eden turned to Connor, wondering what he must be thinking, but his expression was unreadable.

How could he not be disgusted with her parents? By extension, how could he not be disgusted with *her*?

"Yes, *his* fault," her mother repeated. "Because of his stupidity, I shall now have to face the magistrate and explain why I attacked him. I am certain he will understand and absolve me of all blame. But what if he is a boor and does not? Am I to be condemned now as a criminal? And must I be questioned? It is too humiliating to contemplate. Oh, why must I suffer so?"

"You? Papa got the worst of it, since you may have killed him," Eden pointed out, hoping against hope her father had merely been knocked unconscious and was not lying dead on her floor.

"Stop lecturing me, Eden! Must I face your inquisition *and* that of the magistrate? It is too distressing. I shall break out in hives because I am so stressed. Your father's fault, of course."

"Am I to understand the reason for your distress is your annoyance at the possibility of being questioned by the magistrate?" Eden glanced at Connor because he happened to *be* the local magistrate. "Do you feel any remorse for possibly ending his life?"

"He should have moved out of the way! It was an accident, not a crime," her mother said with unwarranted indignity.

Connor cleared his throat. "I've sent a footman to fetch the doctor."

"Thank goodness," Eden muttered.

Connor took hold of her hand and gave it a light squeeze. "I'll take you back to your home…unless you would rather stay here while I attend to your father."

Eden was quite spent from her outing, but this was too important an incident to ignore. "I want to go with you."

Her mother tipped her chin up and snorted in indignation. "Of course, leave me behind and run to your undeserving father. You always liked him best."

"At the moment, I do not like either of you. However, you are alive and my father is possibly dead."

"Exactly," her mother said. "He is dead and I am alive. You should be looking after me."

Eden sighed. "Come with us, then."

"I will not set foot in that house while your father is still there. I am staying here." Mama turned to Connor and cast him an engaging smile. "You seem to have a lovely house party going on. I do adore a good party. I'll have a visit with your mother while the two of you deal with *that man*."

"That man is your husband," Eden shot back, leaping to her feet now that the last vestiges of her patience had been spent. "You'll come with us and—"

Connor was still holding her hand, and gave it another light squeeze as he rose beside her. "Let's you and I deal with this. Give me a moment to fill my mother in on what has happened. She'll take care of your mother until we return. All right, Eden?"

She dreaded the impression her mother would make on his guests, particularly the Lothmere family. It made her cringe to think of her mother going on and on about her father and this being his fault. But was it not better to simply get this inevitable embarrassment out of the way? If Eden's mother did not scare Lord Aubrey away after this, then nothing would. "All right."

Connor took a few minutes to speak to his mother and also ordered his brougham brought around. The elegant open carriage awaited them in the courtyard by the time they were ready to leave a few minutes later.

Connor settled beside her and ordered his driver to proceed.

"Right, Your Grace," the man said, spurring the team to a trot.

Eden let out the breath she had been holding all the while in her mother's company. "I'm so sorry this—"

"Eden, none of this is your fault," Connor said gently, and took her hand again. "Nor do I mind helping you out after all the help you've given me. I just hope your father is all right."

"So do I." She sighed and leaned back against the squabs. "Connor, what makes two people hate each other so much?"

"I don't know." He nudged her to his side and allowed her to lean her head on his shoulder instead of the carriage's metal frame. "Love and hate are not opposite emotions. Love and apathy are opposites. Sometimes, there is a thin line between love and hate."

"I cannot imagine they ever started with love. I doubt they ever felt the slightest connection to each other. Nor do they feel very connected to me. I am more of a truce negotiator—and not a very good one at that, since tensions always flare within an hour or two of my attempted resolution. They never think of me as their beloved child."

She felt like crying, but this was not the time for it. She prayed they would find her father sitting up and breathing when they reached her home.

"Eden, assuming your father is still alive and cannot travel for a while," he said, "you are welcome to stay with us at Lynton Grange, if you ever feel the need to escape. My home is always open to you. Come to us whenever you want, day or night, and stay for as long as you wish."

"And have my parents disrupt your household when they come shouting for me to referee their next match?"

"Is it much different than my boys and their antics?" He cast her an affectionate smile.

"Much different. I like your boys. They will grow up to be fine men, just like their father. My family, on the other hand, is hopeless."

"Well, you are a treasure and more than make up for their failings."

She gave a mirthless laugh. "Well, I... Oh, look! There's the doctor's carriage. That was fast."

Connor nodded. "Your staff probably sent for him after your mother ran to us."

That made sense. Unlike her parents, her staff was reliable and sensible.

To her relief, her father was sitting on the settee in the parlor with a bloodied cloth held to his head while the doctor ministered to him.

Eden greeted the local doctor, a dependable man with army training that she thought would come in handy, since her father probably needed stitches in his head. "Thank you for coming so promptly, Dr. Weaver. What's to be done for my father?"

"Just a few stitches and a bit of rest."

She nodded. "I'll attend to whatever he needs." She turned to her father, noting the lump that was the size of a goose egg protruding from his skull. "She really beaned you this time, Papa. What did you say to her?"

Her father cast her an indignant look. "What makes you think I said or did anything?"

Eden rolled her eyes. "You always do something to set her off. On purpose, I might add."

"She deserves it," he muttered. "The woman is an insufferable banshee. I am the one to be pitied. She almost killed me."

Dr. Weaver's expression remained professional and detached. "Sit quietly now, Lord Darrow. I am going to stitch you up, and you will need to remain still for this."

Eden did not know whether it was the heat of the day, too much time spent under the sun, or merely the strain of thinking her father had been killed that prompted her to suddenly feel ill. Her head began to spin as soon as the doctor withdrew his needle. She felt dizzy, and an odd numbness began to spread through her body in waves.

"Eden!" Connor's arms came around her as she suddenly swayed. "Sit down."

He helped her to one of the nearby chairs, and she sank heavily onto it.

"You're shaking, love," he said, his voice tender and husky.

She nodded. "I need air. Connor, please…"

He glanced around, noted the implements the doctor was taking out of his bag, and hastily agreed. "Let me get you outside."

He put an arm around her waist and kept protective hold of her as he led her onto the shaded terrace that was similar to his in size and view, except hers did not have as beautiful a garden. She loved flowers and had many colorful blooms, but they were no match for his display, known throughout England as one of the finest examples of horticultural excellence.

"Evans, bring out lemonade and any sweet cakes you can find," Connor ordered her butler as the man followed after them, concern for his mistress etched on his face.

"At once, Your Grace."

Connor made certain she was seated in a shady spot that was also in the path of a cooling sea breeze. "You overdid it today, Eden. My fault entirely," he muttered. "I should have gone with you. Or not let you stay out so long."

"On our bird watch? When have you ever had the patience to watch birds? But I do it all the time," she insisted. "It wasn't the length of the excursion that was the problem. I enjoyed it, and so did your children. And you could not have gone with us, or it would have defeated the entire purpose of my taking them out of your hair in the first place."

"But I should have been more thoughtful. I don't know, I should have looked out for you better. We were dancing into the wee hours of the morning."

She smiled at him. "I liked dancing with you."

"Me too." He grinned back. "It was nice, wasn't it?"

She nodded. "You are an excellent dancer. Or was it just the music and moonlight that swept me away?"

He tweaked her chin. "It was my being manly and your being in my manly arms, of course. How does it feel to have danced with a Silver Duke?"

"Almost as good as I will feel after taking a sip of this lemonade." She nodded toward Evans, who bustled out with a lemonade pitcher, glasses, and an enormous cherry pie. "You don't expect me to eat all that by myself, do you?"

"No, I'll make the sacrifice and join you," Connor teased, settling beside her. He frowned when she reached for the pitcher. "I'll do it. Sit back and rest, Eden. Let me take care of you."

"Being waited upon by a Silver Duke. Now, that is something to note in my diary."

He arched an eyebrow as he poured a glass of lemonade and handed it to her. "Do you keep one?"

She sighed. "Yes, and I used to write all sorts of improper things in it."

"But no more?"

"Not really, not all that much lately. I did at one time, but that was ages ago. It turns out my life is very dull and there was never anything of interest to write in it, so I had to make up lots of exciting things."

"Such as?"

"Oh, mostly silly things. Pirate invasions. Dragons. Elves and pixies."

"What about your debut Season? Was this not interesting enough?"

She took a sip of her lemonade. "No, not particularly."

He regarded her dubiously while cutting her a generous slice of pie. "Not even a first kiss? I thought that was a monumental event for a young lady. Better even than encountering dragons and pixies."

She blushed and began to fidget. "Let us speak of something else."

She was never going to admit she had yet to be kissed by a beau. This was perhaps her greatest regret, for she had been young and too uncertain of herself. She was so scared to trust any man that she had trusted no one and never experienced a first kiss. Nor was she foolish enough to allow herself to be compromised by some scheming fortune hunter who would then insist on marrying her to "save" her reputation.

But amid all her wariness and secure defenses, she had missed out not only on the thrill of a first kiss but on the chance of a true and enduring love.

That hurt most of all. She would never marry or have children of her own. She would go to her grave never having been kissed in a romantic and enrapturing way.

Was this not the most pathetic thing imaginable?

Perhaps she would ask Lord Aubrey to kiss her before the house party ended and he returned to London. One kiss before he dropped her like a stone now that he understood the sort of family she would bring along with her, should they ever marry.

Ha! Marriage? Even under the best circumstances, it remained an impossible dream. Her parents were as bad as a plague.

But in thinking of kisses, she knew Lord Aubrey was not the one she wanted for her precious first. She wanted Connor, but how could she ever ask him? He was the only man whose lips she wanted touching hers, the only man she completely trusted. He would always be honest with her.

However, they were friends and neighbors. Could they share one kiss and then proceed with their lives as usual? Or would it change everything and she would lose his friendship, too?

No, it would be too risky. Losing this precious rapport she

had with Connor was too upsetting to consider.

Connor continued to eye her intently, and she knew the moment he became aware of her secret. "Eden, have you never been kissed before?"

She avoided answering the question by shooting out of her chair when her father happened to emit a timely howl. "I had better see to him." The stitches had to be painful as the doctor put them in.

Connor clamped his hand on her wrist. "There is nothing you can do but hover over him, and that will only make him behave worse. He is going to continue howling because he is not the stoic type."

She stopped trying to tug out of his grip that was not tight, merely persistent. "Stoic?" She laughed mirthlessly. "No, my parents shall never be known for their grace under pressure."

"Those stitches will hurt a little, but he will survive," Connor assured her. "The doctor knows what he is doing."

At her nod, he released her.

"Finish your pie, Eden." He refilled her glass of lemonade and then cut each of them another generous slice of pie.

Her father howled again.

Connor placed his hand over hers. "You must have smelled the odd, faintly sickly smell when we walked in. The doctor has already numbed the area of the wound, so I think your father is shouting more out of indignation than any serious pain. I've had stitches myself."

"You have? What happened?"

"My upper arm was sliced during a battle in Spain. The army surgeon sewed me up, and I was back on the battlefield within an hour afterward. I'm sure I was fairly useless to my regiment, but no one ever complained."

"I'm sure you were valiant and your fellow soldiers were heartened to see you back with them. How many stitches?"

"Thirty."

"Oh, Connor. I'm so sorry. I had no idea."

"It was nothing. Others fared worse."

Her hands were shaking as she raised the glass to her lips. "I'm sure it was quite something. But you make it appear insignificant because you are brave and heroic. My father is a spoiled child."

As though to prove her point, her father began bellowing invectives at the doctor. It was yet another humiliation to endure, but Dr. Weaver was familiar with her family by now. She would apologize to him profusely once he was done.

On a brighter note, did this not prove all was well with her father? He was alive and back to his usual bellicose form. His lung capacity was undiminished.

This also meant her mother was no longer doomed to spend her days as a criminal on the run.

Could she ask for a better outcome?

Connor was still watching her. He had forgotten about their prior conversation…she hoped. "Yum, the pie is delicious and the lemonade refreshing. Don't you think so? What is your favorite pie, Connor?"

He leaned closer. "Eden, I see right through you."

"I have no idea what you mean." She had dug through one generous slice of pie and was determined to keep digging into the second piece, and a third if it meant keeping her mouth full and her unable to speak. She was not going to discuss her lack of a first kiss.

But Connor was not through probing her about it.

Why did he care? It was not as though he was ever going to kiss her in the ways she had made up in her diary. Yes, she had written all about his splendid kisses, every word a complete fabrication.

"You cannot choose Aubrey for a first kiss," he muttered.

She coughed. Or was it a sneeze? Maybe something of a snoffle. "Why are you remarking on this? What makes you think I haven't been kissed a thousand times already? Well, perhaps not that many. Do you think I have not been kissed at least once in my entire life?"

He sighed. "It so happens that this is *exactly* what I think."

"Well then, keep your thoughts to yourself," she said, shoving more pie into her mouth.

"Fine, but I will say this… If someone is ever to kiss you, it needs to be me."

Of all the conversations she had ever thought to have today, this wasn't one of them. She hastily swallowed the last of her bite and stared at him. "Why must it be you, Connor?"

And why was she being stupidly defensive when this was exactly what she had been wishing for? Had she not written pages and pages of kissing scenes between them in her diary? Hot kisses. Sweet kisses. French kisses (whatever they were). Tender kisses. Blazing, singe-one's-eyebrows-off kisses.

His kisses.

She had better burn that diary before anyone got their hands on it.

Here he was, offering her the very kiss she had only thought possible in her dreams. And there she was, rejecting it.

"Never mind," he said, drawing back. "It doesn't have to be me. After all, why wouldn't you prefer a younger man? Just don't let it be Aubrey."

"Why not him?"

He raked a hand through his hair. "I don't know. I just don't trust him. Besides, a first kiss should be something special, given by someone who cares for you, someone you trust never to hurt you. I thought you trusted me, that's all."

"I do trust you." She stared at her hands that were now clasped and resting on her lap. "I trust you more than anyone else in the entire world."

She trusted him with her very heart. But what if she gave it to him and he did not want it?

She took a deep breath. To her horror, tears began to form in her eyes. "Oh, dear. Ignore me, Connor."

He reached over and gave her cheek a light caress. "All right.

Forget I ever brought it up. It was a stupid idea. I just did not want you to be kissed for the first time and be disappointed."

"Nor do I. Let me think about it, will you?"

He cast her a Silver Duke smile, the sort that was beguiling and utterly heart melting. "All right."

She cleared her throat. "Well, now that you know my humiliating secret...can you explain what I am missing and why it should not be anyone but you?"

He laughed. "Curious, are you?"

She nodded.

There was not a hint of teasing in his voice as he said, "Because of who you are, Eden. I know you are intelligent and independent, but you are also sweeter than anyone I know. Your heart is soft and vulnerable despite all the barriers you have erected around it. So a first kiss needs to be magical for you. More than that, it needs to be a perfect moment of enchantment. I understand this, and I understand *you*. I am going to do this right for you. Moonlight. Music. Warm summer night."

Her eyes widened as he spoke. "Tonight?"

"Perhaps." He leaned back and stretched his long legs before him. "The moment has to feel right. I'll know it when I come upon it."

"And you will kiss me?"

He cast her another Silver Duke smile. "Yes, Eden. I will kiss you till your toes curl, and it will be unforgettable."

Her heart beat wildly for this. For *him*. For the hope of his kiss.

"Connor, if you are jesting about this, I will dust off my diary and scribble the most terrible things about you in it."

He chuckled. "Just what awful things will you write?"

She laughed along with him. "That it felt as though I was kissing a frog. Or being licked by a dog."

"And what will you write if you like the kiss?"

CHAPTER EIGHT

S INCE EDEN INSISTED on staying with her father for what was left of the afternoon, Connor returned to Lynton Grange without her. But he chose to walk back on his own, leaving his carriage and driver at Chestnut Hill in the hope she would follow soon after him, since there was still the matter of her mother to address. The woman could not be sent back to Eden's home while her husband was still there recovering from her attempt to do him in.

How did Eden endure the pair? How had she turned into the extraordinary woman she was despite all their attempts to damage her? Well, he thought sadly, they had done quite a bit of damage. They had left her wary and distrustful of marriage.

This was a terrible thing for Eden, who had so much love to give.

He strode briskly along the familiar path between their homes, breathing in the country air that was a mix of fragrant woods, damp earth, and salty sea breezes. The sun filtered through the rustling leaves and spread dots of light amid the shaded walk.

"What a coil," he muttered as his conversation with Eden began to sink in.

He had agreed to kiss her. Not just agreed, but actually been the one to raise it first and *offer* to do it out of a sense of moral obligation and other feelings he did not care to think about.

Had he completely lost his mind?

Yes, he must have. How else was he to explain his profoundly apish jealousy? The thought of anyone other than him kissing Eden had his body in turmoil.

Yet a simple kiss between them would change everything, especially if things went further than an innocent touch of their lips.

Ha! There was nothing innocent in the scorching way he meant to ravage that delectable mouth of hers.

But what then? He could not in good conscience turn Eden into a convenient bed partner, much as he found himself aching to do so. "Hell and damnation," he muttered, raking a hand through his hair. When had this come about? When had they gone from merely being friends to…whatever this was?

She deserved better than to be his mistress. *Gad!* That sounded awful. He had never had a mistress in all his years, nor did he desire to take one on now.

Not to mention, it could never be Eden. She deserved to be loved and adored. She deserved to be treated with respect. Indeed, there was no one more deserving than Eden, and no one he admired more. If he ever bedded her, it would be as his wife.

He could never be intimate with her on any other terms. She was his to protect, even from himself.

Was this not precisely how he had gotten himself into this coil? She had wanted a first kiss and meant for Lord Aubrey to be the one to provide it. But that wretch was going to break her heart—Connor just knew it and felt it in his gut. Eden could never let down her defenses and allow him in.

This was the primary reason Connor wanted to step in first and kiss Eden. She was smart, but innocent when it came to matters of love. What were Aubrey's intentions?

"Hell if I know," Connor grumbled, unwilling to consider the other reasons he needed to kiss Eden and keep Aubrey away from her.

Why was he so possessive when it came to her? Did she not

have the right to secure a joyous future?

"But not with Aubrey," he muttered, knowing that lord could not possibly be right for her. He was too slick. Too attentive. Too...*wrong* for her.

His mother accosted him the moment he entered his home. "How is Eden's father? Dare I ask? Is he alive?"

"Yes, alive and howling like a banshee as Dr. Weaver put stitches in his head," he said as they hurried into his study before he was surrounded by the peahens vying for his attention. He closed the door to afford them privacy. "Evans had the presence of mind to have the doctor summoned immediately. He was already there when we arrived. Eden's father required about six stitches on his forehead, but one would think he had to endure six hundred. The man is an infant. Speaking of which, how is Lady Darrow?"

"Eden's other infant parent?" His mother sighed. "Soaking up the attention."

"What a surprise." Connor did not bother to hide his sarcasm. "We'll have to put her up here for the night. She and her husband cannot be left alone together at Chestnut Hill."

"What about Eden? Will she stay with her father?"

Was it wrong of him to hope she would not? He wanted Eden here with him. "I don't know yet. Her staff is fully capable of caring for him, but she might decide to remain by his side on the chance he takes a turn for the worse. Whatever her decision, we will keep her mother overnight and see what comes about tomorrow."

His sharp-eyed mother studied him. "I hope Eden does return to us. Lord Aubrey has been asking after her."

Connor grumbled something apishly unintelligible.

His mother pursed her lips as she studied him. "Why don't you like him?"

He rubbed a hand across the back of his neck, irritated with himself for allowing his feelings to show. "Who says I don't?"

"Oh, let me see. How about your every word and action? I

am your mother, Connor. I don't give a fig about that Silver Duke never-going-to-marry nonsense you keep spouting. Or in your situation, the never-marrying-*again* nonsense. You cannot hide your feelings from me."

"And just what is it you think I am hiding?"

She ambled to his desk and distracted herself a moment with the apology letters his children had written him that were sitting atop his pile of work. He had read them over and over because they were so innocent and heartfelt.

This had been Eden's idea. He now had these precious mementos from his beloved heathens because of her.

His mother looked up at him once again. "You are feeling confused."

He snorted. "That isn't very helpful."

"You like Eden, but have no plans to do anything about her. That is, you *had* no plans until Lord Aubrey came along and trespassed in your territory. It is not right of you, Connor. Eden is not a piece of land to claim as yours. She is a lovely young woman who deserves better than what you have given her...which, I might add, is nothing at all." She approached him as he stood with a shoulder casually leaning against the fireplace mantel. "My son, do not close yourself off to marriage."

He snorted in response.

"Very well, remain stubborn about it. I was hoping you might find a nice girl among my house party guests, but I was mistaken."

"I'm glad you finally realize it. They are—"

"I say this because you have already found the girl. You've had three years since poor Mary died to get to know Eden and fall in love with her. You needed time and distance to get over the loss, but it is now well past time. Oh, I know you and your Silver Duke friends are all about maintaining your freedom. And do not tell me again that you already have your heir and spare, or I will club you over the head just as Lady Darrow did her husband."

He held up his hands in mock surrender. "Why is this conversation suddenly turning violent?"

"It is not violence but frustration," she said with a sigh. "Open your eyes, Connor. Look at what has been in front of you all along. Do not lose this woman you love because you are foolishly equating freedom from the bonds of matrimony with happiness. If you say nothing, then Lord Aubrey will win her hand."

"You think I am in love with Eden?"

"I do not think it. I *know* it."

"Do not presume to know my mind," he shot back for no reason other than to be difficult. He did not like his mother prying into his affairs.

"Fine, two can play at this game." She cast him a fierce look that warned he was not too big to have his ears boxed by his mother, even though he was a full head and shoulders taller than her. "I meant this house party to be for you, but I have changed my mind," she said with a huff.

He groaned. "Could you not have changed your mind *before* inviting everyone here, sparing us all the inconvenience?"

"No, I could not have. If you dislike the intrusion, then take yourself off for the rest of the week. Your presence is no longer required. You are unnecessary, so go away. This house party is now held entirely for Eden's sake. I am going to find her a husband before the week is out."

"A husband? Among that motley lot?"

"They are a *prime* lot, and Lord Aubrey is obviously the best of them. He seems perfect, does he not?"

Now she was just trying to rile him.

"He is young, handsome, and sincerely appears to like her," his mother went on. "So, keep to your Silver Duke pact and live out the rest of your days a shriveled old man. But I am going to do all in my power to see Eden happily matched."

That said, she was about to leave, but turned back to him again. "Consider this a declaration of war."

Before he had the chance to respond, Eden's mother burst in. "At last, you are back!"

Great, now he had to deal with this woman's high drama. Well, she had to be anxious about her husband's condition, even if the reason was merely to save her own hide.

She was followed in by Lord Aubrey and his irritating sister. Yes, Persephone was beautiful and charmingly coquettish, but she was little more than a spoiled child.

She wasn't Eden. She lacked Eden's quiet grace and intelligence.

And he couldn't stand her flirtatious giggles and eyelash batting, as though dust particles were incessantly falling into her eyes.

"Well, Your Grace? Is my wretched husband alive?" Lady Darrow asked, taking on the role of put-upon victim.

"Yes, he lives. Dr. Weaver is with him now, sewing stitches in his head. I think it is best you stay here tonight. My housekeeper will have a room prepared for you, and—"

"Oh, I can take Eden's room. You've given her a lovely bedchamber. I doubt she'll be using it tonight, since she will want to stay with her father. She always takes his side," she said with a practiced pout.

Did this woman believe her pouting would endear her to anyone? Connor itched to toss this irritating woman out of his house. "That chamber is Eden's to use as she wishes for the duration of the house party. You will have a room of your own, and it will certainly not be Eden's."

"I do not see why—" She took a step back in response to his glower.

"Have I not made myself clear, Lady Darrow? That is Eden's room. I will have you sleep in the barn if you dare attempt to take it over for yourself."

Everyone gasped.

He thought he was behaving with remarkable restraint. "I'll send word for your lady's maid to bring over whatever you'll need for tonight and tomorrow morning."

"Let me carry that message," Aubrey said, stepping forward.

The ladies leaped at his offer, both Lady Darrow and his own traitor of a mother eagerly agreeing to the suggestion. His mother cast him a victorious smirk.

"All right," he said between clenched teeth, unwilling to be pushed into declaring himself for Eden. Whatever he felt was between him and Eden alone, and would be dealt with in due course.

He tried to go about the business of playing host for the next few hours, but he was going out of his mind with annoyance by the time supper came around. Neither Aubrey nor Eden had returned, and to make matters worse, his children were acting up again.

His mother must have taken pity on him, for she chose to come to his rescue as he stood in the entry hall with Priscilla crying in his arms and asking about Eden. "I miss her, Papa! Where did she go?"

Why was Eden suddenly everyone's darling?

His mother took Priscilla's hand when he set his daughter down. "Priscilla, why don't you and I draw a pretty card for Eden's father to wish him well? I think Eden will be quite touched by the thoughtful gesture."

"All right, Grandmama. But I can do it myself." His daughter smiled brightly, obviously taking to the idea with enthusiasm. She ran upstairs with Millie. That now took care of his youngest.

"I'll leave the boys to you," his mother said, and sauntered onto the terrace to join their other guests. The older crowd was seated in the shade and sipping tea while the younger guests were playing lawn games.

Unable to think of what to do with his boys, he decided to allow them to participate in a round of pall mall. It seemed harmless enough, just knocking a ball to a wicket.

Yes, harmless—until they started going at each other with their mallets.

Connor quickly put an end to that idea and sent them up to their bedchambers for an early supper while they still had all their teeth intact and did not require stitches. Dr. Weaver had done enough stitching for one day.

They gave little protest, not because his sons respected his wishes—they decidedly did not—but because they were growing boys and could eat an entire bear in one sitting if given the opportunity. They would behave for food.

This left Connor alone once again to entertain Persephone and the other peahens still flocking around him. He could not possibly be all that charming, and his jests could not be all that hilarious. But the women dutifully tittered and giggled and complimented him on his wit. Persephone did not stop clinging to his arm, as though she had taken a proprietary interest in him.

Well, the girl was in for a rude awakening. Nobody had claim to him. He was a Silver Duke.

He finally managed to slip away with an excuse that he had work to do before they met again for supper.

He retired to his quarters and enjoyed a moment of solitude before it was time to wash and dress in more appropriate formal attire for their dinner party, after which there would be dancing, as well as card tables set up for those who did not wish to dance.

Once ready, he happened to peer out his window and notice the carriage he had left at Chestnut Hill for Eden's use now coming up the drive.

By fortunate circumstance, he had his binoculars atop his bureau. He grabbed them and peered at the approaching conveyance. Not that he was in the habit of spying on his guests. He merely had them conveniently at hand because he meant to join Eden and his children on tomorrow morning's excursion and had prepared in advance.

Although who knew what Eden's plans would be now?

He saw the lovely girl seated beside Aubrey, chatting with him and smiling as Connor's team of horses, under his coachman's steady control, made their way into the courtyard. It was not jealousy that had him setting aside his binoculars and hurrying downstairs to greet her.

No, not jealousy. He was too old for that nonsense. Was it not neighborly good form to express concern?

"How is your father?" He reached for Eden and placed his hands around her waist to lift her down, purposely keeping hold of her lithe body a moment longer than was necessary before he released her because he knew it would irk the interloper.

Aubrey noticed. His eyes narrowed and he tossed Connor a challenging frown.

Eden appeared oblivious to the tension between the two men. She answered his question cheerfully and with unmistakable relief. "My father is now comfortably settled in his bedchamber. Cook has prepared his favorite meal. Evans has brought up a selection of books from my library for him, although I think his eyes will strain if he attempts to read on his own. Most of my staff are educated, so any one of them can read aloud to him while he rests his eyes. I have left instructions for someone to sit with him throughout the night. I've left it to Evans to make the assignments. They'll take four-hour shifts this first evening. I'll look in on him tomorrow morning, as will Dr. Weaver." She glanced toward his house. "And how is my mother?"

He arched an eyebrow. "Oh, she's made herself right at home."

Eden winced. "Sorry. I thought she might. How are the children?"

"Completely unmanageable and barely surviving without you," he said with a soft laugh. "Priscilla is preparing a card for your father while the boys are doing their best to eat me into impoverishment."

She happened to smile just as the sun reappeared from behind a cloud.

Yes, this was what Eden was—pure sunshine.

"I'll look in on them before their bedtime," she said with a shake of her head, and then spared a glance at his attire. "Oh, am I too late for supper?"

"Not at all. Run up and change. We'll wait for you to come

down before I have Brewster ring the dinner bell." He noticed a trunk perched in the rear of the carriage. "Your mother's things? One of the footmen will carry it up to her bedchamber. I'll assign Sarah to assist her for the duration of her stay."

"Thank you. That is very generous of you."

He cast her a wry smile. "I've taken the liberty of placing her at the opposite end of the hall from your chamber."

She laughed again. "That sounds perfect."

"I thought it might."

She thanked him once more and hurried into the house.

Connor now turned to Aubrey, who had remained standing by the carriage during his and Eden's brief exchange. He did not like the fellow, nor did Aubrey appear to like him. Nevertheless, they maintained their gentlemanly façades.

He grudgingly thanked Aubrey for assisting Eden. "She seems relieved. Crisis averted. But how is she feeling, really?"

To his credit, Aubrey did not toss back a whimsical response. "Shaken, I think. She hides it well, pretends to take their antics in stride. But I'm sure their constant battles get to her. She has remarkable composure. However, if one looks closely, one can see she is fragile."

"Yes, she is," Connor replied, his tone intended to send this lord a warning. "That's why she will be seated beside me tonight."

"So you can protect her?" Aubrey frowned. "Why? I can assure you, she will be just as safe with me."

"As I said, she stays by me."

"Do you intend to court her, Lynton? Is this what your glowering at me is about? Then consider the gauntlet tossed. From what I gather, you had three years to declare yourself and have not done it. Too bad, old man. You've lost your chance, for I intend to court her...and I do not like to lose."

That said, he marched off.

Connor knew there was a reason he did not like the man. Nor did he trust him, no matter his declaration about honorably courting Eden.

Now in thoroughly ill humor, he joined his other guests in the drawing room.

There was not much of an evening breeze tonight, and the room felt oppressively dank and hot. Even more so as Persephone and the other young women swarmed around him like bees around a hive. He tried to pay attention to their conversations, but it was impossible to manage while they were all chattering at him at once.

Just to be perverse, he made several particularly inane comments and was curious as to how they would respond. He received nothing short of adulation because none of these girls would ever be honest with him and call him an idiot. A *duke* idiot. And this made all the difference to them.

He was a duke and they would endure the labors of Hercules to become his duchess.

Of course, their motives did not excuse his own behavior. He was being an ass tonight. All this fake admiration was getting to him.

He tossed out another ridiculous comment. They clapped and smiled and regarded him with worshipful eyes.

He resigned himself to a long evening.

These ladies were not to blame for his ill temper, but they were doing nothing to make it better. However, he resolved to be on better behavior. He forced a smile and complimented each on their lovely gowns. He told them how beautiful they all looked this evening. "Indeed, you are all quite...sparkly." The array of diamonds was blinding.

"Thank you, Your Grace," they replied in a chorus of giggles.

Then Eden walked in.

His heart soared.

It took her a moment to spot him, even though he was hard to overlook because of his height. He was usually among the tallest in the crowd.

She released a breath and smiled at him.

His heart soared again.

He was about to make his excuses and detach himself from his hen roost to greet her, but Aubrey's parents scurried over to her first. In the next moment, Aubrey entered the drawing room, for he had also needed to change his attire before joining them for supper.

Connor nodded to Brewster to sound the bell.

Aubrey escorted Eden into the dining room but frowned when he realized Connor had indeed placed Eden beside him and stuck Aubrey at the other end of the table between his own mother and Eden's mother. Across from him, Connor had purposely placed two older gentlemen who spoke of nothing but the Newmarket horse races.

Connor had also taken care of seating arrangements at his end of the table, placing an older gentleman who was deaf as a post to the right of Eden and a countess who was already too deep in her cups to remember anything of what transpired tonight to his left. This way, he and Eden could hold a conversation without worrying about being overheard.

Lord Aubrey scowled at him from his end of the table. What did the bounder think? That Connor would ever give Eden over to him?

This was *his* home. *His* battleground.

His Eden.

"I'm all right, you know," Eden said softly in his ear once they were seated and the first course was about to be served. "You did not need to keep me close to you."

Yes, he did. "I wanted a chance to chat with you at leisure and make certain both you and your father are truly all right. Especially you, Eden. No one looks after you."

"And you feel that you must take up the laboring oar? I will survive on my own, as I always have." She glanced up at the footman and smiled as he served her the soup course, a popular white soup in veal stock.

"It is not a labor but a pleasure," Connor replied once he was also served. "I've said it before—you are mine to watch over."

She laughed lightly. "You do not need to be such a protective ape around me, although I will admit it feels nice. Lord Aubrey was just as apish on the ride back here. Has something been added to the drinking water lately? I haven't had this much attention from gentlemen since my debut Season."

"Did he say anything about kissing you?"

Her delicate eyebrows shot up. "My, we are getting personal. You've told me what you think about who should give me that first kiss. I have duly noted your offer. But I do not need you to be a third parent attempting to control my life. The two I was given are more than a handful for me."

Parent? Did she regard him as old and doddering?

He set down his soup spoon, since he no longer had much appetite.

She sighed. "You are glowering at me."

"You called me a decrepit oaf."

She blinked. And blinked again. "I said no such thing. What an arrogant lout you are. How in heaven's name did you come to that conclusion? Merely because I compared you to my parents? My mother would certainly not appreciate being considered old and decrepit."

She cast him a mildly admonishing look. "Connor, you are the handsomest man at this table. Surely you know this. Indeed, I am sure you know it. You would not be thought of as a Silver Duke if you weren't devastatingly handsome. But you are also quite stubborn and arrogant when you want to be. As you are now. Stop scowling at me."

"I am not scowling at you."

"Then what would you call that fierce expression on your face? You will have all the little partridges quaking in fear if you do not start smiling."

"They are peahens, not partridges. Nor do I care what they think of me." But he eased back in his chair and managed a small smile. "You think I am handsome?"

She rolled her eyes. "You know you are. Stop angling for compliments. Do you not get enough from your adoring diamonds?"

"You were a diamond, too. Need I remind you? But all right. It is more important we speak about what happened today. I'm glad your father will survive. Are things back to their normal routine?"

"With us? Are you asking about my looking after the children?"

He nodded. "What are your plans for tomorrow? I'll take them if you need to be with your father. They are my responsibility, after all."

"In truth, I would much rather be with them. Let's keep to our plan. My father will be all right. I'll walk over with the children in the morning just to make certain. Then I'll have Evans order my rig hitched so we can ride to the cliffs to bird watch for an hour or so before I take them into town for the St. Matthew's church fair."

"Will you eat in town? The fair is a major event and the town will be quite crowded. Should I have Cook prepare another picnic basket for you?"

"There will be plenty of food stalls at the fair. But it would be wonderful to have a little something extra, some scones and fruit perhaps, to carry in our pouches for the morning."

"Consider it done," he said with a nod.

"What are your plans for tomorrow, Connor?"

He groaned. "My preference would be to go with you, but…"

"You have your guests to entertain. I understand."

"I'll try to get away for a little while, if I can. Perhaps bring some guests into town for the fair. And I'll postpone my usual morning ride, push it back an hour so that I can walk to Chestnut Hill with you and the children."

He glanced around the table to the men. "The riders among them won't mind an hour's delay. Since I am the local magistrate, is it not right that I should look in on your father?"

"You know it isn't necessary."

"I know, but I would like to be there with you."

She glanced down at her hands. "Um…"

He waited for the footman to clear away their bowls. Neither of them had bothered to finish their soup, which was delicious, but his cook would be overset to learn he had hardly touched it. "What is that sound of hesitation?"

"Lord Aubrey is going to join me and the children tomorrow. He has wanted to spend some time with me and I saw no harm in allowing it, especially since your three children will serve as my chaperones. Not that a woman my age needs to be chaperoned."

"Why did you not mention it earlier? Then you do not need me at all tomorrow? You should have stopped me as I was mentioning my plans just now."

"Your presence is always welcome, Connor."

"And so is Lord Aubrey's, it seems."

"He asked and I saw no harm in it. That is all there is to it. I have not forgotten our earlier conversation about his intentions. I am not going to leap into his arms, and certainly never in front of your children."

"Eden, it should be never at all," he said as the churning in his gut arose once again. This irritation had nothing to do with his food or the general condition of his stomach, which was in excellent shape. He was not so ancient as to require a nightly physic. "I've made a decision."

"Oh? Do you mind telling me what this monumental decision is?"

"We are all going with you. We'll load up the carriages and bring along every guest who wishes to join us for bird watching and then the fair."

"You want to bring your bevy of peahens to watch birds with us? Do they even have sensible shoes? I do not need any of them slipping and tumbling off a cliff."

His eyes widened in horror. "You don't take my children climbing to the top along those precarious ledges, do you?"

"No, of course not. We set up our watch from the beach below, or from a low ledge. One that is secure and has plenty of room for all of us. I would never risk anything dangerous with your children, especially the boys. You know how they always shove each other around. They do it playfully, of course. But they are often quite rough with each other."

"That's boys for you."

"You big boys are no better. Are you going to behave around Lord Aubrey, or must I keep the two of you apart?"

He grinned.

"I'm serious, Connor. You had better be nice to him."

"Or what? I shall be spanked and sent to my room without supper?" His grin turned even more wicked. "I wouldn't mind if the punishment came from you. I find you quite appealing when you talk like a priggish schoolmistress."

"Connor, honestly!" She kicked his shin under the table, which was draped in an exquisite lace tablecloth no doubt smuggled in from the city of Nantes.

The next courses came out. Connor's footmen carried in silver trays stacked with racks of lamb, game fowl baked in ornately decorated pies, and an enormous fish that had been smoked for days, along with the usual array of potatoes, leeks, onions, and peas.

Desserts came out next, an array of cakes, tarts, flummery, and blancmange.

Connor noticed Eden stifling yawns by the time the ladies were ready to retire to the parlor for tea and sherry. He, too, was eager for the evening to end. But it was tradition for the men to remain seated around the table with their glasses of port wine and cognac.

He drew back Eden's chair when she rose along with the other ladies. "There's to be dancing later. Has Aubrey already claimed the first dance?"

"Yes, he has. But I think I am going to beg off and simply go to bed before the dancing starts. I feel so weary."

"You've had quite a trying day."

She nodded. "But I'll look in on the children before I retire. Sarah told me that Priscilla was crying for me earlier. I'll give her a kiss goodnight and make certain she is ready for tomorrow's excursion."

"I'll check on them later, too. But I won't be able to escape before the dancing ends. They had better be sound asleep by then."

"I'm sure they will be. Well, goodnight." She left his side and sought out Aubrey to beg off their dance. Connor knew he was being petty to enjoy Aubrey's disappointment, but he also understood that he could not have it both ways with Eden. If he chased away her suitors, then he had better be ready to stand in their place.

He was ready, but this was not a discussion to be had amid a houseful of guests.

He endured hours of dancing, managing to be snared twice by the ever-persistent Persephone. Finally, as the clock in the entry hall chimed three, Connor completed his round about the house to make certain all doors and windows were secured. Usually, Brewster attended to this duty. But the hour was late and his staff had worked hard all day. They would be working hard again tomorrow and every day afterward until the infernal house party ended.

Feeling quite tired himself, he made his way upstairs to look in on his children before retiring to his own bed.

He peered first into the rooms his sons occupied, his heart warming as he saw their angelic faces in innocent repose. They were such little demons when awake.

He next walked into Priscilla's room.

Blessed saints.

He thought his heart would melt at the sight.

Lying beside Priscilla, her arms wrapped around his daughter, was Eden. Both of them were sound asleep.

Connor had never seen a more beautiful vision in his life.

He did not know whether to leave Eden where she was or carry her back to her bedchamber. As he was debating with himself, Priscilla poked Eden in the ribs. Then again. Eden would be black and blue by morning if she remained in Priscilla's bed.

"Up you go, Eden," he murmured, lifting her in his arms. "Put your arms around my neck."

She did so, but he wasn't certain she was aware of what she was doing, since she clearly was not awake. He carried her down to her room, taking care not to be noticed as he made his way along the hall.

All seemed quiet, no one stirring at this late hour.

Well, some guests might be bed-hopping. But any who were would have hopped to their assignations by now.

At least, he hoped so. There would be questions raised if he were caught with Eden in his arms, especially since they were headed to her bedchamber.

In truth, he did not care if they were caught. Perhaps a scandal was the push he needed to shed his Silver Duke reputation and marry. He could see himself happily married to Eden.

In fact, it scared him knowing just how happy she might make him.

Would Eden feel the same?

CHAPTER NINE

E DEN KNEW SHE had to be dreaming, for how else could she be inhaling Connor's divine musk scent or feeling the strength of his arms around her? If it was a dream, she did not want to wake up from it.

Connor was carrying her down several steps and then along a hallway. He paused a moment to open a door, then strode in and placed her on a bed. She sleepily complained when Connor's arms were no longer around her, for she enjoyed their protective warmth and wanted more of their rock-hard strength surrounding her.

"Hush, Eden," he said, his voice deep and husky. "You fell asleep in Priscilla's bed, and I am merely bringing you back to your own."

She sat up, but was too tired to open her eyes. "What...?"

Connor sank onto the mattress beside her. "You fell asleep in Priscilla's bed, Eden."

She nodded, vaguely remembering. "Where am I now?"

"In your bedchamber. I just carried you in here. Do you need help undressing? I mean... Dear heaven. No, I don't mean it like that. I'll loosen the lacings for you and then leave." As he spoke, he removed her spectacles, which were already falling off her nose, and set them on the small table beside the bed.

He then took out the pins holding her hair in place. Many of them had loosened, and several curls had already slipped free. He set the pins on the table beside her spectacles. Next, he moved away from her and knelt to take off her slippers. "All right," he said after doing so. "Can you stand up a moment and turn your back to me?"

Her hair had cascaded down her back and now tumbled over her shoulders as she nodded, but then she curled up on the bed instead.

"No, love. I need you to stand." His strong, sure hands were on her as he gently lifted her to her feet and began attending to the task of undressing her, his touch exquisite and gentle.

This was the last thing she remembered before drifting off again, this feeling of being safe and protected as never before. This wonderful feeling of Connor's strong, supportive arms cradling her and holding her up so she would never fall.

She loved this man. She loved being in his arms and wished it could be this way forever.

"Connor," she murmured, and fell back to sleep while on her feet, knowing she had nothing to fear while he was around.

➸➸➸◅◅◅

CONNOR REALIZED EDEN had just fallen back to sleep again by the way her body relaxed against his again.

"No, no, no, Eden. Wake up, love," he implored.

Her body began to slide down his, setting off responses he refused to acknowledge here and now. However, he had no choice but to hold on to her more firmly in order to keep her from tumbling to the floor. Groaning, he brushed her silken hair aside to give him unimpeded access to her hooks and laces, and was surprised by yet another surge of desire he experienced in the simple act of undressing her.

He was not trying to seduce her. His only aim was to take care of her. She hadn't been fully awake even while conversing with him moments earlier, and might not remember come morning that he had been the one to carry her into her bedchamber or put her into bed.

In truth, this rush of desire he felt for Eden was not unexpected. He had been warming to her for quite some time now. However, this ache coursing like a hot stream through his body was more powerful than he had ever imagined.

This was no mere lust, if he wanted to be honest about it. Lust was something temporary, and Connor knew his feelings for Eden were enduring.

She felt so right beside him. She, with her buttoned-up gowns and sensible manner, distracted him and drove him wild.

He held her up when she began to sway again. "I'm almost done, love," he whispered. "Can you raise your arm?"

Apparently not, he realized when she veered forward and then careened backward against him so that he had to catch her by the waist to keep her from falling. To his surprise, not even the jolt from her almost toppling woke her.

Perhaps because she was aware on some level that she was with him and this made her feel safe. Having his arms around her comforted her. She trusted him.

He was not so trusting of himself, however.

He was in her bedchamber and undressing her. She had the softest body. She also had the nicest breasts that he tried not to graze as he held her up and awkwardly worked the lacings of her gown, but it was unavoidable.

He had been looking closely at Eden lately, noticing everything about her and liking everything he saw. But right now, with no illumination in the room, he could barely make out the outline of her body. In some ways this was worse than having a clear view of her, because his other senses were compensating for what he could not see, particularly touch and scent.

She was facing away from him and her back was lightly pressed against his chest. Apparently, this was all his body needed to be in a roil. Having to go merely by the shape of her body and softness of her skin—*dear heaven*, she felt good—was a full-on assault on his composure.

Taking in the scent of her was intoxicating, for her skin was warm and lightly flowery. A hint of lemon and fresh country air. This woman, his lovely neighbor and friend, could be his every night for the rest of his life if he dared take the chance and propose to her.

Perhaps it was time to reevaluate his reluctance to remarry.

Yes, it was past time.

He was in the middle of unloosening one particularly stubborn tie when she suddenly lurched forward again.

He quickly caught her. "Eden! Be careful, love."

He continued to speak softly in the hope of keeping her upright until he finished. But the poor thing was dead on her feet and did not respond.

Since this was not going to work without her cooperation, he turned her around so that she faced him and could lean against him while he managed the last of her ties. This also meant her perfect breasts rested against his chest.

He had undressed women often enough to be familiar with the workings of their gowns, and usually showed more prowess when seducing them. Of course, the women tended to dress more scantily than Eden was now. They also tended to be more alert and cooperative.

Yes, being awake was a requirement. Awake and willing to engage in more than merely being put to bed.

Still, there was something to be treasured about this moment, something that made it so much more special to him than any of those previous encounters in a lady's boudoir. This was not about sex, but about heart and happiness.

Eden was endearing, and felt so sweet resting against him.

He stifled a chuckle when he heard a little snore out of her.

Dear heaven! He stifled his laughter. *How the mighty have fallen!*

Here he was, stripping her out of her gown, and she was not in the least interested. Indeed, she was so lacking in interest that she had fallen back into a deep slumber. However, he had confidence in his abilities and knew things would have gone quite differently had she been awake and aware.

"Eden, your gown is unlaced. Can you step out of it, love?" He had not meant to take over the chore of completely removing her gown. But she was not helping herself out of it and would get tangled up in the ties while asleep if they were left on her. Not to mention the wrinkles or possible rips to the delicate fabric that might happen when she tossed and turned.

Sighing, he set about taking the garment off her. This was agonizing because Eden's body was alluring beyond belief and he had to keep his own from responding.

His primal instincts were on fire. Were he a hound, he would do things to her with his hands and tongue that no man ought to do to this wonderful girl outside of marriage.

Was this not the obvious solution? He had to marry her.

He *wanted* to marry her.

Who else would be as good a husband to her? A faithful husband who would never betray his wedding vows.

Why not propose to her?

Well, he needed to get a better sense of her feelings first.

She liked him and trusted him, so that was a good start. Just as important, his family would be no obstacle, because they liked her better than they did him. She was the fairy princess emerging from the woodlands path between their homes to join them each day. She brought sunshine with her smile and enraptured his children, somehow making them behave with her sprinkling of fairy magic.

His mother adored her and already viewed her as a daughter because Eden had come crying to her so many times when she was younger. His mother had been there to comfort her all those times her own parents had let her down.

Why not marry her when it would make all of them happy?

He only hoped Eden cared for him as much as she obviously adored his mother and children. She was so good with all of them, including him.

But this was Eden, so kind and sweet. Her affection was genuine.

When had Mary ever fallen asleep with her arms around Priscilla? Connor could not recall that she ever had. Then again, he had been away so much during their years of marriage. Still, he could see the way the household ran whenever he came home. Everything had its routine, and the one established for their children did not seem to include Mary at all.

Nor did Mary run the household or appear to have any desire to participate in its management. He had asked her about this, concerned that his mother might have been pushing her out, because the old dowager had a forceful presence and Mary was not assertive. He had made certain Mary understood that she was the lady of the house and did not need to cede her authority to anyone.

But no, she was more than eager to give all the responsibility to his mother.

For the most part, Mary existed in the same house as the rest of them. She always had a smile for the children whenever they were in her presence, which they rarely were because she took no responsibility for their upbringing. A pat on their heads before they were sent up to bed was the extent of her involvement. Priscilla got an occasional hug, but only when the little one initiated it.

As for him, he was the opposite, wanting to squeeze Connor, Alex, and especially Priscilla, since she was such a cuddly thing who seemed to crave affection. He hugged all of them probably too much of the time because he was so happy to be home and have them around.

Mary, who was here all the time, never seemed to appreciate how splendid those little devils were. Perhaps she simply did not have the strength to tolerate their exuberance.

Well, this moment wasn't about Mary or his children. This was about him and Eden.

"Eden, I am going to tuck you into bed now," he whispered

as she remained leaning against him, her gloriously soft frontage pressed to his chest. He ran a hand gently through her silky tresses. "Eden? Climb into bed, love."

He tried to ease her into it, but he was shifting her at an awkward angle and she chose that moment to heed him. She slipped out of his arms and fell like a lump across the bed, her legs dangling off it, her adorable bottom sticking up.

Ah, that was accomplished with Silver Duke flair. *Not.* No points for finesse there.

But he could now get a better angle on her body, and managed to tuck her under the covers while refusing to acknowledge she was wearing only a thin chemise. This had to rank among his worst attempts to get a woman into bed. Indeed, the very worst, because women never hesitated to jump into the sack with him.

Most of the time, he did not have to ask. A mere nod was signal enough. Clothes would fly off before the bedroom door had even shut. The advantages of being a duke.

The disadvantages as well.

These sexual escapades had everything to do with his title and nothing to do with any true affection for him.

"Good night, Eden," he whispered. "Sweet dreams, love."

"They'll be of you," she responded so softly that he almost missed it. "My darling... My Beauregard."

Beauregard? She was dreaming of the little spaniel she'd had as a pet growing up?

He had just had his hands all over her. Most women found this arousing. And she was dreaming of her *dog?*

Well, that was a kick in the arse. Eden was going to need a bit of wooing.

But this was part of the problem of being a Silver Duke. He had never wooed a woman before, not even his wife. Mary had been an arranged marriage that he had gone along with because it seemed the right thing to do at the time. Trouble was brewing on the Continent because of that upstart Napoleon, and he intended to go off and join the fight. But he also needed to secure heirs for his dukedom.

Mary had been pretty enough. An earl's daughter. She understood the rules and dutifully produced the requisite sons, and even a daughter when he mentioned how much he wanted one.

Unfortunately, she viewed it as her *only* role. Job done. Heir and spare. Daughter delivered. She never put an ounce more effort into the marriage or raising their children, since she considered her part of the bargain fulfilled.

The door between the duke and duchess quarters had been firmly closed, and remained closed for the duration of their marriage.

But Eden?

She would put her heart and soul into their marriage. She would give all the love she had to give and then give some more, because this was who she was, tender and caring. This was how she would continue to be with him, his children, and any little demons that came later. She already loved his mother. Who else but Eden would make their family whole again?

He wanted her, and he was in desperate need of her love. Was this not the very thing he had missed out on during his entire life?

Now, he had to prove he was up to the task of being a good husband.

He carefully checked the hallway, saw it was quiet, and slipped out of Eden's room. He encountered no one along the way, although he did hear a door shut behind him.

No matter. It was probably someone who dared not be seen either.

Even if he encountered someone now, what did it matter? Getting out of Eden's room unnoticed was the tricky part. Being observed walking down the hall toward his ducal quarters would raise no eyebrows. Even if some were raised, they could only guess which young lady he had been visiting.

Once in his quarters, he removed his clothes and tossed them aside for his valet to attend to in the morning. He was not usually so careless with his clothing, but he was exhausted and knew he would not get more than three or four hours of sleep tonight.

Eden liked to wake early, and so did his children. He was often up at the crack of dawn himself, but today would be a struggle.

Connor was certain his eyes had barely shut before his valet entered his bedchamber to wake him. He heard the distant chime of the hallway clock indicating the seven o'clock hour, and groaned.

"Rough night, Your Grace?" His valet, Holden, shook his head and tsked as he picked up the clothes Connor had left strewn on the carpet, which was something he never usually did because he liked things neat and orderly.

"A bit." Connor rolled to a sitting position with another groan and glanced down at himself. He'd fallen asleep naked atop his covers, too tired to even bother slipping under them. His head was pounding. Sunlight blinded him as Holden drew aside the drapes. "Gad! Close them a little, will you? That's too bright."

"That is sunshine, Your Grace. You always like the drapes thrown wide."

"Not this morning. I need a bath and a shave."

This was his usual morning routine, a tub rolled in at seven o'clock each morning when he returned from his early ride. He had missed that ride today.

No matter—he would have one of his grooms take Achilles through his paces.

He washed and dressed, then headed to the breakfast room in the hope of finding Eden. There were only a handful of people up at this hour, and she, he was pleased to note, was one of them. She was seated beside Lord Aubrey and quietly chatting with him as she had her cup of tea.

"Good morning," Connor said, taking the seat to the right of her, since Aubrey was seated to her left. He motioned for a footman to pour him his usual cup of coffee, and gave a nod of thanks when the chore was promptly done. Steam drifted upward from his cup, and the rich aroma livened his senses that were still too much alive from the memory of undressing Eden mere hours ago.

She cast him a pleasant smile. "Good morning." But her smile began to falter as she studied him.

He arched an eyebrow as he sipped his coffee.

She began to nibble her lip, no doubt wondering whether she had dreamed him up last night. He would tell her later, assure her it was not her imagination running wild. But this was not something to be discussed in front of others.

"Have you seen the children yet?" he asked her.

She nodded. "Millie is helping them get ready for the day. Your boys have already polished off the scones and apples meant for their pouches. We'll gather more before we head out."

"You really needn't join us, Lynton," Aubrey said. "You're not a bird watcher and will only be bored. Besides, I do not see that any other guests intend to join us. Why not do what you must around here this morning and meet us later at the church fair? I'm sure you'll have takers for that outing. My sister, for one. Bring her along with you."

He was about to tell the viscount to shove his idea up his arse, but Brewster rushed in just then and motioned to him. "Excuse me," Connor said to Eden, and immediately strode toward his butler, who appeared quite anxious. "What's wrong?"

"Lord Darrow has taken a turn for the worse, it seems."

His heart tightened for Eden's sake. As bad as her parents were, they were all she had, and she cared for them. "Do you know if the doctor has been summoned?"

"I'm afraid the messenger did not say. He was only told to inform Lady Eden to come home as soon as possible."

Connor nodded. "I'll take her straight over there. Have my carriage readied."

"At once, Your Grace."

He returned to the breakfast room, and had yet to utter a word to Eden before she leaped out of her seat. "It is my father, isn't it? I should have stayed at Chestnut Hill."

Connor put a hand to her elbow to calm her. "Do not dare blame yourself for any of this. You did all you could have done. Sitting with him would have changed nothing. We're not even sure there is a problem."

She looked up at him, her eyes wide and fearful. "But your expression when you walked in…"

He shook his head. "I was thinking, that's all. He appeared to be on the mend when we left him yesterday. I cannot imagine what happened."

Eden nodded and then turned to Aubrey, who had been listening in on their conversation. "I am so sorry, my lord," she said. "We may have to postpone our outing."

To the man's credit, he took the disappointment gracefully. "I'll be here waiting for you. Send word when you have news. I would offer to accompany you, but I think my presence would only be an interference."

"You are too kind," she replied. "Hopefully, it will only be a false alarm and we can be on our way within the hour. This is what my parents do. They thrive on drama and attention. One eventually gets used to it."

Aubrey regarded her with surprising compassion. "I do not know that you have ever gotten used to it, Lady Eden. It takes a chunk out of your heart every time, doesn't it?"

She pinched her lips and nodded.

Connor wanted to dislike this man, but could not while he was behaving kindly toward Eden. He still did not trust him, however. "We'll keep you apprised, Aubrey."

He walked out of the breakfast room with Eden, and was about to escort her out of the house when she stopped suddenly. "I need to get Priscilla's card."

"What?"

"Your daughter drew a card for my father and meant to bring it to him this morning. I won't be a moment. Anyway, the children ought to be told why I must delay the start of our outing."

"You think it will only be a delay?"

She nodded. "Connor, they do this to me all the time. One day it will be real, but by then I don't think I will care. The two of them have worn me out."

He nodded. "I'll run upstairs with you."

The children were disappointed not to join them, but old enough to understand the seriousness of the reason. Eden suggested they observe the birds and animal life in the expansive Lynton garden while they awaited her return. The children liked the suggestion, since they obviously preferred to be outdoors and not stuck in their quarters.

"Let's go, Eden," Connor said as she tucked Priscilla's card into a pocket of her gown. It was one of those sturdy, serviceable gowns designed for practicality rather than style. Eden still looked spectacular in it, even though others would consider it drab by *ton* standards. "The carriage should be brought around for us by now."

The same brougham he had taken out yesterday drew up in the courtyard at the same time they walked out the front door. Eden climbed in, and Connor did the same right after her. However, this time he dismissed his driver and did the driving himself because he preferred to ride alone with Eden. He flicked the reins, and the horse immediately started along the familiar path. "Eden, about last night."

She pursed her lips. "What about last night?"

"You fell asleep in Priscilla's bed."

Her eyes widened. "I did?"

He nodded. "I carried you down to your room."

She laughed softly and blushed. "No wonder I could not remember returning there. Were you the one who…"

"Undressed you? Yes, but it was in the dark. I wasn't trying to look at you. It must have been around three o'clock in the morning by the time I went upstairs to check on my children, and there you were, squeezed into Priscilla's bed. And there was

Priscilla poking and kicking you as she wriggled around."

She smiled. "I wondered how I got that bruise to my ribs."

"Puzzle solved. Priscilla was the culprit. She would have pushed you out of bed at some point during the night. I thought it best to carry you down to your own. But there was no one awake at that late hour to attend to you, so I attempted it myself. I tried to wake you, but you were too deeply asleep and would not rouse."

He thought she would be angry, and was pleasantly surprised when she merely shook her head and laughed again. "Undressed by a Silver Duke and I completely missed it."

He breathed a sigh of relief and chuckled. "You didn't miss much. I wasn't that competent. You wished me pleasant dreams, but I think you were actually saying this to the sweet pet you had as a child."

She stared at him a moment and grinned. "You mean Beauregard?"

He nodded.

Despite her wearing spectacles, her eyes sparkled in the sunlight as she said, "Connor, I would never mistake you for my dog."

He cast her an affectionate smile. "I'm fairly certain you did."

"Any other tidbits of information I ought to know about as you undressed me? I would like to get every scandalous detail entered properly in my diary."

"If you are going to write it all down, then mention that I showed remarkable skill and prowess, and completely lived up to my reputation."

"And yet I mistook you for Beauregard."

"Do not rub it in, Eden," he said, chuckling again.

Their easy banter came to an end as they reached Chestnut Hill. Evans must have been watching for their arrival. He threw open the front door and rushed toward them before the carriage had rolled to a stop. "I'm so sorry, Lady Eden. He has been howling at the top of his lungs for you for over an hour now. I did not know what else to do other than try to calm him by assuring him I would send word to you."

"He's been howling all the while?" Connor stepped forward. "Then he is not unconscious or running a fever?"

"He's perfectly fine, Your Grace. I did not summon the doctor, since he is due to pass by here later this morning and I saw no need to disturb him when there was no medical necessity. Lord Darrow's ailment is boredom and nothing more. But he was insistent, and I could not put off summoning Lady Eden. I was afraid he would pop a vein or suffer an attack of the heart if he did not calm down."

"You did just as you should have done." Eden's lips were pinched and she looked angry. "I'll go up to see him. The wretched man does not deserve sweet Priscilla's card."

Connor waited downstairs, but patience was never one of his virtues. He wore a hole in the elegant parlor rug while pacing back and forth like a restless lion in a cage. All shouting had stopped and he could hear nothing of their conversation, although he knew Eden had to be severely berating her father for disrupting her morning.

After what seemed like forever but could not have been more than ten minutes, Eden marched downstairs. Her hands were curled into fists and she looked livid. "He is fine. Perfectly fine. Recovering beautifully."

"That's good…isn't it? Not that I am excusing his childish behavior, but is it not better than his actually being in dire health?"

"No! I am through indulging him or excusing his intolerable behavior. He would not even look at Priscilla's card when I tried to show it to him. The servants took more interest in it and made the kind comments he ought to have done. He cares not a whit about anyone but himself. So I am going to place your daughter's lovely card right here on the fireplace mantel. I will tell her that he received it and it is now proudly displayed in a place of honor in my home. Not a lie, just a different emphasis on the facts. Do you think it is all right?"

He nodded. "Fine with me. Who knows if Priscilla cares all that much about it? It is just a card to a man she hardly knows."

"It is to my father, and she will care. She equates all fathers with you, and will believe he is as wonderful as you are. Ha! If she only knew what a self-indulgent wretch he was. But his recognition of her card will fill her with pride. She will also view his approval as important to me. So, this matter of the card will be the first question out of her mouth when she sees us."

Connor shook his head and sighed. "If you say so, Eden. Way too complicated for me."

"Oh, yes. Men and feelings. They are not your strong suit, are they? Let's go back to Lynton Grange. I'm so sorry I delayed the children."

"And Lord Aubrey?"

She nodded. "Yes, him too. But mostly your children. Lord Aubrey will be gone in a matter of days, and I doubt I will ever see him again. I think my parents have efficiently ruined any chance of that."

Her father began to bellow again as they were about to leave.

"Impossible man," she muttered, and stomped back upstairs.

Connor followed her because a strong word from him might quiet the man where his own daughter's pleas obviously fell on deaf ears.

But Eden seemed to be in control of the situation as she grabbed his valise and began to pack his things in it. "What are you doing?" her father asked.

"Did I or did I not warn you that I would toss you out of this house at your next outburst? Well, this is my preparing to toss you out."

"But I am ill!"

"You have a lump on your head that you probably deserved, and it obviously has not stopped you from making a nuisance of yourself." She continued to pack his belongings. "If you can shout that loudly, how ill can you be? My staff is going to abandon me if you continue to bellow and disturb their peace. You have disrupted them enough for one morning. Between you and them, I will always choose *them*. They have supported me and taken care of me throughout the years. You have had a lifetime of chances to do this and never did."

"Eden! Child!"

"Because of you, I am a twenty-seven-year-old spinster with no chance of marriage. I repeat, *no chance*. It will be only a matter of days before Viscount Aubrey, the first man to have shown an interest in me in years, is out of my life forever. That blame falls squarely on you and Mama. So, out you go!"

Her father turned to him. "Lynton, talk sense into my daughter! She has no right to do this to her own father."

Connor crossed his arms over his chest. "Oh, I believe she has every right. This is her home, not yours. *Her* home. She sets the rules. She was very clear about what they were. You ignored her and broke them."

The man frowned, obviously not liking Connor's response. "Then where am I to go?"

Connor shrugged. "Not my problem."

"You are having a house party. Surely you must have room for one more. I'll join you."

"Not on your life," Eden replied before Connor had the chance to open his mouth. "Mama is already there and disrupting everyone's enjoyment with her typical flair for the dramatic."

"Then send her here and I will go in her place."

Eden sighed. "Oh, she will love that. No. I am not replacing one unruly parent with another."

"Why do you always take her side? You are as much my child as hers. Have I not always been kinder to you than she has been?"

"Actually, you have both been abysmal." She stopped packing his things and turned to him. "The two of you are the most irresponsible people in existence. Need I remind you how many times you and Mama forgot me at school? Forgot me at end of term. Forgot me at holiday breaks. Forgot me when parents were invited for special family events."

"It could not have been all that often, Eden. We just mixed up our schedules at times, that's all. You know how we try to have as little contact as possible with each other. She thought it was my turn when I thought it was hers. Innocent mistakes. That is all."

"Yes, make your excuses. But do not even once think to apologize to me for leaving me to wander the school halls alone, and do not bother to show any remorse for all the times I was shoved into a mail coach and left to make my own way to our London townhouse, hoping against hope someone would be there to let me in."

She turned to Connor, her expression raw and anguished as she struggled to hold back her tears. "See? Neither of them ever cared. Do you see a scintilla of remorse on that man's face? All he is thinking about is how long he must stay quiet and endure *my* outburst."

Connor reached out to comfort her, but she shook her head and began to unpack her father's belongings that she had just tossed into the valise. "Fine, stay here. But I shall advise Evans *not* to send word to me if you take a turn for the worse. Nor do I care if you take your last breath. He may, however, send word to me once you are gone. *After* you've gone. Whether by carriage on your own two feet or by coffin is of no concern to me."

Her father's mouth gaped open. "Eden!"

"Do not dare feign hurt or outrage. I know you are just faking. What a dense child I was, always convincing myself that you and Mama cared, that you would surprise me one day and take me from school, hugging and kissing me, and telling me how much you missed me as we rode in your elegant coach back to London. But no, it never happened. There's no need for politeness between us anymore, no need for tearful farewells. You will never shed a tear for me, so I refuse to shed a tear for you."

But softhearted Eden looked as though she was about to burst into tears. She let out a brief, curt sob and a few sniffles.

"Eden." Connor wanted to wrap her in his arms and just keep

holding her.

"No, I'm fine."

She did not look it. In truth, she tore at his heart.

"Excuse me, Connor. I need a breath of air to compose myself."

He let her go and listened to her soft footsteps hurrying down the stairs before he turned to her father. "If you have a problem, send word directly to me. I will attend to it. You are done manipulating Eden."

That said, he followed after her.

She had run outside and was standing beside his brougham. "Eden…"

She cast him a shaky smile as he approached. "I'm all right. Just a few tears. Not so bad. I will compose myself in a moment."

"Take all the time you need," he said gently.

"No, I'm good. Just feeling their antics acutely at present. And what of me? I am such a soft touch. I had him packed up and found I could not send him packing after all. What is wrong with me that I allow them to walk all over my heart?"

There was not the slightest thing wrong with her. In truth, she was a marvel because she had turned all the hurt she had endured throughout the years into compassion and not a trace of bitterness.

This made him ache worse, for someone as good as this girl deserved all the happiness in the world. She deserved to be around those who would love and respect her.

He helped her back into his carriage. "Eden, I think it is time for things to change."

She dabbed at her tears with her handkerchief as she smiled at him. "Oh, I am so ready for change. I just don't know how to go about it."

"I have been giving your situation plenty of thought. I think I know a way to make some changes that I think you will like."

Her eyes widened. "You do? Oh, Connor, please tell me. What is your plan?"

CHAPTER TEN

E DEN WAS IN better spirits by the time she and Connor returned to Lynton Grange. She was eager to learn of his ideas on improving her life and had pressed him about it, but he was being quite mysterious.

She shrugged off his reticence because they were almost upon Lynton Grange, and he must not have wanted to start a conversation that would be interrupted. He was surprisingly sweet to her when helping her down, and remained by her side as they searched in the garden for his children. They would be pleased to know their plans for bird watching and then the afternoon fair would proceed according to schedule. Brewster had been told to advise Lord Aubrey, as well.

Priscilla ran over as soon as she heard Eden calling for her. "Did your papa like my card?" she asked.

Connor arched an eyebrow and grinned at Eden. "Amazing. How did you know?"

"Women just know these things." She turned to his daughter. "Everyone thought it was beautiful, and I have it placed on the mantel in my parlor to show it off to one and all whenever I entertain."

It was true, because she had made a point of showing it to her staff and they all had admired Priscilla's handiwork.

The girl beamed with pride. "Can we go find more birds now?"

"Yes, let's gather your pouches and hats. I see you have your binoculars already strapped around your neck."

"And food," young Connor said as he and Alex joined them. "Don't forget we need to pack more food."

Eden tweaked his chin. "Dear me, how could I possibly ever forget that?"

The children ran in ahead of them, leaving Eden once again alone with their father. "Connor, will you be joining us?"

"I'll meet you at the fair. Is that all right?"

She hid her disappointment as she nodded and smiled. "Yes, of course. It's just that you seemed so distrustful of Lord Aubrey accompanying me and the children."

"I may have been a little apish about it," he admitted.

"A little?" she teased.

"All right, I behaved like a big ape. But you ought to know me by now, Eden."

"Yes, I do." She gave her head a light shake. "In truth, it is odd how well I feel I know you."

"Same here when it comes to you. But it could be said we've had a connection to each other almost since the day you were born. Certainly ever since your tumble into the fishpond. Gad, you were such a determined little thing with a mop of fiery red curls."

The memory had her grinning.

Of course, being only two years old at the time should not have left her with a vivid memory. But she did have a vague sense of it, more the remembrance of strong hands fishing her out and then making her feel safer than she ever had felt before or since.

"You spent so much time here when your grandmother owned Chestnut Hill. Then your nitwit parents chose to send you off to one of those fancy boarding schools."

She pursed her lips. "You had gone off to fight Napoleon by the time I inherited the property and moved back here permanently. But I suppose our lives intertwined enough that we got to be friends."

"Dearest friends," he said quietly, and then said no more as Lord Aubrey joined them. A moment later, the children returned with their pouches slung over their shoulders and hats in hand. It was not long before the five of them were on their way.

Eden walked alongside Priscilla while Lord Aubrey walked a little ahead with Connor's boys. They seemed to like the viscount. For his part, he showed remarkable patience as the boys chatted excitedly about all manner of things. They only paused from chatting when they passed the pond and the boys scampered off the lane to chase the geese for no purpose other than to disrupt those poor birds.

Well, at least they were no longer throwing rocks at them. "Boys! Stop it or I'll send you straight back home!" Eden called.

They ran back to her side, laughing as the geese chased them.

Priscilla hugged Eden's skirt and began to cry. "They're going to bite me!"

Eden placed her body between the little girl and the birds. "It's all right, sweetheart. I won't let them hurt you."

One pecked Alex's backside. "Ouch!" he yelped, and began to run down the lane to escape the angry bird.

His brother chased after him, not to comfort him but to tease him. "Chicken!" he shouted, and wrestled Alex to the ground while making squawking sounds.

Lord Aubrey patiently broke them apart. "You had better not behave like this by the cliffs. Your father will be quite put out if we return to Lynton Grange minus two children."

He then resumed walking with the boys but made certain to stand between them.

Eden liked that he was patient with Connor's sons and told him so as they neared their destination and he slowed his step to walk alongside her. "Thank you, Lord Aubrey."

"My pleasure," he said with a jovial tip of his hat to her.

In truth, he and Connor were remarkably alike in many ways, both of them handsome men with an air of confidence and obvious intelligence. They were commanding men but not pompous. She could see Lord Aubrey would make a good father someday, and hoped he would find a nice debutante who made him a good wife.

She knew all hope for herself was lost, even though he seemed to like her.

But what chance had she *ever* had with him?

His family would never approve of an aging spinster who wore thick spectacles and had the worst parents in London. But resigning herself to all hope being lost also freed her to be herself and not care what Lord Aubrey or anyone else thought of her.

To her surprise, he seemed to enjoy his time with her tremendously. "Give me your hand, Lady Eden. Let me help you onto the ledge," he said once they reached the beach and had walked close enough to the cliff nests to observe the colonies of nesting birds.

"Oh, thank you, Lord Aubrey."

These birds were everywhere, some flying over the water and soaring above the cliffs, some resting upon the higher ledges, and others foraging for food to feed their young. Still others were scavenging for twigs to build up their nests.

Lord Aubrey then helped the children onto the ledge, starting with Priscilla, since she seemed to be particularly clingy toward Eden today. "And up you go, Lady Priscilla."

"Thank you," she said most politely while her brothers shoved and pushed each other because each wanted to beat the other onto the ledge. Alex, being the smaller brother, lost out and tumbled onto the sand.

Lord Aubrey helped him up. "Are you all right?"

Alex nodded while scowling at his brother.

Eden frowned at young Connor as well. "Your brother could have been hurt falling off."

"He was only going to fall onto sand," Connor retorted, then hopped down from his perch. "You can have my spot, Alex. Did I hurt you?"

"No, I'm all right," Alex said, and both boys scrambled back onto the ledge.

Chuckling, Lord Aubrey climbed up last and settled beside Eden. "I never had a brother. I see now all the fun I was missing."

She laughed softly. "And all the bruising, all the teasing—all the punching, poking, and wrestling you missed out on? But I know what you mean. They love each other and infuriate each other. I wish I had this, too. I missed out on having siblings."

He nodded. "Having a sister is not at all the same thing. Mine can be quite demanding, and often over the most inane things. Persephone requires attention on herself at all times and is not a good sport when she does not get her way. Still, she is my sister, and I love her even though she often grates on my nerves."

Eden understood what he meant.

All five of them continued to chat while peering through their binoculars.

Priscilla took out her drawing pad and pencil to draw a nest of baby birds. "Eden, what are those birds called?"

"Those are curlews," Eden said. "And look overhead—do you see that goshawk? He is hunting over the water in search of his next meal."

They watched as it dove and came up with a fish in its talons.

When the boys appeared to be tiring of merely watching birds, Lord Aubrey took them for a run along the beach, after which they splashed water on themselves to cool down. By the time they were ready to dig into their pouches for something to munch on, Aubrey sank onto the sand beside her and groaned. "Lord, they are exhausting."

Eden laughed. "Oh, yes. Do not even try to keep up with them. It is an impossible task. The best one can do is keep an eye on them and try to stop them from mortally wounding themselves or wreaking havoc on the others."

"But it is nice, isn't it?" he remarked, leaning back on his elbows as he stretched out beside her while she sat on the warm sand. "Nice having young ones to look after. There is a refreshing innocence even to their mischief. This is what I enjoy most about being in the countryside, this ability to relax and just be yourself. There are so many rules one is required to follow when in London, not to mention the falsity of it all. Everyone approaches you with an ulterior motive."

"Well, a house party may be more casual, but the young ladies and most of the younger gentlemen attend in the hope of finding a match," Eden remarked. "Scheming goes on here as well."

He nodded, his gaze turning troubled as he regarded her. "Yes, that is true. This is certainly my sister's goal, to snare herself a duke for the mere reason he is a duke and she wishes to be a duchess."

Eden tried to suppress the pang of jealousy, because she knew Lord Aubrey's sister had set her cap for Connor for this very reason. Of course, Connor was proud to be a Silver Duke and had no wish to marry anyone. But wasn't it possible for men to be seduced just as easily as women? Persephone, for all her faults, was quite beautiful, and men fell over themselves to court her. "Lord Aubrey, what—"

"Please call me Trajan. Is it too forward of me to request this? And may I call you Eden? The children all do, and I've noticed so does their father."

She shrugged. "I've had a longstanding friendship with the duke and his family. His mother was more of a parent to me than my own."

"And now? Is it merely friendship you feel for Lynton? Or has it grown into something more?"

Her heart twisted. "Oh, it shall never be anything more than friendship between us. But I will not deny wishing for all of this." She motioned to the children, who had now finished devouring their apples and scones and gone off hunting for seashells on the beach. Incredibly, they were on their best behavior. Each boy took a turn holding their little sister's hand, and cheered and complimented her as she found her seashells. "I have plenty of friends and lots of ladies' societies to keep me busy, but it is not the same. How can one's heart not swell with joy upon watching these sweet children? Of course, I will be leaping to my feet in a moment as Connor tries to drown Alex."

Lord Aubrey laughed, but soon sobered and regarded her thoughtfully. "The hour must be approaching noon. How about we head into town and grab a decent meal at the fair? I hear it is to be quite a lively event, one of the largest fairs in this region. Rather surprising for a church fair."

She nodded. "It has been an annual event for as long as I can remember. The vicar takes great pride in it."

"Let me guess, you are on its planning committee."

She laughed. "Of course. The vicar is most persistent about gathering his volunteers, but I don't mind. It is very popular. Everyone has fun, the merchants sell briskly because of the large crowds passing by their stalls, and the church gets a percentage of the gate."

"And I suppose there is plenty of food to be had?"

"Oh, yes. There should be just enough to feed Connor's hungry wolves," she said with a laugh as she watched the boys.

"The others might be there already and waiting for us."

"Yes, I'm surprised the boys have not complained yet that they are starving." When Lord Aubrey held out his hand to assist her up, she took it without hesitation. However, he did not immediately release her.

"Eden," he said gently, "I think you know that I like you. But I haven't dared say anything to you because I was not sure how things were between you and Lynton. But if you are just friends and nothing more, would you permit me to get to know you better? I would like our friendship to turn into something more, something perhaps permanent."

She was taken aback. "Are you asking for permission to court me?"

He nodded. "Why are you so surprised?"

She shook her head and laughed. "You have met my parents, haven't you? Well, you've met my mother and witnessed her theatrical performances. And after this morning's false alarm, you know how childishly my father behaves."

"Oh, they are quite the characters. But they are not you, Eden." He gave her hand a light squeeze. "You somehow managed to survive their pettiness and turn into this beautiful young woman everyone adores."

She blushed. "Young? Now you are shamelessly flattering me. You know my age, my lord."

"Trajan's the name. I do not wish us to be formal with each other. Oh, I know it is a ridiculous name for an Englishman. But your parents are not the only parents in the world who ever embarrassed their children. As for that nonsense about your age, I think beauty such as yours is timeless. You hardly look above twenty, truth be told."

She rolled her eyes.

"But it isn't merely your physical appearance that makes you beautiful. It is the loveliness of your soul that shines in your eyes and spreads light wherever you step." He laughed and released her hand. "That was a bit gushing, wasn't it? I am not in the habit of spouting pretty words like a romantic poet. Forgive me, but this is how I feel about you, and there is too little time to waste being polite or cautious."

The children chose this moment to scamper back to her side and declare they were starving. "Oh, my. We had better hurry into town before you waste away to skin and bones," she teased.

Grabbing their belongings, they all walked on to the town of Lynton.

The church spire was visible in the distance, gleaming in the sunlight. The afternoon had turned cooler than usual, and there was a strengthening breeze blowing off the water that made it perfect weather for hiking. Eden could see Priscilla was tiring, so she suggested they head straight to the food tent and grab a table before doing anything else.

"Good idea," Lord Aubrey said.

The fairgrounds, spread out across the church's expansive

property, were crowded by the time they arrived. Everyone in Lynton and all the surrounding towns had come out for this event. There were plenty of vendors set up in stalls, and some had set up in brightly colored tents. Musicians wandered the grounds playing their lively tunes, and there was dancing for those who wished to dance, and also games of every variety.

"I don't see any of our group here yet," Lord Aubrey remarked. "Let me get us settled, and then I will order food and drinks for all of us."

Eden smiled at him. "Thank you, Lord Aubrey. That would be most helpful."

She had no intention of calling him Trajan whether alone or in company, but liked that he had suggested she could. She also liked his name, finding it quite interesting because of all the history behind the Roman emperor first bearing the name.

Since the food tent was quickly filling up, Lord Aubrey hurried off with young Connor to secure them a table and then assist him in carrying back their pasties, mince pies, and drinks. They kept their eyes on all who came in and out of the food tent, hoping to spot some of the group from the house party, but none had shown up yet.

"My Papa said he would be here," Priscilla said, her voice plaintive.

"He will," Eden assured her. "But let's go have fun in the meanwhile."

After they finished eating, they all walked around the fairgrounds together. But Eden and Priscilla soon split up from the boys, who wanted to partake in the various games of strength offered.

"I'll watch the boys," Lord Aubrey assured her.

She wasn't certain he was up to the task, for the boys were quite devious when they wanted to be. But they seemed to be on their best behavior, so she agreed. She and Priscilla watched all three of them take up a side in a game of tug of war. The ground between the two sides had been muddied so that the losing team was going to get caked in mud.

Oh, well. The mud would wash off.

To her relief, Lord Aubrey and the boys won, so they were spared a mud bath. While the three moved on to attempt other games of strength, Eden took Priscilla through the various stalls that sold trinkets and other wares. She purchased a bracelet for the girl that was made out of colorful beads of glass, and then they watched a glassblower as he shaped his melted glass into delicate animal designs. Eden also bought a glass swan for Priscilla.

"It's so beautiful," Priscilla exclaimed, and hugged her. She immediately put the bracelet on her wrist, but when Eden took the swan to tuck in her own pocket for safekeeping, the girl made a fuss and began to cry. "I can carry it!"

"But you might lose it, Priscilla. It will be safer in my pocket."

"No, no! I want to carry it," she insisted as tears welled in her eyes.

Eden sighed. "Very well, but hand it over to me if you get tired of holding it."

The girl nodded as she sniffled.

They walked on, browsing several other stalls until they encountered Connor and his house party guests. "There you are," he said, striding up to them with a smile on his face. "I found the boys with Aubrey about ten minutes ago. Sounds like you had fun today."

"Yes, Papa," Priscilla replied, her eyes big as she stared up at him in adoration. "We did, but I'm tired now. I want to go home."

"Sweetheart, my guests and I have just arrived. Why don't I accompany you and Eden to the food tent and fetch you both lemonades? You can relax there and wait for us to take a turn about the fair."

"All right," she grumbled, but put her little hand in his without complaint.

The tent was crowded by now, and there was hardly a seat to

be found. Being a duke had its advantages, however. The tent's proprietor hastily directed his boys to set up a table and bench just for them in a quieter corner away from the food line, although this tent was so packed that nowhere was truly quiet. However, they were sufficiently out of the way so as not to be constantly jostled.

The proprietor attended to them himself, bringing lemonades for them and an ale for Connor. "Anything else, Your Grace?"

"No, Mr. Fitchett. This is excellent."

Connor took a sip of his ale, cast a wink at Eden, and then turned to his daughter. "Tell me about your day, sweetheart. What did you and Eden do?"

The girl began to bend his ear, intent on describing every detail from the moment they walked out of Lynton Grange. "And then the goose bit Alex..."

Connor guffawed. "Ah, my boys. They fill me with such pride."

Priscilla went on to describe their bird watching and walk through the fair. "Then Eden bought me this lovely bracelet." She raised her wrist to show her father. "See how it shines?"

"Oh, yes. It is quite beautiful. Did Eden purchase anything for herself?"

"No, Papa. But she also bought me this swan...this..." She began to search around for it.

Eden groaned and did the same, hoping against hope it had merely fallen under the table. Unfortunately, it had not.

Priscilla had lost it.

"Oh, Papa! It's gone!" She burst into tears and would not be consoled even when Connor drew her onto his lap. "I've lost it. And now Eden will be mad at me!"

Eden rose as Connor did his best to comfort his daughter. "Let me go search for it. Priscilla, it must have fallen somewhere between the glassblower's stall and here. I'll try to find it for you."

Of course, she doubted that she would locate that tiny glass swan, considering the number of people who were walking between here and that stall. Someone had either picked it up and kept it for themselves, or the delicate thing had been trodden on and was broken. There was a small chance someone was honest enough to return it to the glassblower's stall. But Eden knew this was unlikely.

The glassblower had made several swans, and she would simply buy a new one for Priscilla after conducting a token search. She wasn't sure yet whether to claim she had found the original swan or tell Priscilla the truth and reveal she had bought her a replacement. Well, she would give it thought.

She carefully retraced her steps and was searching behind a row of crates beside the glassblower's stall when she heard some familiar voices. "Why should I not be angry with Trajan?" Persephone said to her mother, Lady Lothmere. "He was supposed to distract that Darrow girl and keep her away from the duke while I made my move on him."

"He is trying his best, Persephone."

"But it is not enough just to talk to her. He has to pretend to woo her. He promised me he would do this. He just has to keep up the pretense for a few more days. How difficult can that be?"

"Not difficult at all, I would imagine. She is pretty whenever she is without those hideous spectacles."

Persephone laughed harshly. "Ugh, her, pretty? She's old and washed up. Even Trajan declared he would not marry a girl above twenty and five."

"Then all the more reason to be grateful to your brother for the sacrifice he is making on your behalf."

"What sacrifice? A morning of bird watching? We found him playing games with the duke's boys, and that Darrow hag was nowhere in sight."

"Child! She is not a hag, and I do not think I like your behavior. You are getting too much above yourself. Do not think the duke hasn't noticed. I would worry less about her and more about how you are coming across to him. No man wants a wasp for a wife, so you had better curb that sharp tongue of yours."

"Mama, don't tell me you like her." Persephone sounded aghast.

"Yes, it so happens I do. I feel sorry for her because she is a nice person but will never be anything more than a spinster. You are fortunate she is too old even for the Silver Duke. A man like him can have someone young and fresh. Were she a few years younger, I think she might have won his heart."

"Ugh! Do not even suggest it. He is mine, and I will not let her have him."

"Enough, Persephone. He already has three spoiled children to plague him. He does not need a childish wife to make a fourth. Come along, let's look at the jewelry."

"All right, but when we are married I am sending those children off to boarding school. I have no intention of becoming their mother."

Eden remained behind the crates, unable to move as Lady Lothmere's conversation with Persephone sank in. Those beautiful, kind words spoken to her by Lord Aubrey this morning were all a lie.

And she had been foolish enough to believe him.

Was this what was happening to her? Had she grown old and desperate? Deluded enough to believe the handsome viscount's flattery? Gad, he'd been so convincing, so seemingly sincere in word and deed.

So there it was. The bitter truth.

She was to have no happiness. No Silver Duke because Connor was never going to marry her, and now Viscount Aubrey was out of the question because she was just old and used up as far as he was concerned.

"Lady Eden, is everything all right?" the glassblower asked as she approached him once Lord Aubrey's sister and mother had walked out. She nodded unconvincingly and then asked about Priscilla's lost swan. "No, no one has turned it in."

"Oh, then I will purchase another. Can you please wrap it up exactly as you did the first? His Grace's daughter is bereft, and I'm thinking that I ought to pretend to have found the original swan."

He nodded sympathetically. "I cannot give it away for nothing, but you can have it for half price."

They completed the exchange and Eden slowly made her way back to the food tent. She was distracted and jostled by the crowd, but did not care. She just wanted to go home to Chestnut Hill and have a good cry. But she would have no peace there either, since her father was in residence and would start behaving like a spoiled infant as soon as she returned.

She fixed a smile on her face and entered the food tent. Priscilla and Connor were still there, now joined by his sons, Aubrey, and Aubrey's mother and sister.

Oh, just wonderful.

Persephone was glued to Connor, her manner proprietary and aggressively wary as soon as Eden joined them. Indeed, if Persephone had been born a cat, Eden knew the girl would be hissing at her and displaying her claws right now.

Lord Aubrey shifted down to make room for her beside him, but she chose to sit next to Priscilla instead. "Here is your swan, Priscilla."

"You found it?" The girl's eyes shone with relief.

But Eden could not quite get herself to tell a falsehood, so she simply related the truth. "No, sweetheart. When I told the glassblower about the lost swan, he gave me this beautiful one instead. Here it is with his warm regards. He hopes you will love this one, the sister to the first, because this swan needs love, too."

Priscilla was not certain what to make of this. "But it is just made of glass. It doesn't have a heart."

"Perhaps not a heart as we know it, but all things respond to affection. Did you know that flowers do better when people talk to them?"

She nodded. "Grandmama talks to them all the time."

"See?" Eden smiled at the girl. "Swans are no different, whether real or made of glass."

Priscilla nodded and gave her a hug. "Then I will love it. I already do. Thank you, Eden."

Crisis averted as Priscilla now happily showed off her bracelet and the swan to everyone at the table. "It is quite beautiful," Lord Aubrey said, taking a long moment to admire the swan. "And what did Lady Eden get for herself?"

"She didn't get anything," Priscilla replied.

"Oh, that cannot be right." He rose from the bench and came around to stand by her side. "May I escort you back to the glassblower's stall?"

Eden did not wish to be in his company, but everyone was watching her and she did not want them to see how hurt and miserable she felt. Her heart was as fragile as that glass swan, so easily shattered. "It isn't necessary."

Lord Aubrey's eyes darkened. "On the contrary, I think it is quite necessary. Come with me…please, Lady Eden."

She glanced around the table, saw Persephone's smug expression and Connor's resigned glance. Yes, he was resigned to endure all of them for the duration of the house party, and then he would take himself off with his fellow Silver Dukes to do whatever these men enjoyed doing when on the prowl. Persephone would be forgotten, but so would she. "All right."

Lord Aubrey offered his arm to escort her through the throng, but slowed his steps as they approached the glassblower's tent. "You are upset with me."

She glanced at him, sparing but a moment before looking away again. "What makes you say that?"

"Look at me, Eden." He sighed when she did not. "Fine, it is obvious you will not look at me. But I've seen enough to know that you are tense and resentful over something I might have done. If I am at fault, it was inadvertent, I assure you. Please tell me straight out, have I done something to anger you?"

"I am just tired, that's all."

"If you say so. I know this is no place to talk privately, but give me a few moments after tonight's dinner party. Take a walk with me in the garden." When she said nothing, he led her into the tent and insisted she look through the objects on display. "How about this glass dog? I know how much you cared for your Beauregard."

She turned to him in surprise. "You know about my dog?"

He nodded. "Your mother talks a lot. Mostly about herself, but she did manage to tell me a little about you when I asked."

"Why did you bother?"

"Eden, I like you. Is it not obvious? I meant it sincerely when I said that I would like to get to know you better. Was I too presumptuous? I will take it slower, if this makes you feel more comfortable. But I have only a few more days here and would like to spend as much time with you as I can."

Oh, yes. He wanted to worm his way into her heart and then drop her like a stone as soon as his sister had succeeded in her purpose. Was it mean of her to be glad Connor did not like Persephone? Was it mean to hope the girl would break out in hives and be confined to her bedchamber for the remainder of the house party?

She hated to wish ill on anyone, but jealousy did this to a person. Not even she was immune.

"Thank you for the little dog," she said, smiling sincerely because it was a perfect gift even if he was a liar and a hound himself.

"My pleasure."

They caught up to the others, who were making their way through the fair. She showed the little group what Lord Aubrey had purchased for her, trying not to wince as everyone gushed over it, especially Priscilla, who assured her it was as beautiful as her swan.

The men volunteered for several more games, including an arm-wrestling competition between Lord Aubrey and Connor. "Do not hurt him, Trajan," Persephone called out to her brother. "His Grace needs to dance with me tonight."

"Papa can beat you," Alex assured Lord Aubrey.

"I'm not so sure," young Connor exclaimed. "Papa's getting

on in years."

"I'm *what!*" Connor growled at his son.

Young Connor grinned. "Gotcha!" He laughed heartily and playfully poked his father, something no other duke would have accepted from a son, because few of high rank had such open and easy relations with their children.

Connor took it all in stride and ruffled the boy's hair. "I'll take you on after I defeat Aubrey, you smug whelp."

"My bet's on Papa," Alex declared.

Connor ruffled his youngest son's hair, too. "At least one of my boys appreciates me."

"I appreciate you too," Priscilla said, and pushed aside her brothers to hug him.

Connor bent to hug her back. "Thank you, my sweetheart."

Yes, Eden thought, that little girl was the only female who would ever claim his heart. Well, he loved his mother, too. But he was not going to give his heart to any other woman. The sooner Eden accepted it, the sooner she might fall out of love with him.

Perhaps this was what made Lord Aubrey's deception all the worse, this knowledge that no man wanted her. Not a young man. Not an older man.

No man.

Connor ultimately won the arm-wrestling competition, but these two were very closely matched in strength.

Teatime had long since come and gone by the time all the guests scrambled into the carriages and returned to Lynton Grange. Eden hopped into Connor's carriage with Priscilla, while Lord Aubrey and the boys rode in the carriage behind theirs, along with Lord Aubrey's mother and sister.

Eden did her best to pretend all was well, but she was not certain she had fooled Connor, because he kept glancing her way and frowning. She breathed a sigh of relief when his magnificent manor house came into view. The house was enormous, yet the stone façade was as warm as the gold stone of the Cotswolds, and the door was an inviting sea blue framed in white trim. Bright red flowers abounded along the courtyard's borders, adding to the charm of his home. She ran inside, ignored her mother as she approached and began unloading yet another complaint— something about shoe buckles—and hurried upstairs to her bedchamber. "No time to talk now, Mama."

"But Eden, this is urgent! I am bereft! I haven't a suitable pair of slippers to wear to—"

"Then go barefoot, Mama!"

"Eden!"

She dashed into her room, shut the door, and then leaned against it while letting out a sob. Her entire body was shaking from the strain of having to hide her anguish. She did not care about her mother's shoes or her wardrobe, all of which were perfectly fine.

How could she care about these trivial complaints while her heart was tearing in half? Nor was her wrenching sorrow about Lord Aubrey, as nice as he had seemed. He was handsome and titled and everything she should love, but she was not in love with him. That he had so convincingly lied to her was the painful part. For one bright moment, he had given her hope that not all men considered her an unwanted object collecting dust on a shelf.

But that little glimmer was quickly extinguished. She was nothing but an aging spinster, and this was how everyone viewed her.

How everyone *used* her.

Connor himself had only wanted her as a governess for his children. She recalled his shock when she had made the mistaken assumption he was asking her to be his wife, when all he wanted was to have her care for his children during the house party.

Her tears were for Connor and the impossibility of his ever loving her.

It felt as though the entire world was laughing at her.

Yes, quite the jest.

One man who was pretending to adore her for the sake of his

sister's schemes to trap a duke into marriage. And said Silver Duke remained firmly determined never to marry.

Add two incompetent parents. A dozen missed opportunities for happiness. And here she was.

Closer to thirty years of age than twenty, and doomed to a loneliness that would only deepen as time wore on.

She set aside the little glass dog that really was a nice gift, even if the viscount who gave it to her was a bounder, threw herself onto her bed, and cried in despair for a heart—*her* heart—that would never know love.

CHAPTER ELEVEN

C ONNOR SAW HIS children settled in the care of Millie and Sarah and then returned downstairs to the parlor, where several of the older ladies had congregated and were listening to Eden's mother complain about shoe buckles.

Dear heaven.

How was it possible this empty-headed woman and the lovely Eden were related?

He quickly moved on before he was roped into their conversation. "Just hang me from the yardarm," he muttered, and hurried away despite their calls to have him join them.

Other guests were on the terrace enjoying the late afternoon breeze, and still others were playing lawn games.

He returned inside, once again hastening past Eden's mother and her circle of friends, who were still talking about her confounded shoe buckles.

A few of the gentlemen had settled in his billiards room for a game, while others looked on and drank his scotch.

They still had a few hours before supper, and he had now taken stock of everyone but Eden. Where was she?

Aubrey stopped him as he marched down the hall to return to the parlor for another look. "Lynton, did you say something to Eden to overset her?" he asked. "She raced into the house, and I haven't seen her since."

"Me? I've hardly seen her all day. You were the one with her since morning. What did you say to upset her? And do not bother to deny it, for the culprit had to be you."

"Me?" Aubrey furrowed his brow in genuine concern. "I give you my word, Lynton. If I am to blame, then I do not know what I could have said to rile her."

Connor's apish instincts began to take over. "Did you attempt to kiss her?" He was going to rip this man in half if he had tried.

The two faced off against each other like two dominant bulls fighting over the same pretty heifer, both of them refusing to back down.

But Connor was going to win this bout because Eden was his to love and protect, and no one, especially not *this* bloody arse, was going to take her from him.

"No, I did not kiss her," Aubrey finally admitted with a sigh. He rubbed a hand along the nape of his neck. "She is a respectable girl. But I did tell her that I cared for her. Perhaps I revealed too much of my feelings. She seemed not to mind at the time. However, she was not herself when she came back to the food tent after searching for your daughter's lost trinket."

Connor uncurled his fisted hands and nodded. "Yes, I noticed that too."

"Something must have happened between the food tent and the glassblower's stall. I'm worried about her, Lynton."

Connor truly wanted to detest this man, but could not. Aubrey was his stiffest competition for Eden's affections, but who was he to blame but himself for even making it a competition? He should have said something to Eden months ago, when these deep feelings had fixed themselves so deeply in his heart that they could no longer be denied.

And still, he had denied them.

"I'll talk to her," Connor said with a sigh. "She's probably hiding in her bedchamber."

Aubrey's eyebrow shot up. "You cannot go up there alone. I'll go with you."

"And this will make it less scandalous?"

"Perhaps not," Aubrey muttered. "Then ask her maid to summon her to you. No one is in your study at the moment. We can speak to her in there."

"*I'll* speak to her," Connor insisted. "Go about your business, Aubrey. I'll summon you if you are needed."

Aubrey obviously was not pleased, but Connor was his host and also had claim to a title superior to his, so the obstinate lord was not going to win this battle of wills. Now realizing Connor would not relent, Aubrey gave him a stiff nod. "Lynton, I will call you out if you hurt her."

"Rest assured, I will do the same if it turns out you have offended her in any way."

"Fair enough," the viscount said with another curt nod, and went on his way.

Connor strode into his study and rang for his housekeeper. The ever-efficient woman scurried in almost immediately. "Your Grace," Mrs. Dayton said with a swift curtsy, looking so harried that he almost felt guilty for piling another chore upon her overburdened shoulders.

"I believe Lady Eden is in her bedchamber. Kindly ask her to come into my study right away."

He waited impatiently for Eden to join him, but it was Mrs. Dayton who hurried in a short while later. "Your Grace," she said, wringing her hands, "Lady Eden refuses."

"She *refuses*?" When had anyone other than his unruly children ever defied his requests? Was it possible Eden was angry with *him*, and this had nothing to do with anything Aubrey might have said or done?

"Yes, Your Grace." His housekeeper nodded and then cleared her throat. "She said to tell you that she is not coming downstairs now or ever. She added that you can command her to appear until you are blue in the face and she still will not come down."

"She said that? Lady Eden's exact words?"

Mrs. Dayton nodded again. "Yes."

He gave a curt laugh of disbelief, although he did believe this was something Eden would say. But to him? Why?

"Shall I try again, Your Grace?"

"No, it won't be necessary. Thank you, Mrs. Dayton. I'm sorry I distracted you from your duties."

"Not at all, Your Grace." She bobbed a curtsy and hurried off.

Connor decided to march upstairs and confront Eden. Not that he was angry with her in the least, but she was clearly avoiding him, and he meant to get at the reason why. This behavior of hers was worrisome, especially since it seemed to have stemmed from something *he* had done. But Aubrey thought she was upset with him, too.

What in blazes had either of them done?

Eden was the calmest person he knew. Nothing ever rattled her.

Well, that was not quite true. She had been more overset than usual by the behavior of her parents. But how was he to blame for that? Nor did he seriously believe this was the reason she had locked herself away.

Come to think of it, had she bothered to lock her door?

He had the pass key to every room in the house and could retrieve it to let himself in if she attempted to shut him out.

He knocked on Eden's door.

"Go away!"

"It's me. Lynton."

"I know who it is. Go away!"

How could she tell it was him merely by his knock? "I need to speak to you, Eden."

"I am through speaking to you, so save your insincere words of sympathy because I do not wish to hear them. I have nothing to say to you. Nor to Lord Aubrey. Nor to my parents. Nor to anyone else," she said between sobs and sniffles.

Had he made this sweet girl cry? "Eden, please open up."

"Stay out! In fact, I would like everyone to stay out. Just leave me alone. I do not want to see any of you ever again."

"I'm coming in."

"Don't you dare! As soon as I stop crying," she said, her voice etched with pain, "I am going to pack my things and go home to Chestnut Hill."

"Your father is still there," he reminded her, trying to gently point out she would only be exchanging one headache for another.

He heard more tears as she said, "I am sending my father to you. And do not dare send him back to me or worse, exchange him with my mother and send *her* back to me. I am leaving both of them for you to handle because I want nothing more to do with them. Or with you. Or Lord Aubrey," she repeated.

Yes, she was making it quite clear that he and Aubrey were the culprits. Her parents were irrelevant, because they were a longstanding heartache and this was not how she ever dealt with their misbehavior.

So it was down to him and Aubrey. And both of them were at a loss to understand what they had done.

"But I do not mind your mother and your children," she went on between hiccups and sniffles. "I love them. They are wonderful."

"They love you too. Shall I send my mother up to—"

"No! I cannot bear to face her just now. I cannot bear to speak to anyone yet. Why will you not leave me in peace? All I want is to be left alone," she said with a sob, "and I do not want to talk to you. Definitely not you. Go away."

She repeated that she was going to pack her things and leave.

For someone who was through speaking to all of them, she certainly had a lot to say. "Eden, I'm coming in."

"No!"

He placed his hand on the doorknob. "Are you dressed?"

Several seconds passed before she finally responded. "No! I haven't a stitch on."

Gad, the girl was a terrible liar.

Even if it were true, what would it matter? He was going to marry her. Yes, it was highhanded of him, and the last thing he wished to do was place her in a compromising position and force her hand. But was he not the one who would be hurt most if he had to spend the rest of his life without her? "I don't believe you, Eden. I'm coming in."

He tried the door, relieved to find it unlocked, and entered cautiously on the chance something would come flying at his head. Fortunately, nothing did. Had Eden been anything like her mother, there would have been objects crashing all around him right now.

But she was all goodness and kindness, nothing like either of her spoiled and childish parents.

"Eden, love. What happened?" His heart tugged when he spotted her curled up in a little ball on her bed, her back to him. He shut the door behind him and crossed the room, taking a seat on the bed beside her in order to remain close. The mattress dipped, rolling her toward him.

He wanted to draw her into his arms and hold her, but had not expected her to look quite this wounded and was now at a loss as to what to do. "Eden, I am not going away, so you may as well talk to me."

She sat up and turned to him with a tearful glower. "You cannot be in here, Connor! Are you mad? If anyone saw you come into my room or notices you coming out of it, I'll be ruined and then you will have to marry me! Do you hear me? Marriage. Wedding vows. Church bells."

She studied his expression, no doubt surprised he wasn't flinching or trying to hurry away. "I will not let you destroy my reputation and blithely ignore the consequences. So get out now before you find yourself trapped in marriage to an aging spinster."

"Are you through berating me?"

She gasped. "I am not berating you. I am trying to warn you of a dire circumstance that you seem to be taking far too casually. Or do you think so little of me that you do not care if I am shamed and you will never do the honorable thing?" She turned away from him and sank back into her curled position, emitting another sob.

"Eden, have I not said I will always protect you?"

"I don't recall."

"I'm sure I have said it many times," he muttered. "Will you turn around and look at me?"

"So I can be blinded by your Silver Duke brilliance? Your Silver Duke I-am-never-going-to-marry brilliance. No, I prefer to wallow in darkness."

She had not drawn her drapes, so the afternoon light was pouring into the room. Nor was Eden's heart or soul even remotely dark. The girl was pure sunshine.

"I can *feel* you mocking me, Connor."

"I am not mocking you, just trying to figure out what happened to leave you so undone. Just talk to me. Don't you know by now that you can tell me anything?"

"Ha!"

"You can, Eden. I will listen and never judge you harshly."

She gasped. "Judge me? *Me?* What right have you to judge me?"

"None whatsoever. You are right, of course," he said, feeling quite exasperated because he had not a clue what was wrong with her. "Let's try this again. Have I said or done something to upset you? Or is it Lord Aubrey who has upset you?"

He was met with silence.

"Eden, I will not let you leave my home until I have the truth out of you. So you may as well start talking. Who upset you? Me or Aubrey?"

"Both."

"Ah, both." Connor ran a hand through his hair in consternation. "What have we done?"

She gave an indignant sniffle. "Oh, plenty!"

Connor still had no idea what she was talking about. However, she was the last person on earth he ever wished to hurt. "For pity's sake, Eden. Just give me a hint, will you? And do not tell me that I ought to know what I did, because I don't have an inkling.

Consider me dense and too stupid to figure it out on my own. Tell me what terrible thing it is that I have done and I will apologize and promise never to do it again."

"You are not stupid."

"All right, then, I am dense."

She sat up again, turned to face him, and spared him no more than a glance before bursting into tears again.

"Oh, Eden," he said with a wrenching ache, and drew her onto his lap. "Do not fight me. Just let me hold you."

He thought it might have been the wrong thing to say, because she moaned and cried some more. But she also leaned her head against his shoulder and wrapped her arms around his neck as though holding on to him for dear life. Was this not a sign of trust on her part?

"Love," he said gently, his heart truly aching because he had never seen her looking so frail or hurt, "tell me why you are so sad."

"How can you not see it, Connor? Is the truth not obvious?"

He wrapped his arms more securely around her. "No, love. As I said, I am dense and still do not understand what happened."

"*Love.* That's just it. Nobody loves me. Nobody wants me. And I was so stupid...so incredibly stupid to believe... But he just lied to me and was using me. He was going to drop me like a stone as soon as the week was out."

She sobbed some more.

"Eden, are you speaking of Lord Aubrey?"

She nodded against his chest. "He told me this morning that he cared for me and wanted to pursue a courtship. I believed him. I *believed* his lies. He had me completely fooled. Have I gotten so pathetic that I should fall for false words and think for a moment, for one stupid moment, that someone truly liked me?"

"Dear heaven... Eden, what makes you think he lied to you?" His heart sank, for he had not seriously considered that Eden might fall in love with someone else in the span of a house party, and now she would never consider his own feelings that he had stupidly never revealed to her.

She was still crying into his chest and clinging to him as she spoke. "I overheard his sister talking to their mother about me. It was all a trick, a setup to keep me away from you. She told her brother to woo me in order to keep me distracted while she pursued you. This is exactly what he did."

"I'll call him out. The bounder, I'll challenge him to—"

"Don't you dare do anything so foolish. You are a father and have your children to think about. You cannot get yourself hurt over me."

"Who is to protect you if not me, Eden?"

"You? Connor, you are just as bad as he is."

"What?" Lord, this was why he had chosen to remain a Silver Duke. Casual liaisons. No complications. Walk away without hurt feelings. But he could not walk away from Eden. He did not ever want to walk away from her.

She was in his heart to stay.

"How am I as bad as Aubrey?"

"He said too much and you said *nothing*. Not a thing in all the years we've known each other. Well, you can keep your Silver Duke reputation and you can keep your moonlight kisses, because I do not want to be kissed by someone who does not love me. I am not that pathetic… Well, maybe I *am* pathetic. But I still have my pride. I will endure and go to my grave with the ache of never having been kissed."

He took out his handkerchief and began to gently dab away her tears. "Eden, were you hoping for Aubrey to be the one to kiss you?"

She merely glowered at him. Now what had he said wrong?

"Did you fall in love with him? Is this why you are feeling so hurt?"

"Him? You think I fell in love with him? *Him?*"

Gad, why was she getting so angry? Should he not be asking about her feelings for his rival? Should he not be worried that he might lose her to Aubrey? He was so many things that Connor wasn't. Younger, fitter. Perhaps handsomer. Just as wealthy. Just as titled. Although of a lesser rank, and holding only a courtesy title of viscount. Still, he was an earl's heir and next in line to become earl. "Eden, help me out here. What am I not understanding? Just tell me straight out. If it is in my power, I will give you everything your heart desires."

"And you assume it is *him* that I want?"

Lord, his head was spinning. "Isn't it?"

"Well, if this is what you are hoping for in order to wriggle out of kissing me, then I hereby free you from all obligation in that regard. No kiss. Not ever. Not in daylight. Not in moonlight. Not in rain or sleet or snow. You do not have to kiss me ever."

Yes, he did have to kiss her. He had to kiss her because he loved her, and it was past time she knew it.

"Blessed saints, Eden. You are the most exasperating woman I have ever met. You also happen to be the most endearing. I do not care if you have freed me of the obligation to kiss you. It was never an obligation for me. You will have your moonlight kiss tonight."

She frowned at him. "Do not concern yourself. I just told you I want to be kissed with love or not at all."

He tucked a finger under her chin to tip it upward and keep her gaze firmly on his. "And I just told you that you will have your desired kiss."

"A moonlight kiss? With love? From you?"

"A moonlight kiss. A daylight kiss. A million kisses," he said in a husky murmur. "A kiss every morning and every night, and all of the hours in between if you will have me, Eden. Will you?"

There!

He had just proposed to her.

Dear heaven.

He had just proposed to Eden.

Gad, he hadn't meant for it to happen this way.

This girl was in desperate need of romance, and he had planned to provide it tonight by way of a moonlight kiss followed by a marriage proposal.

Now everything was rushed and had come out backward. He had not even spoken to his mother or children yet about his remarrying. Well, his mother had contrived this house party for the sole purpose of pushing a new wife on him. Surely she could have no objections over his choosing Eden, since she had already accused him of immense stupidity in not seeing what was before his very eyes.

His children adored Eden and would cheer loudest upon learning he wanted to marry her. They would likely insist on having the wedding take place tomorrow, before he said or did something else idiotic to chase her away.

She was staring at him as though he had just spoken to her in a strange foreign tongue unheard for a thousand years. "Eden, will you?"

"Will I what, exactly?" She looked utterly confused, but his words had to be sinking in, because she was no longer sniffling and her lips were no longer trembling.

Was that the hint of a smile at the corners of her very kissable lips? Those beautiful, bow-shaped lips that were slightly pouty, slightly turned down at the corners, and slightly plump, so that they would feel deliciously soft as he sank his mouth onto hers, which was something he had ached to do for ages now.

"Will you marry me, Eden?" He'd said it again. How much clearer did he have to be?

Silence stretched between them.

Was she going to accept him or not?

What an idiot he was. He had not considered that she might refuse him. But she would if she was in love with Aubrey, even if that wretched man had dashed her hopes.

"Eden?" What was she waiting for?

Then he realized what else needed to be said, because this was Eden and love was the very thing she had been deprived of all of her life. This was the reason she had been crying her heart out moments earlier.

Love.

He cleared his suddenly tight throat. "I am not asking you to marry me because I find the situation most convenient. I can see how you might mistake it, considering how well you get along with my children and my mother."

She nodded.

"In fact, my feelings for you are most *inconvenient*. I had fallen into an easy routine and was comfortable living the life of a Silver Duke. I thought I had my heart securely protected behind thick walls, and for the most part, it was true. But I found I had no defense against you. Your beauty, your wit and charm, your kindness and intelligence. There is not one wall left standing because you have demolished them all. You conquered my heart quite some time ago, Eden. I simply did not know how to broach the subject with you. Sometimes it is hardest to be honest with those you care for most. But here it is now. I love you."

"You love me?"

Her voice was so fragile, it made him ache. "Yes. Quite fiercely and irrevocably."

"Are you certain you love me in the way a man loves a desirable woman and not because I would make a good governess for your children?"

Her eyes were big and wide as she stared up at him, revealing all the hurt she had endured over the years—and just how vulnerable she felt right now.

"Yes, I love you with embarrassing desperation," he assured her. "I cannot think straight when I am around you, and miss you with a cavernous ache whenever you are not around."

He sighed and continued, because there was no turning back now and he may as well make a complete arse of himself, pour out his heart until there was not a drop left to drain. "You are so beautiful, you leave me breathless. I was in torment as I undressed you last night."

She shook her head and laughed softly. "You shouldn't have done it."

"And left you uncomfortable all night? Priscilla was about to push you out of bed. Besides, your gown would have been wrinkled beyond repair."

"It could have been ironed out."

"You might have torn it while tossing and turning."

"It could have been sewn...maybe. Well, it is a delicate fabric."

"And had more tapes and lacings than I've ever seen on a gown," he said with a groan. "Eden, you were asleep and I was not going to touch you in any inappropriate way. You would have laughed at me had you seen the contortions I went through trying to avoid any impropriety."

Although it could not be denied that she had fallen against him a couple of times, her soft bosom pressing against his chest and roiling him in unmentionable ways. This did not bear mentioning at the moment, especially since her perfect breasts were once again pressed against him as she remained on his lap and holding on to him.

She felt nice against him. He liked that she was comfortable in his arms. They fit so well together.

He wanted it to be this way for them always.

"It is quite ironic," he said, breaking the momentary silence between them, "that someone with a Silver Duke reputation has trouble stringing romantic words together. What I am trying to say, rather ineptly, but speaking sincerely from my heart, is that I do not want you for my children. I want you for myself. I want you for a lifetime, and I want you for my wife."

Her tears flowed again.

He rubbed his thumb along her cheeks as he spoke. "Eden, I've loved you for quite some time now, but never dared let on because...I don't even know what was going through my head these past few months. More than a few months, for I've had these feelings for you for well over a year now."

"Why did you never say anything to me?"

He gave a short, mirthless laugh. "You were so perfect, it

scared me. And our friendship was so precious to me, I feared to lose it by saying something you did not wish to hear from me."

"Me? Perfect?" She shook her head insistently. "You are the perfect one, the unattainable Silver Duke. I am just the eccentric spinster."

"Hopefully, soon to be my eccentric duchess. Honestly, Eden, what more must I say to convince you that you are the only one for me? I love everything about you, even your owlish spectacles. In truth, I adore the way you look in them. Yes, you are beautiful without them. But your true beauty shines through when you are being *you* and not London's notion of some fashionable ideal."

"Fashionable?" She laughed softly, which was another thing he loved about her, the gentle warmth of her laugh. "I am certainly not that."

He caressed her cheek. "You set your own style."

Her body had remained relaxed against his as they spoke, and he hoped this was a good sign.

Her smile seemed genuine as she said, "I will forgive you if you are not enamored of this hideously drab gown I am wearing."

He smiled back. "It is quite practical for bird watching. Completely unfashionable. But my point is, you could be wearing a sack and still look stunning. You do not need silks or satins or fine jewelry to sparkle like the diamond you were and *always* will be."

Finally admitting he loved her was surprisingly freeing. "I am going to kiss you now."

She shook her head to stop him. "No!"

"No?"

"I do want you to kiss me," she said with an emphatic nod, "but…should you not have done it before you proposed to me?"

"No, I already know how it will turn out."

"You do? How is that possible? What happens if you are wrong and decide you were mistaken about our kiss?"

"Eden, it is never going to happen."

"Never?"

He nodded. "I am going to like it and so will you. Trust me on this. It will only deepen my feelings for you. Hopefully, it will do the same with regard to your feelings for me. Do you have any idea how long I've ached to kiss you?"

She laughed softly. "Apparently not."

"My fault entirely," he said, knowing they should have been honest about their feelings months ago. Their deep friendship would be the basis for a good marriage going forward, but it had also held them back and caused needless distress because both of them were so afraid of losing that precious friendship if their feelings were not reciprocated.

He was sorry it had taken heartbroken tears from Eden before they found the courage to reveal what had been in their hearts all along. It was done now and had led to this happy result.

Well, he hoped it would be a happy result. She had not accepted him yet. Why hadn't she accepted him yet?

"Close your eyes, love."

She pushed against his shoulders. "Don't kiss me yet, Connor."

"I thought we cleared the air. Why don't you want my kiss?" Being a duke and never being refused by anyone had not prepared him for this rejection. Was she rejecting him? No, he could not be reading her body wrong. A woman's body was something he knew quite well. Eden still had her arms around his neck and was leaning into him again, exhibiting all the signs of attraction and desire.

"I do want it, I assure you. Have I not waited *ages* for it? But will you be angry with me for wanting my first ever romantic kiss to be a moonlight kiss?"

No, how could he ever be angry with her? She asked so little of him.

"A moonlight kiss it shall be, then."

"Tonight?"

"Yes, tonight."

She laughed. "You had better make it worth my while."

He cast her a rakish smile. "Is that a challenge?"

He was going to kiss her with heat and passion, and all the fire of love in his soul. He was going to kiss her until her legs turned soft as pudding and could no longer hold her up. But she would never be in danger of falling while he had his arms around her to always keep her safe.

She was his to love and protect from this day forward. All he had to do was give Eden her moonlight moment.

Yes, he'd give her moonlight and starlight and every bit of enchantment she deserved to have. Being a Silver Duke had its advantages.

Despite his exaggerated reputation, he did know how to kiss a woman. Eden was going to experience a kiss to carry in her heart forever.

She blushed as he regarded her. "Will it set fire to the pages of my diary? I am going to write down every detail as I describe it in my entry."

"Yes, love. Scorching inferno," he said, casting her a steamy look.

Her blush deepened. "I am looking forward to it."

"So am I," he said with a chuckle, knowing she was already affected by the rakish smolder in his eyes. But he was affected, too. Despite his experience and familiarity with a woman's body, he had too much at stake with Eden because he cared for her so deeply. Their kiss needed to end all doubt they were meant to be together for a lifetime. "Eden, you haven't answered my question."

"What question?"

"Will you marry me?"

CHAPTER TWELVE

A FTER LEAVING EDEN'S bedchamber, Connor strode out of his house by the kitchen door in order to avoid encountering anyone and having to answer questions. He was hot under the collar, and it had nothing to do with the heat of the day. The air was still warm, but a light breeze off the water offered modest relief. It rustled through the silvery leaves as he walked along the woodland path between Lynton Grange and Chestnut Hill. But he was headed in no particular direction, just needed to shake off his frustration.

"She'll give me her answer *after* our first kiss?" he muttered while striding along and feeling completely disgruntled.

Who said that to a duke? Why would she not leap at the chance to be his wife, kiss or no kiss? After all, he was the prize everyone wanted.

Come to think of it, she had not said she loved him... Well, not in so many words. But he *knew* she loved him.

He had seen it in her eyes. And in her smile. Not to mention the way her exquisite body had molded to his as though they had been cast from the same lot and designed to be a pair.

The afternoon shadows were lengthening to mark the few hours of daylight left. He was not far from the infamous goose pond and could hear their honks and light splashes as they fluttered their wings in the water.

Why had he waited so long to reveal his feelings to Eden?

And now, she was making him suffer while awaiting her answer. Not on purpose, because Eden did not have a wicked or vindictive bone in her body. No, she was making him wait because she wanted her moment of magic first.

A Silver Duke's moonlight kiss.

Was there a doubt she would accept him afterward?

First of all, he was a wealthy duke. That alone was all any other young woman needed to know to be swayed. His name was irrelevant. His looks, also irrelevant. But not for Eden. She had no need to marry someone merely because they were a bulging coin purse.

Eden needed to marry for love.

In truth, he knew she was in love with him. But she was insisting on that kiss to be certain he loved her. Knowing Eden as well as he did, she was going to reject his proposal if she thought *he* did not truly love *her*.

Well, if the problem arose, he would just have to convince her that he did care. Weren't there many facets to a good marriage? Friendship, for certain.

This led him to the second reason why she should marry him. They were good friends. The best of friends. Was this not the solid foundation for any successful marriage? Trust and friendship. He had learned the importance of both the hard way when realizing Mary had no desire to share anything of his heart or ever allow him to share any of hers. Their marriage, while producing his beloved children, had not been built on any foundation at all.

Quite the opposite would be true with Eden. She had shared so much of her heart with him over the years, and in his own way, he had done the same with her. How often had he confided about his children and his worries that he was failing them as a father? Their conversations at times were quite intimate, exposing his deepest concerns and trusting her not to violate his confidences. He did the same for her.

The only unanswered question between him and Eden concerned the bedchamber, and this was one area in which he had no doubt at all. Eden obviously had passion and would respond to his touch.

Nor was there any doubt about his ability to have her respond, or about the fact that she liked his touch. He would always get the truth with Eden, and the way she had held on to him while crying her heart out revealed all.

Despite her reluctance to accept his offer of marriage before that first kiss, her body had already accepted him.

"Lynton!"

Connor recognized who was calling out to him and turned to await the man as he caught up. "Aubrey," he responded with cold reserve.

"What did Eden tell you? Why was she so upset?"

"Because of you, you bloody arse." Well, perhaps he was not quite as cool as he intended to be. He curled his hands into fists, struggling to keep his temper in check, because he meant to give Eden her first kiss and did not wish it to be done while nursing stitches to his lip after he and Aubrey bloodied each other in a brawl.

"For the life of me, Lynton, I don't know what I did to anger her." Aubrey raked a hand through his hair, apparently frustrated and doing a good job of pretending to be distraught. "Did she give you a reason?"

Connor nodded. "She knows your courtship was a ruse, so do not bother to pretend you care for her, because she knows the truth and will never believe you no matter how many times you deny it."

"A ruse? I *will* deny it!" Then he groaned. "Did my foolish sister say something to her?"

"Eden overheard her talking to your mother. The two of them were standing by the glassblower's tent and did not realize Eden was there."

Aubrey groaned again. "I knew something was not right when she returned to us with that glass swan. And Eden believed what my peahen of a sister said?"

"Why wouldn't she? Do not bother to deny you pursued Eden just to give your sister a chance with me. It was a wasted effort, I can assure you. Spoiled, manipulative debutantes are not, and have never been, my cup of tea."

"I am quite aware of my sister's failings. But she is still my sister, and I will admit that I steered Eden away from you that very first day to give Persephone her chance. But it took me only a few minutes to realize she had no prayer of gaining your notice or affection. So, if giving my sister those few minutes makes me guilty of conspiring in her scheme, then yes, I am guilty."

"And you think this absolves you of hurting Eden?"

"My pursuing a courtship with Eden has nothing to do with my sister's wishes. It has everything to do with the fact that I like her. I sincerely like her, Lynton. I'll tell you straight out that my feelings for her run far deeper than merely a temporary acquaintance. If she will have me, I intend to marry her."

Connor shook his head and laughed, for if he did not look upon the remark with humor, he would punch this man. "She will not have you. Nor will I give you the chance to spout more lies in her ear. Aubrey, I want you and your family out of here first thing tomorrow morning. Do not approach Eden tonight either, or I will toss you out the moment I find you within arm's length of her."

"Is she saying this, or is it you?"

"It is *me* saying it," Eden said, coming upon them as the two men stared each other down. They had been so busy glowering at each other that neither heard her approach.

Connor's heart lurched, for her eyes were still red from crying and she looked quite pale in the afternoon light. Still beautiful, but as fragile as the glass swan she had purchased for his daughter. "Eden...why are you out here?"

She came to his side. "I was watching from my window when I saw you leave the house, and realized there was something important I should have told you. Then I noticed Lord Aubrey follow you out and thought I had better see what was going on."

"Nothing is going on," Aubrey insisted. "I have no intention of raising my fists to an old man."

"Old man," Connor growled, knowing he was being baited and falling for it nonetheless. "I'll show you—"

Eden placed a hand on his arm. "Honestly, Connor. You both need to behave yourselves." She turned her back to Aubrey, completely ignoring the man while she concentrated her attention on Connor. "I will not accept you if you are damaged goods. Got it?"

He grinned as he caressed her cheek. "Yes, love. Got it."

Aubrey gasped. "Love? Eden, is this true? Has he lied to you and told you that he loved you?"

She curled her hands into fists as she turned to face him. "Lied to me? You dare accuse him of lying to me when you are the knave who has done nothing but falsely flatter and deceive me from the moment we met? You pretended to court me. You pretended to *like* me. They were all lies meant to give Persephone a chance to snare her duke."

He held his arms out in supplication. "Eden, let me explain—"

"No! Why bother to lie to me at all? It wasn't necessary. You already had me occupied bird watching this entire day. That's all you had to do. Keep me away from the duke so Persephone could sink her claws into him. Or did your cruelty extend so far as to plot with your sister to ruin me? Was this your wicked scheme? To seduce me and then abandon me as damaged goods, knowing the duke would never marry me once he found out?"

"Never! Eden, damn it. I would have to be the lowliest of bounders to consider something so vile."

"Are you not?"

"For pity's sake. I am in love with you!"

She placed her hands on her hips as she laughed in dismissal. "Ha! Am I supposed to believe you fell in love with me after a day of bird watching?"

"No," Aubrey said, sounding obviously pained...or was he the consummate actor? "I fell in love with you within ten minutes of meeting you. Today was just meant to be enjoyed. My mind was already made up about you. I intended to propose to you at the end of this house party, but there is no point in putting it off now. Will you marry me?"

She gasped. "Oh, this is surely a divine jest. Two proposals in one day. Are either of them real?"

Having said that, she returned to the house.

Connor watched her walk away. Aubrey did the same. "You proposed to her? Why? To preserve a convenient governess? Do you even love her?"

Connor ignored the question.

Since he was not going to get any peace while Aubrey followed him around and tossed him questions, he marched back to the house. To his annoyance, Aubrey maintained his stride beside him. "Eden has every reason to be angry with me. But just because my sister asked me to distract her, doesn't mean I agreed. Well, I did agree at first, as I admitted. But Eden is an angel. Anyone with a decent pair of eyes can see it." He stopped and moaned. "She'll never believe me, will she?"

Connor paused as they reached the courtyard. "No. How can she ever trust you now?"

"Help me make this right, Lynton."

Connor laughed. "Me? You do realize I am your competition, don't you? Why should I help you out?"

"Because you are a decent fellow. And you know my sister is a manipulative, headstrong nuisance of a girl who would not give me a moment's peace until I agreed to distract Eden for five minutes. That's all I intended. Everything else was real."

"Real? Even if what you say is true, am I supposed to believe you fell in love with Eden in the span of a day?"

Aubrey frowned at him. "Why wouldn't you believe it? Is she not obviously charming, intelligent, and achingly beautiful?"

"Yes, but…" Lord help him, it had taken Connor years to notice Eden. He'd known her practically from the moment she was born and seen her turn into the lovely young woman who was going to break hearts in her debut Season. But he had been married back then and could not ever permit himself to develop feelings for her. "Of course, she is all those things. Leave me alone, Aubrey. I'll think about your request."

Well, he had probably loved her all along but convinced himself it was nothing. Was he not a master at repressing and denying? Even after being free to acknowledge his feelings, he had kept silent. Why? To enjoy the life of a Silver Duke? In truth, just how much had he, Bromleigh, and Camborne enjoyed their notoriety? Not very much, for his part. He could not even bring himself to bed other women once he admitted to himself that he had feelings for Eden.

And yet he had said nothing to her and allowed his exaggerated reputation to take a life of its own and grow out of all proportion. "Thank you, Lynton. It is only fair that she knows the complete truth and makes her decision with all the facts before her. If she chooses you, then know that I will wish you both every happiness, because it would never be my desire to see her unhappy. Unfortunately, I expect she will choose you. Despite my bravado, the painful truth is that I have little chance competing against a Silver Duke." Having said what was on his mind, Aubrey walked off.

Connor could not deny that he and his friends were treated as mythical gods. This would no longer do.

Eden needed a man to love her truly and sincerely. A real man of flesh, blood, and grit, with strong arms to hold her and protect her through good times and bad. She did not need some idol on a pedestal to be worshipped from afar. That Aubrey saw her worth so clearly in a trice was unsettling.

And yet was anything this man said true?

Connor was fairly good at spotting schemers. A man in his position always had to be on the alert. His gut instinct told him Aubrey could be trusted, but his own jealousy was skewing his opinion, and he was never going to trust this man. It was much easier to ignore the truth and consider him unworthy. Aubrey was very good in the role of lovelorn suitor, very believable, and had perfected the ability to cast sincere looks. Yes, he was quite polished.

Connor sighed, knowing he could not deny the obvious.

The poor sod had fallen in love with Eden.

What was he to do now? Tell Eden the truth? Let her be the one to choose?

Aubrey was equal to him in so many ways. Both held titles. Both were wealthy. Indeed, the Lothmeres were perhaps even wealthier than he was.

Aubrey was younger and fitter. Yes, fitter, even though Connor had beaten him at arm wrestling. He would never admit it, but his entire body ached after that exertion.

"Bah," he muttered.

Most of his guests had retired to their quarters to prepare for tonight's supper and dance. He was on his way up to the children's quarters to speak to them about Eden when he remembered she had approached him on his walk because she had something important to tell him. Aubrey's surprising marriage proposal had interrupted them.

He marched down the hall to her room and knocked at the door. "Eden, it's me."

"Go away!"

Oh, not that again. He knocked once more. "You had something important to tell me."

"Yes, but I cannot tell you now."

"Why not? Are you dressed? I'm coming in."

"I'm not dressed!"

And that again, too. "Too bad. You have to the count of ten to make yourself decent. One...two...three..."

The door to her bedchamber flew open, revealing a bespectacled Eden wearing a plain brown robe not even an elderly grandmother would deign to wear. The thing was hideous, and yet heat shot through his veins, for she'd hastily wrapped it around her lithe body and left one shoulder slightly exposed.

His heart was banging like a hammer in his chest.

She had also unpinned her flame-red hair, no doubt preparing for her maid to fashionably style it. But for now, it flowed in a fiery cascade of red-gold fire down her back. "You are a beast, Connor," she said, but a smile teased at the corners of her mouth. "You do know this."

"I do," he replied, nodding. "What was so important that you followed me out of the house to tell me?"

She sighed. "My maid will be back at any moment. You cannot be found in here."

"I am only at your door. And what does it matter even if I were found naked in your bed? I've already told you that I love you and wish to marry you."

Her eyes had widened at the mention of him naked in her bed, and now her cheeks showed a hot blush. "Now that is something I would love to write about in my diary. A Silver Duke without a stitch of clothes on in my bed? Would you mind if I embellished the moment?"

He laughed. "Go right ahead. Embellish to your heart's content. Although my Silver Duke reputation is not completely unearned. I don't think much embellishment will be required if ever you were to join me in that bed."

Her cheeks burned redder.

"However, when it comes to speaking from my heart...I'm sorely lacking in that regard. I'm sorry I waited so long to reveal my feelings for you. I almost lost you because I was such a fool."

She placed a hand to his cheek and looked up at him. "No, Connor. There was a reason you waited. Your heart simply wasn't ready."

He hoped that was affection he saw in her beautiful hazel eyes, and not pity because she had decided to reject him. "Let me come in, Eden. What was it you had to tell me?"

"No, you mustn't come in." She placed her hand on his chest to hold him off. "You are going to try to kiss me after I tell you what I need to tell you."

"Then it is something good?"

She nodded. "But it doesn't change a thing. I want my first kiss to be a moonlight kiss."

"Eden, I—"

She took a deep breath and groaned. "I love you, Connor."

CHAPTER THIRTEEN

E DEN STROLLED DOWNSTAIRS to join the others in the parlor before supper. Evelyn's maid had gone out of her way to make her look pretty this evening, no doubt sensing something was in the air. Had she noticed Connor standing outside her door and seen the two of them speaking intently to each other?

Perhaps it was the starlight in Eden's eyes as she had washed and dressed that gave her away.

She hoped Connor would admire her in this gown of sea-blue silk that had several diaphanous layers of matching blue over the silk to give the gown an ethereal sway and movement. She rarely concerned herself with matters of fashion, but she wanted this night to be special in every way.

Her mother was seated amid a circle of older guests and still complaining about her shoe buckles. Never mind that she had almost cracked open her father's head—to lose a buckle, now that was a true crisis.

Eden merely smiled and hurried past her and her friends before she was caught up in that excruciating conversation. But as she moved further into the room, she suddenly stopped and blinked, not trusting her own eyes.

To her surprise, her father was also here. "Papa?"

"Ah, Eden. Lovely party Lynton has thrown, isn't it?"

She nodded numbly, wanting to glance back at her mother but not daring to do it while these two were in the same room and actually behaving. Fortunately, her father stood on the opposite side of the room from her mother with drink in hand as he engaged in conversation with Lord and Lady Lothmere. She greeted them warmly, for she liked them even if their son was a hound.

But what was her father doing here? Had Connor invited him?

Perhaps he had invited himself over. Yes, this was just the boorish sort of thing her father would do.

But she was glad he felt well enough to be up and about, and no doubt enjoyed showing off his stitches to all who would look and listen to his harrowing account.

Connor had become used to her parents after all these years and long since accepted the inevitability of their constant rancor.

Still, Eden was never going to speak to her mother or father again if they ruined this night for her. She wanted nothing to interfere with her moonlight kiss or the celebration that would occur when she accepted Connor's proposal of marriage immediately thereafter.

She was about to look for Connor on the terrace when he strode into the parlor and immediately captured everyone's attention with his commanding presence. He looked incredibly handsome in his formal attire, black tie and tails that accentuated the darkness of his hair that had a light sprinkling of gray, and his eyes that were hawk sharp and could pierce a girl's soul.

She certainly was not immune to his stunning good looks. Nor were any of the other ladies in the room. Sighs could be heard floating all around.

Ah, yes. The Silver Duke aura on full display. His shoulders were broad, and he exuded power and danger as he started in her direction.

Eden's heart was now pounding and her legs were in danger of buckling as she watched him move toward her with the lithe grace of a jungle creature. His eyes, the deep blue of a May sky, remained focused on her with predatory precision.

She had been wearing her spectacles and now hastily took them off and tucked them in the cleavage of her bosom, because these elegant gowns did not have any convenient pockets and she did not know where else to stick them where they would remain secure.

Connor grinned wickedly as his gaze darted to her breasts. "Let me know if you need my help retrieving your spectacles," he teased upon coming to her side.

She laughed. "People will talk if you continue to stare at me like that."

"Let them. By the way, Sir Nero Arnulfson was looking and also noticed you tucking your spectacles away. Well done, Eden. He's just spilled his drink all over Squire Hartley."

She laughed again. "You are making this up."

"Not at all. Every word is true. Look."

Indeed, a footman had a cloth in hand and was wiping wine off Squire Hartley's jacket while another footman was hastily sweeping up the shattered shards of Sir Nero's fallen glass.

"Good thing your staff rolled up that beautiful carpet for tonight's dancing, or else it might have been ruined," she said. "Red wine is no easy stain to remove."

"Ah, ever the practical lass. But it is my duty as host to point out that your body is spectacular and every man here is completely besotted and cannot tear their gaze away from you."

"Oh, Connor, stop. You are being ridiculous."

"No, love. I am being honest, and kicking myself ten times over for waiting this long to tell you what has been in my heart for eons now." He glanced around to make certain no one was close enough to overhear them, although all eyes were on them for certain. "Eden, I want to announce our betrothal tonight. Immediately after our kiss. Is that all right?"

"Are you certain this is what you want?" she asked him.

"Yes, don't you?"

She had always had feelings for Connor. First loving him as her savior when she was barely able to toddle. Then in friendship and admiration. And now in full awareness of him as a man who might soon be her husband.

Was there any doubt she was eager to share his bed?

"Yes, Connor. I am certain."

He nodded. "This is what I want, too. Not a single doubt. That first kiss is for your satisfaction, not for mine. I know how delicious you are. I've already kissed you a thousand times in my dreams."

She let out a soft breath. "You have? You are impossible to resist, you know. Every woman in the room is wishing they were standing in my place."

"Perhaps, but you are the only one I hope to claim. I've told my children about my feelings for you."

She was glad he had done so, for they were so much a part of who he was. It was right that they should be told and given the chance to voice objections. "What did they say?"

He grinned. "They berated me for being so dense and waiting this long to realize you were perfect for us all. They want me to send for them when I am ready to announce our betrothal."

"Oh, yes. Please do."

"I had already planned on it. They think you are marrying all of us and consider it their moment, too. They love you, Eden."

"The feeling is quite mutual. I hope they know how much they mean to me. Connor, have you also told your mother?"

"I'm sure she suspects, but I decided not to tell her beforehand."

"Oh? Why not?"

"She'll interfere. Is this not what she always does?"

Eden frowned, for this would hurt her so much. Evelyn had always been so loving to her. A valued mentor, mother, and friend. "How would she interfere? Do you think she will object to your choosing me?" After all, this party was Evelyn's idea, and she had selected the *ton* diamonds to be invited. Perhaps she wanted someone younger and fresher for Connor.

"No, Eden. She adores you and will be delighted. But I do not want to tell her anything until after you have received your kiss." Having made that declaration, he bowed over her hand politely and moved on to chat with his other guests.

Lord Aubrey came in shortly after she and Connor had finished chatting. Eden was now talking to the dowager duchess, who had pounced on her the moment Connor left her side because she knew something was in the offing. "Eden, what did my son say to you?"

"He said I looked pretty tonight. Evelyn, I—"

The dowager suddenly turned away and gazed toward the doorway. "That one," she muttered as Lord Aubrey walked in and began to stroll about the edges of the crowded room.

Eden was hardly surprised when he did not acknowledge her or attempt to approach her. Connor had warned the viscount to keep away and would go after him like a rampaging bull if he dared disobey.

"What about him?" Eden asked, curious to know why the dowager was scowling at Aubrey and appeared to dislike him as much as Connor did.

"He is trouble."

"How so?" She hoped he would not be so brazen as to cause a scene. Some women might not have minded having two handsome men fight over her, but Eden was not of that mind. She had been raised in a household of constant fighting and knew how hurtful it was not only to the combatants but to those who witnessed it.

These men were too evenly matched, and both would be bloodied if fists flew. Connor's daughter especially would be undone if she saw her father bruised and sporting a black eye.

Eden breathed a sigh of relief when Lord Aubrey noticed Connor chatting with her father and turned to walk in the opposite direction. He approached a young lady and bowed rakishly over her hand. The girl, the wealthy Miss Olivia Applegate, tittered and blushed as the handsome lord turned on the charm.

Eden breathed a sigh of relief and continued her conversation with Duchess Evelyn. "Why do you say he is trouble?"

"It is only gossip, but is there not always a bit of truth in every rumor? Your mother told me that he was quietly pursuing several heiresses at this party and intended to purposely compromise one of them to force a marriage."

"Pursuing several?"

"Oh, yes. I noticed the way he circled you. Margaret Wallingford and Olivia Applegate appear to be his current prey. Perhaps he has been eyeing others, too."

"And he meant to compromise one of us?" Had he intended her to be the one compromised, but then realized Connor was onto him and would protect her? Well, so much for her Helen of Troy "conquering the hearts of kings" moment. She was nothing but a coin purse for Aubrey to steal, after all. Only one among other pretty coin purses. "Evelyn, will you excuse me a moment?"

"Yes, of course. Is everything all right?"

"Quite perfect. I will only be a moment."

She stepped out onto the terrace and took in a refreshing breath.

Thank goodness Connor loved her.

Thank goodness she loved him with a deep and abiding conviction—something she ought to have made clear earlier, but she hadn't, and needed to give him more than a delayed acceptance of his proposal and the tame *I love you* she had given him seemingly as an afterthought.

She had loved him for so long that when the moment was upon her, she froze.

But her love had never wavered. Of this she was certain. Even when Lord Aubrey had shocked her by proposing, there had not been a moment when she was tempted to marry him instead of Connor.

And a good thing that was. She would have lost everything had she fallen prey to his charms. Lost her beloved Chestnut Hill, her funds, and everything else she owned. Most of all, she would have lost Connor forever.

"Eden, I need a moment of your time," the very fiend himself said, stepping onto the terrace after her. "I won't approach you, I promise. I'll step no closer than this. But there is something I must say to you."

"Haven't you said enough already?"

He sighed. "I just tried flirting with Miss Applegate, but could not endure more than a minute in her company. She laughs like a goat."

"That is a cruel thing to say."

"Perhaps, but is it not important that one not cringe when speaking to a potential wife?" He held up his hands in a gesture meant to forestall the next remark she was about to toss at him. "Eden, to my dying day I shall regret not being honest with you from the start. Losing your trust is quite a severe punishment for what I thought was a harmless deception in giving my sister a few minutes with Lynton. But in doing so, I have lost all chance with you."

She said nothing, intending to walk away before he could spout more lies.

"Don't go. Please," he said when she took a step toward the parlor. "Just one more moment of your time. I'll be leaving tomorrow because it is best for all. My family will be staying on. You'll be pleased to know that Persephone has given up on the duke and will now set her cap for the Marquess of Rathburne's son."

"Damien?"

"He's a bit of an idiot," Lord Aubrey said with a wry smile, "but he's a better match for her than Lynton. She'll rule that roost, and Rathburne's son will be all the better for her firm guidance. Lynton is not a man she could ever tame."

"Is this what you came out here to tell me?"

"No, although I do not know why you would ever believe me. Perhaps one day you will. Here's what I wish to tell you." He raked a hand through his hair and cleared his throat. "I know a treasure when I see it, and I do not mean your house or your trust funds. I mean *you*. Not that you need my assurance that you are beautiful and wonderful. But you need to know that my affections were not false. They were never false. That is all I am going to say. It was a pleasure spending the day with you. I shall never forget a moment of our time together."

"Oh." She did not know how to respond to that. However, if he was telling her the truth, then she wanted to know more. "Lord Aubrey, I am hearing gossip that you had your eye on every heiress at the party. Are you here to hunt fortunes?"

He laughed. "No, my family is filthy rich. Most of the wealth has already been settled on me, since my grandfather seemed to think I showed promise and would make a better earl than my father, who was too intellectual for his liking. When my parents named me Trajan, that was it for my grandfather. He had hoped I would be named William after him. But no, when he threatened my father and told him the unentailed properties would be left to me unless he bent to my grandfather's will, my father refused to bend. For the record, my full name is Trajan Hercules Ramses Aubrey."

Eden laughed. "Ouch! But good for your father. Three cheers for standing his ground."

"Do not tell him so—he's already too stubborn by half."

She nodded. "Your mother spoke kindly of me when she was arguing about me with your sister."

"Yes, both my parents liked you very much."

"I suppose they liked the other heiresses, too."

He raked a hand though his hair again. "There were no other heiresses of interest to me. That is nonsense. Where did you hear that rumor?"

She shrugged. "Just floating around. So why did you bother with Miss Applegate just now?"

He released a sigh to mark his exasperation. "To see if I could settle for something other than love. Apparently, I cannot. It took me less than a minute to figure that out. So I will take myself off in the hope that someday, sometime in the near future, I will meet the right girl and find that ever-elusive, enduring love. I thought you were the one, but I do not think I ever had a chance with you. Lynton has always had your heart."

She nodded. "Ever since I was two and fell into his fishpond."

"Since you were two? He's had that long a head start?" Aubrey gave a mirthless laugh. "I really never stood a chance then. Farewell, Eden. I wish you every happiness."

"I wish the same for you, Lord Aubrey," she said with all sincerity.

She watched him stride away, but felt no satisfaction in regaining her Helen of Troy moment. Perhaps his affections were genuine, but having a bevy of men interested in her was not what she'd ever wanted. There was pain in not being loved, and she did not wish this on Lord Aubrey or anyone else.

To her surprise, Connor stepped out from behind one of the pillars as soon as Lord Aubrey had disappeared back into the crowded parlor. "You saw him?" she asked, surprised Connor had not made his presence known sooner.

He nodded.

"And you did not rush at him like an angry bull?"

He shook his head. "I wanted to, but you would not have approved."

"Did you hear what he said to me?"

He nodded again. "Every word."

"I'm glad you did not stop him. He isn't worth a fight. I'm sure it was all lies he was still spouting anyway."

Connor frowned. "No, Eden. He was sincere and every word he said was true. I was wrong about him."

"But your mother heard he was chasing every young lady at your party."

He laughed lightly. "Yes, and she heard it from *your* mother. We all know what a reliable source she is."

"Oh, that's true." She winced. "Then he was never chasing

heiresses?"

"No, only you. And he was not interested in your fortune, since he is already a wealthy man. His interest in you is why I've had my eye on him from the moment he arrived here. Persephone may have viewed you as her competition, but I viewed her brother as *my* competition. I have been in complete and utter agony, and apishly jealous from the moment he walked up to you and introduced himself."

She cast him a tender smile. "Why are you telling me this now, Connor? You could have let me continue to think ill of him."

He rubbed a hand along the nape of his neck. "Yes, I could have done that. But I don't want you to make your decision about marrying me based on the mistaken belief that Aubrey was a cad. Especially if you did have feelings for him."

"I see."

"I do not want us to enter into a betrothal upon a lie, Eden. Whatever the outcome, I want you to follow your heart and find your true happiness. I hope you will find it with me, a dense, arrogant clot whose only saving grace is that he loves you and will always regret not telling you sooner."

"I did a bit of denying, too." She had poured her feelings into her diary while hiding them from Connor even once he was free to love her. Much of that time, she had denied them to herself, too. She had almost convinced herself that loving him was merely a fantasy and could not be real. Then the party had started and all those beautiful debutantes began to flutter around him.

Oh, that pain of losing him was quite real.

What would have happened had her parents not arrived when they did? She might have remained at Chestnut Hill trying to pretend she did not care if he chose someone else. She would not have been here for Connor to finally accept these feelings he had for her. Persephone would not have had any competition and might have weaseled a marriage proposal out of him.

No, it would not have happened. Likely he would have remained a Silver Duke, ever resistant to marriage.

"Your happiness matters more to me than my own," he said. "There should only ever be honesty between us. Well, there it is. The honest truth laid out before you. I haven't said anything yet to my mother, so no harm done if you choose Aubrey over me."

"But your children know."

"They only know that I meant to propose to you. They will get over the disappointment if you reject me. Is this not what children do best? Recover and move on. But the champagne toast is ready...whether it is me or Aubrey that you choose."

"That is awfully generous of you," she remarked, moving into his arms, which he closed around her, his expression clearly one of surprise and relief. "You do recall that I told you I loved you."

He cast her a wry smile. "Yes, Eden. But you may have said it because of a false impression about Aubrey."

She shoved at him lightly.

"What?" He laughed when she gave him another gentle push. "Am I not being gallant and admirable even though my heart is at risk of being ripped to shreds?"

"For someone with your reputation with the ladies, you really know nothing about us." She took his hand. "Come with me."

She led him into the garden and the fishpond tucked away in a far corner.

"All right, here we are. The original scene of the crime," he teased. "What happens next?"

"What happens next is that you kiss me, Connor."

He glanced up at the sun hanging low on the horizon and still shining. Sunlight glistened upon the waves so that the water shimmered blue and splendid. "It is still daylight."

She nodded. "I'll have my moonlight kiss now, if you please."

"Now?"

"Yes, because I have belatedly realized it isn't the moonlight that provides the magic. It is you, and only you. The time of day is irrelevant. Although moonlight is awfully nice, isn't it?"

He smiled and drew her into his arms again. "Yes, it is nice. But so is this... Close your eyes, Eden. Imagine a thousand stars twinkling overhead. There's also a moon shining full and bright above us. Do you see it?"

She closed her eyes. "Yes, I see it shining very brightly in my heart."

"I'll give you starlight and moonlight every night for the rest of our lives, if you wish it," he said in a throaty whisper, before lowering his head to hers and capturing her mouth with possessive heat as he proceeded to make her dreams come true.

She had waited a lifetime for his kiss.

This kiss.

Butterflies fluttered in her stomach as Connor sank his lips onto hers with all the confidence of an experienced rake, pressing warmly, deeply upon hers and proving he was right. She was going to love all his kisses. This first one and all those to come throughout their lives. She was going to love them because she loved *him* and always would.

She kissed him back with all the sincerity and hope in her heart.

He had to know that she would respond this way, trusting him and his Silver Duke prowess as he unleashed all the sensual power under his command.

Dear heaven.

It was considerable, a full assault on her senses.

Her skin tingled and her senses reeled, for he made her entire body thrum and spring to life with every light graze of his hand along her spine and the subtle shift in pressure upon her lips. She gave herself over to these new sensations, amazed at the complexity of a single kiss. There were so many nuances, and Connor understood them all, for his kiss showed both sides of him. Rough and yet tender. Conquering and yet protective.

And so blazing hot.

His mouth moved over hers with confidence, never a doubt

he was going to win her heart. And yet he offered up his own heart in surrender as well.

His splendid lips continued to press firmly but gently over hers. She had spent pages in her diary describing their fullness and perfect shape. When he smiled, his lips were as beautiful as sunshine and capable of melting a frozen wasteland.

His tongue dipped into her mouth, gently invading when she opened for him. Until this very moment, she had not realized there was more to a kiss than the mere press of one's mouth to another. In truth, they were a splendid assault on one's being, a magnificent invasion of the soul.

It was also the introduction to the intimacy of their bodies joining physically. She looked forward to it, for he made her feel desired and safe within the circle of his muscled arms.

She moaned as she breathed in his divine musk scent.

"Eden, dear heaven." He laughed softly afterward, smiling at her as they eased apart. "I knew it would be good with you."

"Just good?" She leaned her head against his chest when he drew her closer again. She felt his strong and steady heartbeat, while hers was wildly racing.

Had she made a cake of herself? Shown herself to be inept?

"It was spectacular, love," he whispered against her ear.

"Yes. I thought so too." She gazed up at him, melting again when he smiled at her. "I saw moonlight and starlight. It was even more incredible than I ever imagined a Silver Duke's kiss could be. But I learned something important, something that you probably knew all along."

"What is that?"

"Your kisses will always be moonlight kisses, the best sort of kisses because they are given in love."

He gave her an exquisitely tender kiss on the cheek. "There are plenty more in store for you, if you wish it."

She nodded. "I do wish it."

"Good," he said, releasing a light breath as he studied her intently. "Do you need more convincing? Or have I removed all doubt? Eden, love. Will you marry me?"

She had never felt so much joy in her life as she responded, "Yes."

CHAPTER FOURTEEN

C ONNOR HAD ALLOWED his children to stay up late so they might join him and Eden in celebrating their betrothal. It was hours beyond their usual bedtime, but they were too excited to care. He even allowed the boys a glass of champagne each. Priscilla took a sip of Eden's, but she did not like it when the bubbles ran up her nose.

"Yick," she muttered, unimpressed by perhaps the finest selection from one of the most revered chateau vineyards in the Champagne region of France.

But he'd never seen happier children, and knew their lives would forever change for the better now that Eden was to become a part of their family. In truth, they had accepted her years ago.

His namesake, young Connor, hugged him fiercely. "Thank you, Papa. You made the best choice."

Alex was next to hug him. "Took you long enough," he grumbled, and then hugged him again.

Priscilla tore at his heart and also managed to insult him. "I wished so hard upon every star at night, hoping you would make Eden our mama. We all loved her so much, and she loved us. Why did you wait so long, Papa? You made Eden so sad. But it's all better now."

Yes, it was better.

And he was never going to be so foolish as to hide loving

Eden ever again. She would get his affection by the bucketful.

After the betrothal announcement, and once the children scampered back upstairs to their bedchambers, he and Eden took his mother and her parents into the study for a moment of privacy. The food and champagne flowed freely and would keep their guests happily occupied. If that wasn't enough, the orchestra hired throughout the week was playing a lively reel, and the card room was open for those who wished to play instead of dancing.

Connor closed the door to the study to allow the five of them privacy. He hoped against hope that Eden's parents could behave like adults for the next ten minutes while details of their betrothal and wedding were discussed. As for his mother, she had quite the smug expression on her face.

"What is that look about?" Connor said, arching an eyebrow as he settled in a chair beside Eden, facing the three parents, who sat in a row on the sofa. His mother sat between Eden's parents, of course. It was never safe to have that battling duo within arm's reach of each other.

"I was beginning to despair you would ever come around," his mother said. "So I had to prepare a battle plan."

He nodded to acknowledge he had been quite difficult these past few years. "I suppose you had reason to despair that I would marry again."

His mother cast him another smug look. "Oh, I knew you would eventually. But I fretted that it might not be to Eden. You see, I knew it had to be Eden for you. No one else would ever do."

"Me?" Eden's eyes widened. "This was your doing all along?"

Connor regarded both in confusion. "All right, I am being dense again. Why invite every simpering peahen to this party if all you wished me to see was Eden?"

His mother cast him a long-suffering look. "The two of you have been in front of each other all along, and neither would say a word to the other. I had to shake things up, make both of you open your eyes and find the courage to reveal your feelings."

Eden shook her head and laughed. "It was no coincidence that my parents arrived at Chestnut Hill on the same day, was it, Evelyn?"

Connor's mother, looking every inch the elegant and wise dowager duchess, cast her a warm smile. "No, my dear. I hope you will forgive me for forging your signature to those letters inviting each of them here. I knew they would never behave, and this would chase you straight to Lynton Grange to escape them, and hopefully into my son's arms."

She turned to each of Eden's parents. "Do forgive me, Lord and Lady Darrow. But I love your daughter and had to do something drastic."

"You are quite forgiven," her parents said at the same time, perhaps the only time they had ever had a compatible thought.

Eden was obviously pleased they approved, but not above gently admonishing them. "Let it be noted that you did not fail Duchess Evelyn. Indeed, you behaved exactly as she'd hoped. Mama, you almost killed Papa within minutes of your arrival."

Her mother's chin shot up in indignation. "He should have ducked."

"He survived and the matter is concluded," Connor insisted, not wishing to dredge it up again when they ought to be talking about wedding plans.

His mother cast both of her parents another apologetic look. "Well, I did not wish for your mother to almost kill your father. But I was truly afraid my son would never let Eden know what was in his heart. And I knew she had always loved him."

Eden blushed. "You did?"

His mother cast her a doting smile. "Yes, my dear."

"How could you know when I did not always know it myself? I would never have acted upon my feelings or acknowledged them while Connor was still married."

"My dearest, you've been in love with him since you were two and fell into that fishpond." She turned to study Connor, and he felt the force of everyone's gaze on him. "And as for you..."

"What in blazes did I do but pull her out of that pond?"

"A mother feels these things... Well, I certainly did. It was in the way you looked at her."

Connor was still confused. "How did I look at her?"

"As though you had silently resolved in your heart that you were always going to protect her."

He laughed and shook his head. "I was barely fifteen, and she was an irritating two-year-old. I made her cry because I told her that if she fell in again, I would let the fish eat her."

Eden gasped. "You said that to me?"

He grunted. "Well, I didn't *mean* it."

She playfully swatted his shoulder. "All these years, I remembered you as my savior and protector."

"I was always going to protect you," he said. "But you were sobbing and howling in my ear, so I told you the first thing I could think of to make you stop crying. Gad, you were such a little duck. Pudgy cheeks and pudgy legs that held you up as you waddled around. You had the brightest red hair. Biggest hazel eyes."

He laughed in recollection and continued. "When you stopped crying, I assured you I would always rescue you if you fell into the pond again. You made me promise. You did not know a lot of words, since you were so young, but *promise* was one of them. So I did."

"The two of you were still stubbornly staring at each other as we all rushed to you," his mother added. "A fifteen-year-old marquess being stared down by a strawberry-haired, stubborn two-year-old. I knew it then. You two were going to fall in love."

Connor tried to deny it, but his mother would not hear of it. "I was so happy for you both, so hopeful that in the fullness of time you would realize you were in love with each other. But my biggest heartbreak happened several years afterward when you went off to fight Napoleon."

"I had to do it," he said. "Was it not my duty to defend England?"

"Others had bought their way out, but I knew you never would. You were always courageous. And always had a strong sense of duty. This is why you chose to marry Mary, out of duty to the ducal title. I understood why you decided to, for there was a great risk you would be killed in battle, and you wanted to secure the Lynton line."

"You got three beautiful children from the marriage," Eden said. "They were meant to be. It was all part of a divine plan, I suppose."

"One I almost wrecked because of my refusal to recognize my obvious feelings for you," he muttered.

"How was I any better? I was so afraid to say anything to you, so terrified it would destroy our friendship if you did not feel the same about me. I could not bear to lose you completely."

"This held me back, too. You were not the only coward." He arched an eyebrow and grinned at Eden. "But I was not going to let the situation continue beyond the yuletide season."

Eden stared at him, no doubt wondering what his grin was about. "You weren't?"

He shook his head. "I had it all planned out, my own grand scheme to get you to notice me."

She chuckled. "Notice you? Dear heaven, *everyone* noticed you. I was a stuttering idiot every time you approached me."

"So what was your grand plan, Connor?" his mother asked. "And why did you not tell me about it before I went to all the trouble of putting together this house party?"

"Serves you right for scheming behind my back. I am a grown man, too old to confide in my mother. But as I said, yuletide. I was going to have mistletoe positioned in every room of the house and kiss Eden the moment she walked under one of the sprigs. Not just any kiss, either."

Eden laughed. "A Silver Duke kiss?"

He nodded. "Only the best for you, love."

"I liked my plan better," his mother insisted. "Inviting wholly unsuitable girls to a country house party at Lynton Grange so you could see what a gem Eden was and finally do something about it."

"Right, and I almost lost her to Lord Aubrey, who also happened to fall in love with her," he grumbled.

His mother did not appear repentant in the least. "Whose fault is that? Certainly not mine. I've been trying to get you and Eden together for the past two years, to no avail. Honestly, you were both so stubborn. And Aubrey was a cad, wasn't he? He was only pretending to admire Eden."

Connor turned serious. "No, there was not a word of truth to the gossip. He fell in love with Eden at first sight."

Eden's mother spoke up. "But I saw him flirting with both Miss Wallingford and Miss Applegate just this evening. Who knows how many other girls he set his cap for? The man is an unworthy rake."

Connor never thought he would be defending his rival, but he had to speak up. "Lady Darrow, he sincerely cared for Eden and was ready to marry her."

His mother groaned. "Oh, dear. That was not foreseen in my plan."

"Why would it be?" Eden said. "I was firmly on the shelf."

"Never, Eden," his mother insisted. "There is no one more beautiful or charming than you. Now, it is time we discuss betrothal terms and make wedding plans."

"No negotiation," Connor said. "Eden gets whatever she wants and keeps full control over the assets she brings into the marriage."

Eden smiled. "I don't want anything from you but your love. I have all the material wealth I will ever need. Your assets are for your children."

"Including any we may have from our marriage," he said with a satisfied nod.

"Yes, ours." This caused her to blush, especially as everyone immediately turned speculative eyes on her at the mention of producing children.

Well, it was no one's concern but his and Eden's.

"As for the wedding," Connor said, clearing his throat, "I intend to obtain the license first thing tomorrow morning and marry Eden within an hour after that. Any objections, Eden?"

She grinned. "None whatsoever."

Connor spared a glance at the elders, waiting for any objections, but none were voiced. "Good. All settled. My cook already has the ovens at full blast preparing for tomorrow's round of entertainments. We'll just turn it into a day-long wedding breakfast. My boys will enjoy the chance to stuff their faces until their spleens burst."

After another round of congratulations, Connor's mother and Eden's parents left to rejoin their guests and share in the evening entertainments. Now finally left alone, Connor took Eden's hand in his, rubbing his thumb softly over the top of her hand. "I know I was highhanded in making these plans."

"I would have said something if I had any objections."

"Then you are all right with marrying me tomorrow?"

She reached up and kissed him lightly on the cheek. "I can think of nothing nicer than having a Silver Duke in my bed tomorrow evening."

He cast her a rakish smile. "Why wait until tomorrow?"

Chapter Fifteen

C ONNOR ENDED UP getting nowhere near Eden that night because his own meddlesome mother put a guard at her door to protect his fiancée's virtue. What difference did it make if he ravaged her luscious body tonight, since they would be married within a matter of hours?

Nor did any of the women allow him anywhere near Eden the following morning. Again, his meddlesome mother and Eden's prevented him from approaching her when he returned from obtaining the marriage license. "Botheration," he muttered when even Priscilla scolded him.

"Get yourself ready, Papa!" She had the audacity to wag her finger at him. "You have to get to the church before Eden does."

"Why?"

He got no answer, just a little *harrumph* before she scampered back into Eden's bedchamber and slammed the door in his face.

His little girl was going to be a bossy bit of goods.

But goodness, she looked so happy even as she excoriated him.

Standing in the hall was becoming dangerous, he realized as he was unceremoniously bumped out of the way while his mother's maids rolled in a tub, another carried Eden's gown, and yet another had Priscilla's gown and flowers in her arms.

A score of other items were also brought into her bedchamber. Ladies were scurrying in and out.

Priscilla shouted at him again when he once more attempted to enter. "Papa! Delia is fixing Eden's hair and then she is going to attend to mine. You have to keep out!"

He laughed and raised his hands in surrender. "All right. I give up."

Eden was naturally beautiful, so he did not understand what all the fuss was about. Little was needed, or so he thought, to get her ready for the ceremony that was due to take place shortly before noon.

It was just after nine o'clock in the morning now. This gave Eden easily two hours to prepare.

It would not take him very long to get ready—a half an hour at most, since he had already shaved this morning before obtaining the license.

But he was *persona non grata* according to Eden's helpers and his own daughter, and that was made quite clear to him.

He went upstairs to check on his boys.

His only regret in rushing the ceremony was that his dearest friends, Bromleigh and Camborne, would not be with him on his wedding day. Despite their reputations as confirmed bachelors and rakes, he knew this was not who they truly were. They were all hoping to find the love of a good woman, although Camborne was quite hopeless when it came to selecting women. The leather-tough Scot always chose the firebrands to take on as mistresses, although he'd given up on keeping a mistress ever again since that last debacle.

However, Camborne still escorted ladies of the *demimonde* around town, the indecent sort of women that matchmaking mamas disdained. This would ensure every sweet young thing with marriage on the brain stayed clear of him. Camborne lived hard and his breakups were always fiery.

Well, perhaps one day he would meet a woman who could tame him.

Bromleigh was another matter altogether. He had been burned in love in his younger days and never trusted any woman again. For this reason, he had resolved never to marry. He never wanted to give anyone the chance to break his heart again. No doubt, this was why he was so determined to see his nephew settled with the right young woman, one who was never going to deceive the lad or ever be unfaithful to him.

Connor shook out of thoughts of his friends as he looked in on his boys. Alex and Connor had just finished washing up and were about to begin dressing. His own valet, Holden, had made certain to lay out their finest attire, freshened and pressed, on their beds.

"Papa, you need to get ready!" Alex admonished him, wagging a finger.

What was with all the finger wagging?

When Holden rushed in, finger wagging at him too, he realized his own valet was the culprit. "Your Grace, I've been looking for you everywhere."

Since his sons did not need his hovering over them as they prepared for the wedding, he returned to his chamber and readied himself with Holden's assistance. Indeed, his valet was not letting him out of his chamber until he looked worthy of his ducal title.

He was met with admiring glances and approving looks as he strode downstairs a short while later.

He and his children took the first carriage to St. Matthew's Church.

He was ready and waiting at the altar when Eden arrived. She was escorted by his mother and her parents, who were not fighting with each other for once. No doubt, his mother had threatened them with death if they ruined this day for Eden. Having plotted for years to match him with Eden, the determined dowager duchess was not going to let anything or anyone interfere with this happy day.

Connor could have told her not to worry, for nothing was going to keep him from exchanging vows with Eden.

His children ran up to her with cheers and squeals of glee. Eden had a big smile and a hug for each of them. Priscilla was beaming.

His heart tightened while he watched his little girl. She had been in such need of a mother's care, and Eden had provided it to her these past few years. Just as Eden used to come crying to his mother, Priscilla would run into Eden's arms whenever she was sad and crying.

His boys looked quite handsome, he noted with pride.

As for Eden, she looked spectacular in a gown of cream silk and a simple circlet of flowers in her hair, which was done up in soft waves.

The church was soon packed to the rafters with house party guests, villagers, and Eden's entire domestic staff, who all gasped in admiration when she walked down the aisle, a majestic faerie queen draped in a circle of light as the sun filtered through the stained-glass windows and seemed to follow her the entire way to his side.

He took her hand, breathing a quiet sigh of relief when her mother and his, as well as his children, took seats in the Lynton family pew to his right while her father took a seat in the Darrow family pew to his left. "You're not wearing your spectacles," he whispered.

"Your mother hid them from me," she whispered back, laughing softly. "Apparently, she did not want your new wife to march down the aisle looking like an owl."

The vicar, who was also noticeably relieved the Darrows were on their best behavior, cleared his throat to gain their attention and proceeded with the ceremony.

Although it was not commonly done, Connor held Eden's hand throughout the ceremony and continued to hold it through their exchange of vows. He heard the joy in her words as she said, "I do."

He felt a contentment such as he had never experienced before when his turn came, and he repeated, "I do."

Cheers rang out the moment the vicar pronounced them husband and wife.

Ah, yes. Those were his little heathens hopping out of their seats and reveling like pagans in the aisles.

Connor led Eden out of the church and into the splendid sunshine. They remained in front of the church to accept well wishes from all in attendance. Everyone would now return to Lynton Grange for the wedding breakfast that was to include a feast, entertainments, and drinks flowing until all hours.

Everyone wished them well—even Persephone, who hadn't taken long to put a tether on the Marquess of Rathburne's son, Damien. The amiable dolt scurried forward on her command, offered congratulations on her command, and gave his arm to escort Persephone to the Lothmere's waiting carriage—also on her command.

He appeared happy as a lark.

Yes, Persephone was perfect for that good-natured clot who did not have much going on between his ears.

Lord and Lady Lothmere approached them next to offer their good wishes. Lady Lothmere appeared quite sad as she said, "We would have welcomed you into our family, dear Eden. But I think you are exactly where you are meant to be. I only hope my son finds another such as you to love."

Eden gave her a kiss on the cheek. "I also wish this same happiness for him."

Sir Nero approached them next, appearing quite disgruntled as he stepped forward to offer his congratulations.

Eden noticed, too. "He will have to find someone else's bottom to pinch now that I am your duchess and he fears you will cut off his hand if he dares try it again."

Connor frowned. "I'll do much worse if he ever dares."

Eden gave his hand a light squeeze. "Completely unnecessary. Merely a fierce stare from you will do. See? Perfect. Just as you are staring at me now."

He laughed. "I am staring at you with love. It isn't at all the same thing."

She stared back with her big hazel eyes shimmering.

The memory of that fishpond rescue came back to him. Her eyes. Those very same eyes that had touched his soul all those years ago.

Yes, he should have known they were bound together in that moment.

Later that evening, after all the feasting and dancing had ended and everyone had retired to their bedchambers, Connor led Eden into his ducal suite, where they would spend this first night together and all others to come.

He was already familiar with the exquisite feel of her body from his hapless attempt to undress her the other night. Tonight, he hoped to exhibit a bit more prowess. He had dismissed Holden for the evening, for Eden would assist him if required, although there was nothing he could not manage himself.

As for her, he was *quite* capable of assisting her out of her clothes. After all, was this not his reputation? And she was awake and willing this time, so there was that too.

She stood in the center of his large, elegantly appointed chamber with her hands clasped, uncertain what to do. "Eden, the duchess quarters are attached to mine, with an interior door between them. That suite of rooms is yours to settle in, for I'm sure you'll prefer not having Holden rush in and out as you wash and dress. You'll have your privacy and ample space for your entire wardrobe. But I hope that door will always remain open between *us* and that you will share my bed from here on out. Or I do not mind sharing yours, if that is your preference," he said, motioning to the adjacent room.

"I won't care which bed we share, as long as we are together." She came to him and wrapped her arms around his neck. "Can you believe we are married?"

He nodded. "Yes, it is the fact that I took so long to ask you that has me shaking my head in dismay."

He kissed her as he began to undo the ties and tapes to her gown. Having her awake and not about to topple if he dared release her allowed him to work at his leisure and soon have the gown and corset off her, leaving her in a sheer shift.

He smiled upon gazing at the softness of her body and feeling the silkiness of her skin. She sighed when he kissed her neck and moaned softly with pleasure as he began to suckle lightly on one of the tender pulses. "Your turn," she whispered, shifting in his arms so that she faced him.

He had only removed his jacket, but now took off his waistcoat and cravat. Eden helped him with the cuff links, and soon his shirt was off, too. Her eyes widened as she took in the width and breadth of his shoulders, and the light spray of dark hair dusted with silver across the broad length of his chest. But she inhaled sharply upon noticing the jagged scar along his arm. "Connor! You said you were wounded in battle, but I never realized it was such a serious injury. You might have lost your arm." She leaned closer to examine it and then lightly kiss it.

"It healed years ago, Eden. What I did not realize is that my heart had yet to fully recover. But it will now, with you by my side."

They both disrobed completely, for they both felt this strong connection to each other. To reveal hearts, bodies, and minds was the only way they knew to be with each other. He was not bashful by nature, but Eden was. However, not with him, because she trusted him so profoundly. When he took her to bed and began to explore her body, she was eager to learn what to do. "Let me lead the way this time, love," he said.

He took it slow with her—at first.

But it was not long before their passions were aroused. She responded to the flick of his tongue across the tips of her breasts, and the slide of his hand to the sensitive spot between her legs. She was ready for him when he entered her, wrapping her slender legs around his hips and impatiently lifting herself upward to take all of him in when he meant to use care this first time. "Eden, love," he said with a groan, quickly shedding that plan and giving her the passion she desired.

He watched her beautiful face as she responded with awe and

heightened arousal when he began this mating dance, moving in and out of her with primal confidence and an ease gained from experience. He knew when she was close to the edge, knew how to enhance her pleasure, and exactly when she tumbled to her release. He kissed her on the mouth as she cried out in ecstasy, feeling the waves of pleasure ripple through her body, and waiting for his turn to take his.

The look of her, with her wild red hair splayed across his pillows, her creamy breasts thrust into the air as she arched her back and felt the climax of her desire, did him in. He'd never seen a more beautiful sight. In two quick thrusts, he followed suit.

Afterward, as she rested in his arms while he stroked her hair, she asked him for a full report. "How was it for you, Connor? Was I terrible? It was only my first time."

"Eden, sweetheart, do I look displeased?"

She glanced up at him and grinned. "No, you look quite smug and triumphant."

He chuckled. "It was wonderful. Truly. Better than anything I've ever experienced before."

"But you do have a lot of experience. Was I better than your worst? You do not have to be tactful about it. I'd rather know the truth."

He wasn't going to deny his years of experience. Nor did he intend to lie to her. There was no need, because he loved everything about her, down to the lovely scent of her skin that stirred him on a primal level.

Eden was perfect, and he told her so. "You were better than the *best*, Eden. There is not a one who can compare to you. I know you love your scientific studies, and there is no denying intimacy has an important biological aspect to it. But it is most of all about feelings, and not at all based on common sense or logic. How are you feeling about what we just did?"

"Very good," she assured him. "I'm quite happy. Well satisfied."

"Same for me, but..." He rolled her under him. "As for satisfied... I am certainly well pleased, but not yet done. I still crave you."

She smiled at him, obviously delighted by his remark, and drew him closer.

He'd always loved the rich, dark-red earthen color of her hair that also had hints of gold in it. She was on the tall side of average in height, but this suited him fine because he was tall himself. She was the perfect shape, too. Full breasts, long and slender legs, and a smile that filled one's heart with sunshine.

No one had a lovelier mouth or more beautiful eyes that held starlight in their irises.

At her encouragement, they made love again.

He wasn't certain who was the more eager, her or him. They fit together like long-lost lovers who'd been searching through eternity for their mate and had now found each other. There was no holding back, and they were both grunting and laughing as they tumbled over the precipice of ardor together, each of them more deeply in love and more bonded in unity than when they started.

Eden had wanted her moonlight kiss.

He had wanted *her*.

Yes, he had wanted her and would always want her because she, he had finally come to realize, was his moonlight.

EPILOGUE

Lynton Grange
North Devon, England
September, 1817

B ARELY TWO WEEKS had passed since his wedding to Eden and an aura of happiness had settled over his home, Connor thought as he and his wife entered the children's quarters to speak to them. His boys were quietly playing marbles, trying to knock each other's aggies and cat's eyes across the room with gleeful ruthlessness. Priscilla was seated at a small writing table with paper and pencil, drawing birds. Well, it looked something like birds. Bless her little heart, she was never going to be an accomplished artist, he thought with some amusement.

Eden winked at him, knowing exactly what he was thinking.

Unaware of their exchange, Priscilla glanced up and cast him a beaming smile. "Look, Papa! I drew a picture of you."

Dear heaven. That was meant to be him? The figure more resembled an ostrich.

Eden must have thought the same, for she coughed and turned away. "Oh, dear. Excuse me. Tickle in my throat."

He chuckled. "It is beautiful, my little sweetheart. I shall treasure it always. But hold on to it for now. We'd like to speak to all of you. Boys, gather round. I have something important to discuss with you."

"Is Eden with child?" young Connor asked, sounding remarkably grown-up and sophisticated about such matters.

"What?" Connor was aghast. His eldest was on the cusp of understanding how a man could feel about a woman, but to ask such a question? Fortunately, the lad still had a few years before raging lust took over and he turned into a complete idiot.

The boy regarded him earnestly. "Papa, did you compromise Eden and this is why you married her?"

Connor struggled to retain his composure. "Where are you hearing this nonsense?"

"No," Eden said calmly, trying not to choke on a burst of laughter. "Your father did not compromise me. Do you actually know what that means?"

They all nodded.

Connor was even more aghast. "You all do? Even you, Priscilla?"

"Yes, Papa. It means that you took Eden to bed before you were married," his daughter replied, shocking both of them.

"Oh, dear," Eden whispered.

Connor was mad enough to spit fire. "Priscilla! Who taught you this?"

"We overheard Sir Nero talking to Grandmama Evelyn," Alex replied. "You needn't growl at us."

"That wretched man," Eden muttered. "And did your grandmother box his ears for his impertinence? Honestly, the gall of that man. Your father never did any such thing. He has always treated me with the utmost respect. In any event, it is too soon to tell whether I am with child or not now that we are *lawfully* married. But we digress. Our talk has to do with your father's upcoming trip to London."

Connor was hoping to broach the matter of taking Eden with him, but he had no sooner mentioned the possibility of their being without their new mother for an entire month while he took care of certain pressing Lynton estate matters in London—yes, he had not even fully gotten out the words "London" and "Eden"—when they all began to protest.

"We love Eden," young Connor said. "Why would you take her away from us?"

"Did she accept to go?" Alex wanted to know. "Or did you browbeat her into agreeing?"

Eden laughed. "Alex, your father did not browbeat me. You have an excellent vocabulary for a ten-year-old."

"Dear heaven," Connor muttered. "Do the three of you think I am an ogre?"

"No, Papa," Priscilla said, looking up from her ostrich portrait that she was trying to pass off as him. "We love you. Can you not see it in my drawing of you?"

He choked on his words, desperate to keep himself from laughing. "And I love you, my little sweetheart." He was touched by her big eyes and adorable smile, even if she could not draw to save her life. "Eden is my wife, and I would like to have her with me in London."

He could have told them that the matter was not up for discussion, but it very much *was* to be discussed, since Eden had expressed concerns about leaving the children so soon after they had wed.

"Oh, Papa!" Priscilla frowned at him. "Don't make her go with you. We need her here." The boys agreed.

Eden regarded him helplessly.

It made sense to leave her behind, he supposed. He would be caught up in Lynton business most days and have little time to spend with her. Also, many of the *ton* families would not be in London yet.

"Or we could all go," Eden suggested. "While you are occupied with your business affairs, I could show the children around London. There are museums and gardens to see, bookshops and sweet shops to pass the day. Puppet theaters and boat rides. Perhaps your mother would join us, too."

Alex did not think the dowager duchess would go for the idea. "Grandmama doesn't want to go to London."

"Why not?" Connor asked his son.

"Because Sir Nero positioned her, and she is thinking about it," Priscilla replied.

"What in blazes does that mean? There's no such thing as—" Connor inhaled sharply. "Did that old goat *proposition* my mother?"

"That's the word, Papa!" Priscilla replied excitedly.

"Oops," Eden said, daring not to laugh while he stood there scowling and with the proverbial smoke pouring out of his ears.

"He is a dead man," Connor said with a growl. He started to storm out, stopped, and then turned to face them all. "We are *all* going to London, and that includes Grandmama Evelyn. I'll *bloody* be damned if I let that *bloody* lecherous goat put his hands on my mother. Everyone, start packing!"

The children cheered.

Eden followed after him. "You cannot force your mother to come with us."

"Oh, yes I can. That fiend is not going to pinch your bottom or ever touch my mother again." He marched down the hall. "Evelyn! In my study! Now!"

His mother hurried out of her bedchamber. "Connor, what on earth? Why are you shouting loudly enough to bring the rafters tumbling down on us?"

"I forbid you to see Sir Nero. He does not set foot in this house again. Nor are you to set foot in his home that he probably runs as a house of sin."

His mother's eyes rounded in surprise. "Good heavens, have you gone mad?"

"The children overheard him propositioning you, Evelyn," Eden explained in response to her look of utter confusion.

Evelyn burst out laughing. "Oh, dear. Is this why you are so enraged? Do not be absurd. I have no interest in that lecherous old toad. But it is rather fun to be chased after at my age. I would never agree, of course. I fear my wrinkles would shock him into an apoplexy. Besides, your father and I were a love match. Having known love, I cannot imagine ever giving myself away so cheaply to the likes of Sir Nero Arnulfson."

"Oh, thank goodness," Eden muttered.

Connor let out a breath of relief as he raked a hand through his hair. "Bloody gave me a scare."

His mother frowned at him. "Connor, your face is purple. Your little demons ought to have listened in on the entire conversation. They would have heard me refuse his flattering proposition. But I assure you, he was most insincere about it. It is Eden he really wants, and now he cannot have her."

"Bloody right he cannot have her," Connor replied.

"Crisis averted," Eden intoned, her arm resting lightly on his to calm him.

Surprisingly, it worked.

Yes, Connor thought, she certainly had the ability to soothe him. In truth, everything felt right when she was beside him. This was why he wanted her to accompany him to London. Otherwise, what was he to do? Normally, he would have spent his time with Camborne and Bromleigh. But this was out of the question now that he was married to Eden and was going to remain faithful to her. At best, he might share a drink with them at one of their clubs before returning to his townhouse while they went off carousing.

He had sent letters to his friends telling of his marriage, but he was not certain those missives had reached them yet. Certainly not Camborne's, since he was all the way north in the Highlands. Bromleigh might have received his, for Connor had sent word to him at Lady Shoreham's estate. However, who knew if he was still visiting his cousin or had gone back to London?

Well, if his friends had not heard yet of his marriage, then he would tell them when he saw them in London. Would it not also be sensible to introduce them to Eden at the same time?

And if his children wanted to come along, why not? These men were godfathers to his sons and ought to be better acquainted with them now that they were growing up so fast.

"Will you join us in London, Evelyn?" Eden asked her.

His mother nodded. "It will be nice to catch up with old friends I haven't seen in a while. Also, I'll be there to keep an eye on the children whenever you and Connor step out. I'm sure the invitations will come pouring in once the *ton* realizes you are in residence."

Connor led Eden to his study so that they could discuss their trip while he wrote to the coaching inns and sent word to his London housekeeper to have the townhouse readied for his miniature army. Eden sank down on the sofa to make herself comfortable while he took a seat behind his desk and set out his writing paper, ink pot, and sand shaker.

He had yet to put quill to paper when Brewster entered. "Your Grace…"

"Yes, Brewster?"

"This letter just came for Her Grace."

"For me?" Eden smiled up at his butler as he handed it to her. "Thank you, Brewster."

"Who is it from, love?" he asked once Brewster had returned to his position by the front door. His curiosity was roused while he watched the changing expressions on her face as she read her missive.

"My parents."

He arched an eyebrow. "Your parents? Why wouldn't they just walk over to talk to you? By the way, do you think they will be all right if left unattended at Chestnut Hill while we are in London?"

"You will never believe this. Apparently, they have gone off to Italy together."

"Italy? When? We saw them just the night before last."

"They left this morning." She shook her head in amazement. "Can you believe it? I fully expect to read newspaper accounts of war breaking out wherever in Italy they happen to be staying. How odd. Together? I cannot understand what suddenly brought them around after a lifetime of hating each other."

Connor shrugged. "Perhaps our happiness has set the example for them."

She stared at him. "Do you think so?"

"No, love. Not really. But one can always hope."

"Perhaps almost killing my father made my mother reconsider her feelings toward him." She rose and came to his side to sit on the arm of his chair.

He eased his chair back a little in order to take her onto his lap. "Are you worried about them?"

"No." She hugged him. "It is time I stopped serving as their referee and let them deal with their problems on their own. What they do or do not do to each other no longer torments me. I've found my happiness with you and the children. Evelyn, too. We are a true family, aren't we?"

"Yes, love. Even though my own daughter thinks I look like an ostrich."

She emitted a merry trill of laughter. "If so, you are a very handsome ostrich. A Silver Duke ostrich."

He smiled. "Is there such a thing?"

"I'm sure there must be." She kissed him softly on the lips.

He deepened the kiss, took control of it and added heat to it because his feelings would never be tepid for his wife. "I love you, Eden."

"I love you too," she said with a breathy sigh of pleasure.

By her inviting smile, he knew she wanted him to kiss her again.

So he did, giving her a kiss filled with all the splendor of the heavens as he could muster.

Deep.

Intense.

Because he always wanted her to feel the moonlight in his every kiss.

THE END

Also by Meara Platt

FARTHINGALE SERIES
My Fair Lily
The Duke I'm Going To Marry
Rules For Reforming A Rake
A Midsummer's Kiss
The Viscount's Rose
Earl of Hearts
The Viscount and the Vicar's Daughter
A Duke For Adela
Marigold and the Marquess
The Make-Believe Marriage
A Slight Problem With The Wedding
If You Wished For Me
Never Dare A Duke
Capturing The Heart Of A Cameron

BOOK OF LOVE SERIES
The Look of Love
The Touch of Love
The Taste of Love
The Song of Love
The Scent of Love
The Kiss of Love
The Chance of Love
The Gift of Love
The Heart of Love
The Promise of Love
The Wonder of Love
The Journey of Love

The Treasure of Love
The Dance of Love
The Miracle of Love
The Hope of Love (novella)
The Dream of Love (novella)
The Remembrance of Love (novella)
All I Want For Christmas (novella)

MOONSTONE LANDING SERIES
Moonstone Landing (novella)
Moonstone Angel (novella)
The Moonstone Duke
The Moonstone Marquess
The Moonstone Major
The Moonstone Governess
The Moonstone Hero
The Moonstone Pirate

DARK GARDENS SERIES
Garden of Shadows
Garden of Light
Garden of Dragons
Garden of Destiny
Garden of Angels

SILVER DUKES
Cherish and the Duke
Moonlight and the Duke
Two Nights with the Duke

LYON'S DEN
The Lyon's Surprise
Kiss of the Lyon
Lyon in the Rough

THE BRAYDENS

A Match Made In Duty
Earl of Westcliff
Fortune's Dragon
Earl of Kinross
Earl of Alnwick
Tempting Taffy
Aislin
Genalynn
Pearls of Fire*
A Rescued Heart
*also in Pirates of Britannia series

DeWOLFE PACK ANGELS SERIES
Nobody's Angel
Kiss An Angel
Bhrodi's Angel

About the Author

Meara Platt is a USA Today bestselling author and an award winning, Amazon UK All-star. Her favorite place in all the world is England's Lake District, which may not come as a surprise since many of her stories are set in that idyllic landscape, including her award winning, fantasy romance (romantasy) Dark Gardens series. If you'd like to learn more about the ancient Fae prophecy that is about to unfold in the Dark Gardens series, as well as Meara's lighthearted, international bestselling Regency romances in the Farthingale series and Book of Love series, or her more emotional Moonstone Landing series and Braydens series, please visit Meara's website at www.mearaplatt.com.

Milton Keynes UK
Ingram Content Group UK Ltd.
UKHW020436261124
3104UKWH00064B/442